# CATALYST

## Also by Sarah Beth Durst

*The Girl Who Could Not Dream*

*Journey Across the Hidden Islands*

*The Stone Girl's Story*

*Spark*

# CATALYST

SARAH BETH DURST

CLARION BOOKS
HOUGHTON MIFFLIN HARCOURT
BOSTON NEW YORK

Clarion Books
3 Park Avenue
New York, New York 10016



Clarion Books is an imprint of Houghton Mifflin Harcourt Publishing Company.

hmhbooks.com

The text was set in Fairfield LT Std.

*Library of Congress Cataloging-in-Publication Data*
Names: Durst, Sarah Beth, author.
Title: Catalyst / by Sarah Beth Durst.
Description: New York : Clarion Books/Houghton Mifflin Harcourt, [2020] |
Audience: Ages 10 to 12. | Audience: Grades 4–6. |
Summary: Twelve-year-old Zoe's rescue kitten quickly becomes a giant, talking cat that Zoe and her friend Harrison must keep hidden, especially since there are rumors of other strange creatures in their town.
Identifiers: LCCN 2019028712 (print) | LCCN 2019028713 (ebook) |
ISBN 9780358065029 (hardcover) | ISBN 9780358063629 (ebook)
Subjects: CYAC: Cats—Fiction. | Magic—Fiction. | Family life—Fiction. |
Friendship—Fiction.
Classification: LCC PZ7.D93436 Cat 2020 (print) | LCC PZ7.D93436 (ebook) |
DDC [Fic]—dc23
LC record available at https://lccn.loc.gov/2019028712
LC ebook record available at https://lccn.loc.gov/2019028713

Manufactured in the United States of America
DOC 10 9 8 7 6 5 4 3 2 1
4500796091

*For Uncle Greg, Aunt Pat,*

*Emily, David, Ella, Brooks,*

*Laura, Jake, Johnny, and Anna*

# CHAPTER 1

"**No kitten is that small,**" the text from Harrison read.

Zoe texted back, "Smaller than my hand." She crouched next to the tiny ball of fluff. Shivering, it had wedged itself between the trash can and the garage door. Zoe had spotted it when she'd dumped a bag of crumpled wrapping paper and used party plates into the can.

She cooed at the kitten, "It's okay. Don't be scared. You'll be all right." Checking around the garage, she searched for a mother cat or any other kittens, but didn't see anything. She heard the chirp of crickets, cars on a distant highway, and the hum of her family's voices through the open window of the brightly lit kitchen. But no meows.

Her phone binged with a one-word text: "Photoshop."

"If Photoshop," Zoe typed, "kitten would be riding a velociraptor."

*Bing.* "Sweet." Then: "Still Photoshop."

"Come see."

"Busy."

She sent him an eye-roll emoji. He wasn't busy. She knew for a fact that he was camping in his backyard, next to her own, and that he was most likely "busy" separating the raisins from the M&M's in a bag of trail mix. Laying her hand flat, palm up, she waited as the kitten stuck out its little pink nose and sniffed her fingers. Zoe whispered, "Let me help you."

The kitten crept forward into the light from the garage, and Zoe decided to think of it as a she, because the fuzz above her eyes looked like a cartoon cat's eyelashes. She was trembling, which made her orange, black, and tan fur quiver all over. Her ears were flattened, and her tail was tucked between her hind legs. She looked so miserable and so hopeful at the same time that Zoe felt her heart melt. *Poor little thing,* she thought. "I can't keep you," Zoe warned. "My parents said no more animals in the house, not after the mix-up with the skunk."

"Mew?" the kitten said.

"Long story," Zoe said. "Tonight you'll be my secret, and tomorrow I'll help you find someone who can take care of you."

She stayed still while the kitten sniffed her hand some more. Her nose and whiskers tickled, but Zoe didn't laugh. Gingerly, the kitten placed one paw on Zoe's palm. "You can trust me," Zoe whispered. "Everything's going to be okay. Promise."

Cupping her other hand behind the kitten, Zoe scooted her fully onto her palm. *She really is smaller than my hand,* Zoe thought. She stood, cradling the kitten close. The kitten tensed and then relaxed as Zoe carried her inside.

Zoe heard the clink of glasses being loaded into the dishwasher in the kitchen as her parents and brother cleaned up from her birthday party. Her cousins, aunts, and uncles had all swarmed to their house for the usual hamburger, hot dog, and cake celebration and had left after Zoe opened her presents. Zoe was supposed to be in the kitchen, helping to clean. She tiptoed past and up the stairs to her bedroom.

Tucking the kitten against her with one hand, she used her other hand to drag a cardboard box from her closet, dump out her old rock collection, and line the box with a sweater. Lowering the kitten inside, Zoe told her, "Wait right here."

"Mew?"

The kitten looked up with such wide eyes that Zoe didn't want to leave her. She'd never had anything look at her with so much instant adoration. Certainly the box turtle—one of her last rescues prior to her parents saying *no more*—hadn't cared. "One minute," Zoe promised.

She hurried downstairs and into the kitchen. "Just thirsty!" she sang as she fetched the half-finished carton of milk from the refrigerator. She also plucked a bowl of mostly eaten popcorn off the counter. "And hungry!"

"Fine, but that's it!" Mom called after her. "You've had enough snacks for one day."

"Besides, you have to leave room for leftover cake!" Dad added.

Zoe's older brother, Alex, cheered from the sink. "Second cake!"

It was a family tradition: second cake after the relatives had left. You ate a wedge with all the cousins, and then afterward, once cleanup was done, you could have whatever part of the leftover cake you wanted: just the frosting or just the innards or all the icing roses from on top . . . Zoe was not going to miss that. *Those roses are mine,* she thought.

"Don't you think she's getting a little old for second cake?" Mom said to Dad.

"*I'm* not too old for it," Alex protested.

"Remember when we started second cake?" Dad said. "Alex was four, and it was the only way we could think of to keep him from scooping all the icing off the cake before the relatives finished singing 'Happy Birthday.'"

*I'm never outgrowing second cake,* Zoe thought. That was a horrible thing to suggest. She was just getting taller and older, not transforming into some weird non-cake-loving person. "I'll be right back," she promised. "Don't eat all the cake without me."

She ran back up to her room, dumped the extra popcorn in the trash, and poured milk into the bowl. Kneeling, she nestled the bowl in the corner of the box. She hoped the kitten didn't try to swim in it.

On wobbly legs, the kitten was prowling around the confines of the box. Reaching out a finger, Zoe stroked between her ears. "You don't seem as scared as you were. That's good. You don't need to be scared with me."

The kitten leaned against her finger as if she were so happy that Zoe was petting her. Most of the cats Zoe had met were standoffish, but not this kitten. *She likes me!* Zoe thought.

"I like you too," Zoe whispered to her.

Climbing onto a mound of sweater, the kitten teetered, then toppled onto her side. Zoe laughed and helped her stand. Gazing up at Zoe, the kitten rubbed her cheek against Zoe's fingers. She then got her paws underneath her and continued with her exploration.

Chin in her hands, Zoe watched the kitten reach the milk. She sniffed it and then looked back at Zoe. "Go on. You'll love it," Zoe told her. Extending her paw, the kitten batted at the milk. The surface rippled, and the little cat skipped backward. She inched forward and then swatted at the milk again, clearly fascinated.

Zoe heard a soft knock at her window. "Visitor," she told the kitten. She climbed across her bed, unlocked the window, and lifted it.

Harrison, her best friend, stuck his head in. "Happy birthday. Or birthday-party day." Her actual birthday was in two days, on Monday. Harrison liked to be precise about facts.

"Thanks. You know, you could have used the door. My parents would have been happy to see you." She helped him climb in. As skinny as a skeleton, Harrison didn't need much space to squeeze himself through—he was mostly elbows and knees. He was also not very graceful. He tumbled onto her pillow, much like the kitten falling onto the sweater.

"Gotta keep in practice for Everest." He'd been talking about his dream to climb Mount Everest since kindergarten. There was zero chance his parents would ever let him do it, or that he'd be able to survive the required video game withdrawal. Untangling himself, he stared off the edge of the bed into the box. "Whoa. That's a small kitten!"

"Yep, she is." She avoided saying "Told you so," because that was obvious.

He adjusted his glasses, as if that would make the kitten's size change. "Like seriously newborn-baby-kitten small. Do you think she was just born? Are you sure she's a she?"

"Not sure. And not sure. It's not as if she or he could tell me, so I'm going with 'recently born' and 'she.'" She liked the awe in Harrison's voice. That was how she felt every time she looked at the kitten. So much cuter than a stray turtle. "Cutest thing you've ever seen, right?"

"Beyond cute. There needs to be a new word for how stupendously cute she is. *Cute-ificent. Cuterageous. Cutextraordinary.*" He reached in to pet her, and she fluffed up her fur and gave him a tiny, sweet hiss.

He withdrew, and the kitten returned to the milk. She circled twice around the bowl. Wrinkling her tiny nose, she sniffed at it. Zoe wanted to cheer. "Go on. Drink the milk. You can do it!"

"I thought cats drinking milk was a myth," Harrison said. "Makes them sick."

"Kittens drink milk. Grown cats don't."

"Are you sure?" He pulled his phone out of his pocket and began typing. "Yep, once they're grown, they lose the enzyme to digest lactose, and it makes them vomit. Kittens are fine, though—you're right. But you're supposed to feed motherless newborn kittens milk with an eyedropper. They can't feed themselves."

As they watched, the kitten began to lap at the milk.

"Or maybe they can." Harrison frowned at his phone. "When kittens are first born, their eyes are closed and their ears are flattened back. They can't see, hear, keep themselves warm, or eliminate waste on their own. You're supposed to rub their butts until they poop."

"What? You're making that up." She craned to see his screen.

He showed it to her. "See?"

"Huh." Her kitten was much perkier than that. Her ears were upright triangles, and her blue eyes were fully open. Zoe pointed to another photo of a several-week-old kitten. "She's more like that. She must not be a newborn."

"She's too small to be that many weeks old."

"Maybe she was born premature," Zoe said. "You were small when you were born." They'd known each other since they were both in diapers, and she'd heard all the stories, how Harrison had been in newborn intensive care for weeks, so tiny he couldn't breathe on his own at first. Mrs. Acharya, Harrison's grandmother, had always told the story by comparing her grandson to a honey cake taken out of the oven too soon. He had to bake longer before his parents were able to bring him home. That's why he's so delicious, she'd always concluded, pretending to gobble his shoulder.

"Wait—Look." He scrolled through his phone and showed her another photo. "She could be twelve days old. At twelve days, their eyes are open and their ears are up, but they're still super tiny. Plus, if she's been on her own without much food, that would explain why she's on the small side. Now that you're feeding her, she'll grow."

Harrison, she knew, liked it when he could understand the how and why of a thing. He was happiest when everything was neatly labeled in its own box. His idea of a fun Saturday was reorganizing his bookshelves. Currently his books were sorted alphabetically by topic, which meant revenge stories came after pirates but before superheroes. She had no idea what he did with revenge books about pirate superheroes. It was better not to ask. Now that he'd labeled the kitten as an underfed, twelve-day-old female, he was content, even if Zoe had no idea whether he was right. She decided it didn't matter. All that mattered was the kitten was here, and Zoe was going to take care of her—at least for tonight.

"So, what are you going to do about your parents?" Harrison asked. He knew about her history with animals. Up until six months ago, she'd brought home nearly every animal she found, convinced it needed her help. Her mom had put a stop to that after Zoe had smuggled a baby skunk into the house, thinking it was a cat. Prior to that, Mom had said no to a baby squirrel, an injured bird, and a garden snake—as well as the box turtle—but the skunk was the last straw.

"They were pretty serious after the skunk," Zoe admitted.

"You can't get rid of her! She's cutextraordinary!"

Zoe sighed. She wished she could keep the kitten. She hadn't known it was possible to get attached to anything so quickly, especially something that was basically a walking cotton ball, but all she wanted to do was gaze at the kitten's adorableness.

"Mom will just insist we give her away, like every other animal I've ever tried to bring home," Zoe said. "I think she still has the animal rescue center number memorized."

The kitten lifted her tiny head out of the bowl. Beads of milk clung to her whiskers, weighing them down so they drooped, making her look like she had a mustache. Zoe snapped a photo of her with her phone.

"You could try to change your parents' minds," Harrison suggested. "You're not a little kid anymore." He mimed craning his neck to look up at her, as if he were so much shorter. "Literally."

She glared at him. She'd spurted up in the last year and was now a good four inches taller than Harrison, a fact she didn't like being reminded of. Mom had tossed out all her favorite jeans just because they were "a little short," and at her party, her uncle kept making basketball jokes.

"I'm serious!" Harrison said. "You should at least try!"

"Maybe." Zoe reached into the box again, and the kitten leaned against her finger as Zoe rubbed her tiny, milk-soaked cheek. The kitten seemed to be vibrating. "She's purring!" It was so sweet that Zoe couldn't stop smiling.

"See! You have to make it permanent," Harrison said. "She hissed at me, but she adores you. She's meant to be with you."

*Maybe he's right. But . . .*

From downstairs, Zoe's brother called, "Zoe! Second cake!"

Zoe withdrew her hand from the box as Harrison clambered over her bed to the window. "You know you could come downstairs and have second cake and leave through a door like a normal person."

"Told you: it's practice. Plus I'm going to make s'mores—after I light a fire using only two sticks." He mimed rubbing sticks together, then added, "And a match."

"Didn't your parents ever tell you not to play with fire?"

"Yeah, but my grandmother overruled them." His voice was wistful. The older Mrs. Acharya had died last fall, and Zoe knew how much he missed her.

"Your grandma was the best," Zoe said, "but she still would have told you not to burn down the neighborhood."

He shot her a grin, as if to say he'd never done anything reckless in his entire twelve years of life, which she knew for a fact was not true, and then he climbed out the window and lowered himself onto her porch roof. Before hurrying downstairs, Zoe checked the kitten one more time. She was settling in, kneading the sweater with her little claws.

Zoe felt like bursting with the news. A kitten was in her room! *I may have saved her life!* Even if she hadn't really saved her from anything but a summer night outside, Zoe still felt like something wonderful and special had happened. As if she'd found an extra birthday present.

A secret birthday present.

*It won't do any harm to keep the kitten just this one night,* she told herself. She'd do the responsible thing tomorrow and take her to the animal shelter, but tonight she could be the kitten's hero.

Rounding the corner, Zoe skidded into the kitchen with a giant smile on her face. Mom, Dad, and Alex were already at the table with their plates of cake: a center square for Dad, only frosting and filling for Mom, and a wad of cake that looked like he'd clawed it out with his bare hands for Alex. They'd left the cake itself on the counter. It was vanilla with raspberry filling, decorated with clusters of pink and purple roses, and it looked as if it had been gnawed on by a beaver. Fetching a plate, Zoe scraped off several clumps of roses.

"You look happy," Dad noted. "Did you have a good birthday?"

"Very good." She carried her plate to the table.

"Get everything you wanted?" Mom asked.

"No one gave me a pony," Zoe said. She thought again of the

kitten hidden in her room. It would have been a great birthday present. If there were any chance they'd say yes . . . *But there isn't.* They'd been very clear about no more rescues. "Or a jetpack," she added.

"Or a teleporter," Alex said cheerfully.

"Or a dinosaur," Zoe said.

"Not a single mystical object."

"Not one enchanted sword. Or a lightsaber."

"I want a lightsaber," Alex agreed.

"You'd cut your arm off," Mom told him, then asked Zoe, "Do you like the necklace Aunt Evelyn gave you?" Her eyes were twinkling, and Dad snorted a half-disguised laugh.

"It's amazing," Zoe said honestly. The necklace in question was made of rhinestone letters that spelled out the word *FUN*. She was certain if you tried to find a necklace that tacky and absurd, you'd fail. "I'm going to wear it ironically to every funeral, final exam, and dentist appointment for the rest of my life."

Dad beamed at her. "I love that we raised a daughter who uses the word *ironically* correctly." Leaning over toward Mom, he held out his hand for a high-five. She slapped it.

Alex raised his eyebrows. "Did they just high-five their parenting skills?"

"I think they did," Zoe said.

Alex regarded their parents with mock pity and said to Zoe, "Do you want to break the news about how badly they did, or should I?"

Zoe heaved a sigh. "Earlier today, during the party . . ." She paused for dramatic effect. "Alex ate a potato chip that fell on the ground."

"But surely . . ." Dad said, his voice trembling, "he only let it sit for five seconds."

Zoe covered her face as if in shame. "It was ten seconds!"

Dad wailed. "The horror!"

They all burst out laughing.

"If that's the worst either of you do," Mom said, "I'd say we've done our job well." Dad held out his hand for another high-five, but Mom ignored him in favor of passing out napkins to go with the cake. She herself had eaten so neatly there wasn't a crumb left.

*This is how it's supposed to be,* Zoe thought. *The four of us, together.* Her laugh faded as she thought about what would happen at the end of the summer. *I wish it could last.*

"Hey, no sad face!" Alex said. "I think it's illegal to be sad while having second cake."

"What if you aren't here for my next birthday party?" Zoe stared at the kitchen floor as she asked. Her eyes felt hot, and she thought that if she looked at Alex, she might start crying, which she did *not* want to do on a day that had been so nice. Thanks to the distraction of the kitten, she had almost managed to forget that Alex, the best brother in the world, was leaving for Europe in September.

"Aw, Zoomaroo, I'll always come back for your birthday! Exams are in May. I'll be home every June. And of course I'll visit before then too."

He was supposed to go to college at one of the hundreds of schools within driving distance, close enough to visit whenever he wanted. Somewhere in Boston. Or New Hampshire. Maine would have been fine. Even New Jersey. But no, he had to win a scholarship to study in France. He wouldn't be back for months, and even though Zoe was proud of him, it was difficult to pretend to be happy about having to say goodbye. His choice affected her life too, and no one seemed to care about that. She wasn't asking for a pity parade, but it would be nice if someone acknowledged that this was a big deal for her. "It won't be the same."

Dad's voice was quiet. "Zoe, things never stay the same. That's just the way life is. It doesn't mean it's all bad. Change can be good. Even exciting!"

*Not for me,* she thought. *Everything's fine the way it is!*

But Zoe plastered a smile on her face and squished her feelings down. She was *not* going to be upset on her birthday, especially on a day she'd saved a kitten. And *especially* during second cake. "You're right, Dad. Everything will be fine."

# CHAPTER 2

**Zoe woke to the sound** of purring in her ear. She wished Dad wouldn't mow the lawn so early on a Sunday morning. Flopping her arm over her face, she mumbled, "Murph-mrrr."

Sharp pins pricked her arm.

*That's not a lawn mower.*

Her eyes snapped open. She turned her head and stared directly into the face of a purring kitten. Claws retracted, the kitten tucked her paw under her fuzzy belly.

"Mew?"

Zoe suddenly remembered yesterday, sneaking the kitten up to her room before second cake, and a rush of joy flooded through her. *My kitten!* Except she couldn't keep her. *My temporary kitten.* "How did you get up on my bed, you cutie?" she asked. When Zoe had gone to sleep, the kitten had been safely nestled in the sweater in her box.

The kitten nuzzled her cheek. Her fur felt as soft as velvet. Zoe stroked between the kitten's ears, which made her purr even louder, an extraordinary volume for a creature her size, and it made Zoe want to laugh. She held it in so she wouldn't startle the snuggling kitten.

"Did you sleep all right?" Zoe asked.

Sitting up, she looked down at the box. The bowl of milk was empty, and there was a tiny kitten poop in the corner of the sweater.

That wasn't quite as cute as the kitten herself.

"On the plus side, at least I don't have to make you go—the way Harrison said they did for newborns," Zoe said. "Don't worry—your new owner will have a litter box." She wished that new owner was her with an ache so strong that tears pricked her eyes.

Plopping the kitten back into the box, Zoe showered and dressed. When she returned, the kitten was looking mournfully at the empty milk bowl. "Mew?"

"You want breakfast? I can do that. Wait here."

Leaving the kitten in the box, she closed her bedroom door so the little cat couldn't escape, even if she crawled out of the box again. Carrying the empty bowl downstairs, Zoe heard voices: Alex, Dad, and Mom. Everyone was awake.

*It will be tricky getting the kitten out without anyone noticing,* Zoe thought. If it was a weekday, no problem, but on a Sunday? *Also, how do I explain needing a bowl of milk?* But it was too late to turn around now.

"Good morning, almost-birthday girl!" Dad called.

"Happy last day of eleven to you," Alex sang. Off-pitch. "Happy last day of eleven to you." He kept going. "Happy last day of eleven, dear Zoe!" And going: "Happy last day of eleven to you!" Ending in a shout: "Countdown!"

Entering the kitchen with the bowl behind her back, Zoe announced, "It is one day until I'm officially twelve!"

Alex roared, "Let her eat cake!"

It was a silly ritual they'd invented when they were both little kids and couldn't wait until their "real" birthdays, but she loved it. "Thanks, but I think I'll just have some cereal for now." She held up the empty bowl, as if she intended to fill it with Cheerios.

"Very grown-up of you," Mom said approvingly, and Zoe was tempted to grab a piece of cake just because she said that. But Mom's attention had already shifted back to her laptop.

Alex had finished his breakfast. A plate with bagel crumbs was sitting on the table next to printouts. Glancing at the papers as she passed, Zoe saw they were course offerings. Alex was choosing his classes in Paris.

Returning to their conversation, Dad waved a printout in Alex's face. "You can't skip Impressionism. It altered the world of art forever!"

"I already picked French Painting from the Seventeenth Century to the Nineteenth Century," Alex protested. "That includes Impressionism."

"Van Gogh's *Starry Night* changed how we see the sky itself!"

"You do realize that *I'm* the one taking the classes, right?" Alex asked, amused. "You already did college. It's my turn."

"I'm just excited for you," Dad said. "You're embarking on a new adventure, a once-in-a-lifetime opportunity! You have to embrace it!"

The study-abroad scholarship Alex had applied for was supposed to have been a pie-in-the-sky long shot. Zoe firmly told herself she should be feeling happy for him, like Dad was.

Thinking about another long shot, she wondered if maybe she *should* tell her family about her pocket-size kitten. Yes, Mom had been furious about the baby skunk, and she hadn't reacted well to the mess the squirrel had made, but it had been a while since Zoe tried to take in a lost animal. And the kitten was different from all those others! For one thing, she wasn't a wild animal, which had to be a plus. For another, she was absurdly cute and sweet and wonderful. Zoe glanced at Mom to see if she was in the right mood for such a reveal.

Mom was sitting by the window, typing on her computer. She'd just started her new job at the mayor's office, and she had to work weekends now. Yesterday had been a rare exception, a day off for Zoe's birthday party. *I guess the day-before-my-real-birthday isn't a holiday anymore.* They always used to celebrate day-befores. She felt bad moping about it. After all, Mom's new job was important, and Zoe was proud of her, but she'd liked that family tradition.

Worse, Mom did not look in the right mood for meeting a kitten.

"Do you have to go into the office today?" Zoe asked her.

"Not today, but I do have a lot to get done," Mom said without looking up from her screen. To Dad, she asked, "Did you call the contractor?"

"Yes. They'll start two weeks from tomorrow!"

It was Dad's new project—overseeing the construction of a new laundry room. He'd wanted to be an architect before he became an engineer, and so he got overly excited about any kind of home-building project. They were converting a chunk of Alex's closet, since he wasn't going to need it anymore. He wasn't even out of the house, and already they were acting like he was gone and never coming back. *Why can't a new laundry room wait?* Just because his scholarship saved them money they would have spent on tuition didn't mean they had to do it now. Zoe didn't *want* any more changes!

Suddenly the same horrible feeling she'd felt last night came crashing back. Taken separately, all the things that were happening this summer weren't terrible. In fact, you could argue they were all good things, especially Mom's job and the impact she could make with the new environmental policy she was working on, but taken together . . . Zoe felt as if a tidal wave were coming at her and she was stuck in the sand. She couldn't do anything about Alex and Paris, or Mom and her extra work, or the carving up of Alex's bedroom to make a new laundry room, or growing taller, or the prospect of voluntarily choosing cereal over cake. *But I* can *do something about the kitten up in my bedroom waiting for milk,* she thought.

She made a decision.

In the middle of Dad and Alex discussing the pluses and minuses of art history classes and Mom typing on her laptop, Zoe said, "I found an abandoned kitten out by the trash last night, and I want to keep her."

The typing stopped.

Dad and Alex broke off mid-sentence.

"You what the what?" Dad asked.

"Cool!" Alex said.

"Zoe, what did you do?" Mom said, a warning note in her voice. "I thought you outgrew this. Please tell me there isn't another skunk in your room."

"She's definitely a kitten," Zoe said. Belatedly, she thought she should have eased into the request. Or at least given it more than three seconds of thought. She should have written out her arguments. Or made a poster. "Wait here. I'll show you."

Her heart was racing as she pounded up the stairs and into her room. She scooped up the kitten, cradled the little cat against her chest, and carried her more slowly back down to the kitchen. Staring up at her, the kitten said, "Mew" and laid a soft paw on Zoe's throat, as if out of concern. "They'll love you once they see you," Zoe whispered, wishing she were sure about that.

Her parents and brother stared at her as she deposited the kitten on the table. Zoe poured her a bowl of milk. The kitten splashed the surface with her paw happily. Zoe saw Mom wince as drops spattered across the table, and then the kitten plunged her face into the bowl and began drinking.

For a long minute, the only sound was the *lap-lap-lap* of the kitten's tongue.

"Are you sure it's not a really large caterpillar?" Alex asked.

Zoe glared at him.

"It's cute," Dad admitted, "but we agreed that you weren't going to bring any more animals home. We made it a rule." Dad didn't like making rules—he liked to be the "fun" parent—but this was something he and Mom had both agreed on.

"Rules can change, can't they?" Zoe said. "You said yourself last night: change can be good." She held her breath and hoped this worked.

Alex laughed. "She's got you there. And it *is* the day before her birthday. By the tradition of the sacred day-before, you're obligated to grant her wishes, if possible. It's not like she's asking for a pet lion. Or a skunk."

Zoe gave him a grateful look. Alex had always been the kind of big brother who stood up for his baby sister. She remembered playing catch with a teddy bear in the living room—she must have been five or six years old—and her aim was terrible. She had thrown the bear into a lamp and knocked it over. The lamp had shattered, and when their parents rushed in, Alex said it was his fault. She should have known he'd help her now.

"You all have something you're excited about," Zoe pleaded. "Alex has his scholarship. Mom, your new job. Dad, the laundry room. I think . . . I need something that's mine?"

"Excellent argument," Alex said approvingly. "I'm going to Europe. Why shouldn't Zoe have something special too? Besides, she isn't asking to foster a wild animal this time. She wants a proper pet, and she's old enough to care for one. You don't want to be like those parents who stunt their children's growth by denying them the milestones of independence and personal responsibility."

Zoe nodded vigorously in agreement, and Alex winked at her.

Both of them turned toward their parents.

Mom opened her mouth, then closed it.

Dad began to laugh. "We raised clever children."

"Too clever," Mom grumbled, but she wasn't fully frowning. "If we keep it, and I said *if,* then Zoe, it has to be entirely your responsibility."

Dad jumped in. "You feed it, water it, walk it—"

"You water plants, and you walk dogs," Zoe said, knowing he was teasing her but unable to resist correcting him. "But yes, I promise I'll take care of her." *Please, let me keep her!* She needed this kitten. She couldn't even explain why.

"You clean its litter box," Mom added. "You take it to the vet. You pay for whatever it needs with your own money. Use your birthday money. Save your allowance."

"I'll do all of it!" Zoe promised. She held her breath again and watched her parents' expressions as they shifted from exasperated to amused to resigned.

"Well, since, as Alex pointed out, it *is* your day-before-your-real-birthday . . ." Dad began.

"Yes!" Zoe said. Cooing at the kitten, she said, "You're mine, and I'm yours. And I will take care of you forever and ever."

Both her parents simultaneously sighed, and she knew she'd won.

"Fine," Mom relented. "She's yours, and you're hers. *But* you need to keep her out from underfoot. She stays in your room. And as soon as she's big enough, she becomes an outside cat. I don't want cat hair and hairballs all over the house. Do you understand, Zoe? We're trusting that you've grown up enough for this level of responsibility. If you can't handle it, then she finds a new owner who can take proper care of her."

"Yes!" Zoe couldn't believe it—they'd agreed! She wondered if it was because they felt guilty about all the changes lately, or they wanted to make her feel better about Alex's leaving . . . Or maybe they just saw how cute the kitten was and couldn't resist. Whatever the reason, it *worked!* She wanted to cheer and dance. Instead she hugged each of them. "Thank you!"

"What are you going to name her?" Alex asked. "Hey, how about Tiny? Or Shrimp? Or if we're going for irony, the Hulk or Godzilla?"

"Skunk?" Mom suggested.

Zoe made a face. "Very funny, Mom."

"Fluffy?" Dad said.

Alex snorted. "Do you know how many cats in the history of the world have been named Fluffy? Your naming privileges are revoked, Dad. How about Minnie, short for *minuscule?*"

"Mew!" the kitten said, a sound so tiny it was like a squeak.

"I know," Zoe said fondly. "Her name is Pipsqueak."

Cradling Pipsqueak, Zoe hurried across her yard, squeezed through the gate (which wasn't so much a gate as a loose board in the fence that Harrison's dog wasn't clever enough to move), and let herself in through Harrison's back door. She couldn't wait to tell him the news!

Harrison's older cousin, Surita, didn't look up from her cereal. She was seventeen, with purple-streaked hair and cat-eye glasses. Zoe's parents and Harrison's were paying her to keep an eye on Zoe and Harrison this summer—at least while she wasn't off being a camp counselor—but she was off duty on weekends. "Don't slam it."

Zoe caught the screen door on her foot and let it close gently.

"Is Harrison in his room or still in the backyard?" she asked. "I didn't see his tent." He was going to be so amazed they'd said yes! *I'm still amazed.*

"Yep." Surita was reading a magazine with the title *Unexplained Mysteries* scrawled in neon orange over a grainy photo of Bigfoot.

Both Surita and Harrison loved those kinds of magazines. Harrison claimed he liked that they tried to explain the unexplainable, even though he knew it was mostly nonsense. Ten points to them for trying to give answers, he said.

"Is that 'yes, he's upstairs,' or 'yes—'" Before Zoe could finish the question, Pipsqueak began to squirm. "Whoa!" Zoe said, lunging forward and holding out her hands so that Pipsqueak, when she wriggled free, plopped safely onto the kitchen table instead of plummeting to the floor. She immediately started exploring. "You have to be more careful!" Zoe scolded her.

"Excuse me?" Finally, Surita looked up and saw Pipsqueak. "What is *that?*"

"It's my new kitten."

"It's a chipmunk."

"She doesn't look anything like a chipmunk." Zoe was offended on Pipsqueak's behalf. Meanwhile, the kitten was wobbling her way across the table, around salt and pepper shakers shaped like elephants, a stack of unopened mail, and a ping-pong paddle, toward Surita's cereal bowl. She looked so determined that Zoe didn't try to stop her. She deserved her prize.

"Hamster? Gerbil? Meadow vole?"

"She's not a rodent. She's my cat." *Mine!* Zoe loved the sound of that. *I have my very own kitten! Best birthday present ever. Or day-before-birthday.*

"Rodents make good pets. I've heard rats are very smart." Surita picked up her cereal bowl just as Pipsqueak reached it. She held it two feet above the table.

Pipsqueak mewed indignantly.

"She likes milk," Zoe said apologetically.

"She can't have mine," Surita said. "I'm allergic to baby rats." She was eyeing Pipsqueak as if she expected the kitten to turn rabid, leap off the table, and sink her tiny teeth into her jugular.

"Wow, I've never met anyone who doesn't like kittens." Zoe went to the cabinet and took out a bowl. She knew where Harrison's family kept them and knew his parents wouldn't mind. She'd spent so much time at Harrison's house that it felt like an extension of her own. She poured milk into the bowl and set it in front of Pipsqueak. "Don't worry, Pipsqueak—I think you're adorable and amazing. It doesn't matter what some kitten haters think."

Pipsqueak splashed the milk delightedly, then stuck her face in and began lapping loudly. She seemed so happy with her second bowl of the morning that Zoe felt as if she'd done something heroic. *I did do something,* she thought. *I saved a kitten.*

Softly, Zoe stroked between her ears, and Pipsqueak paused her drinking to lean against Zoe's hand and nuzzle her fingers before she returned to her milk.

"Disliking kittens is a sign that I'm an evil mastermind who will someday take over the world," Surita said. "I also hate puppies, rainbows, and unicorns. Especially pink, fluffy ones."

Zoe pointed to Surita's magazine. "But fluffy Bigfeet are fine?"

"Bigfoots," Surita corrected.

"Pretty sure it should be Bigfeet. Foot, feet. Goose, geese."

"But their species name—oh, never mind. Yes, Harrison is upstairs and awake. He claims to have camped out last night, but he's inside now. On his computer, of course. I don't think he ever sleeps. He could be part robot. You know he alphabetizes his bookshelf regularly *for fun?* His parents periodically move books around when he's not looking so that he can have the joy of re-alphabetizing them."

"He doesn't always alphabetize them. Sometimes he sorts by color. Or theme."

"Inexplicably weird." Surita waved the magazine in the air, gesturing vaguely in the direction of Harrison's room. "See, the magazine doesn't lie. Unexplained mysteries, such as my cousin's personality, are all around us."

Pipsqueak, her face wet with milk, gazed up at Zoe. "Mew!"

It felt as if she were saying "thank you." Or "I love you." Focused on Zoe, the kitten ignored Surita entirely.

Zoe scooped her up, deposited the empty bowl in the sink with the other unwashed dishes "left to soak" (which probably meant it was Harrison's turn for that chore), and then trotted upstairs around the stacks of books destined to be returned to a shelf.

She found Harrison in his room. "I get to keep the kitten," she announced, "and your cousin doesn't understand pluralization."

Intent on his computer, Harrison didn't move. "Level eighteen."

"How was camping?"

"Great. Ate six s'mores."

He looked as if he'd slept outside. Actually, he looked as if he'd slept in a bird's nest. His hair was sticking up at all angles. His sleeping bag had been dumped on his bed, balled up next to the pillow with a heap of blankets and his comforter.

"Did you hear what I said about the kitten? I named her Pipsqueak, and my parents said I could keep her!"

"Wow! Really?" He stopped playing momentarily to gawk at her and Pipsqueak. "That's awesome! What made them change their minds?"

"I think they think saying yes to the kitten will make up for Alex going to Europe."

"Does it?" Harrison asked.

She considered it for a moment, smiling down fondly at Pipsqueak, who snuggled against her, kneading her tiny claws into Zoe's shirt. "Well, no. But I'm not going to tell them that."

"When my grandmother died, mine thought a new video game would cheer me up." Scowling at the monitor as if this were its fault, he went back to playing. Zoe knew better than to ask whether it had worked. Obviously it hadn't. And just as obviously, that didn't stop Harrison from playing. Or from missing his grandma.

Zoe sat on the edge of his bed, watching his game. Pipsqueak crawled out of her arms and began sniffing at Harrison's pillow. Glancing over, Harrison said, "Guess they're going to make friends."

"Who's making friends?" Zoe asked.

Suddenly Harrison's pillow moved. Or, more accurately, the large dog, which had been hidden by the mound of blankets and sleeping bag, shifted.

Pipsqueak squawked.

The dog's head shot up, and his tongue lolled out.

Letting out a *mew,* Pipsqueak barreled off the bed and onto the carpet. She rolled about a foot, scrambled until her tiny paws were underneath her, and then bolted across the room.

"Pipsqueak!" Zoe cried. She lunged for the kitten.

Harrison's dog was a Labrador retriever. He was large, friendly, and not very bright, and he loved beyond all else to fetch. Especially to fetch furry moving things that looked a bit like tan, black, and orange tennis balls.

"No!" Zoe shrieked. "Stop!"

"Fibonacci!" Harrison cried. He lunged for his dog.

Pipsqueak bounded to a bookcase and proceeded to leap up to the third shelf. She fluffed out her fur, posed sideways, as if that would make her look intimidatingly big, and hissed. It was a kind of musical hiss, changing notes in between spewing out tiny bits of spittle.

Harrison and Zoe jumped onto the dog, pulling him away from

the bookshelf and shoving him out the door. They slammed the door shut behind him and leaned against it, panting. Exiled to the hallway, Fibonacci whined and scratched at the door.

On the shelf, Pipsqueak quit hissing and began licking the fur on her back. Zoe felt as if her heart was beating faster than after a race. "Guess this wasn't the best idea."

"Sorry," Harrison said. "I didn't think he'd try to chase a kitten. Fibonacci is actually scared of full-grown cats. Cowered behind the couch for hours when the neighbor's cat hissed at him through the screen door."

"I'm the one who promised to keep her safe." Her first test as a pet owner, and she'd nearly failed! She should have checked the bed. "It's my fault." Next time, she'd be more careful. *Pipsqueak is depending on me.* "Sorry, Pipsqueak."

"My dog, my fault," Harrison said. "But maybe you should keep her at home until she's a little bigger?"

"Good idea," Zoe said.

Pipsqueak meowed, as if in agreement.

# CHAPTER 3

**On Monday morning, Zoe woke** next to a full-grown cat.

Sitting up in bed, she stared at the cat, blinked, rubbed her eyes, and stared some more. She began to feel the kind of nervous, sweaty-hands feeling she had when she was on the verge of making a mistake, like just before she dropped an entire bowl of pasta on the floor.

The cat looked *exactly* like a grown-up version of Pipsqueak. Same orange, black, and tan fur in the same pattern. Same pink nose. Same whiskers and eyebrow whiskers. Less kitten fluff and a more grown-cat face. But otherwise . . .

"P-p-pipsqueak? Is that you?"

The cat nuzzled against Zoe. "Mew?"

*It's her!* Her meow was a little deeper, a little fuller, but at its core, it was the same sweet, chirplike *mew*. But how could her kitten have become a cat overnight?

Oblivious to Zoe's distress, Pipsqueak lifted one leg and began to lick between her toes. She gnawed carefully and methodically at each claw as Zoe continued to gawk at her.

*Don't panic,* Zoe told herself. Maybe with some breeds, this was how fast they grew. Or Zoe could have overfed her. Or fed her the wrong foods?

Zoe picked up her phone, snapped a photo, and then texted Harrison. While she waited for him to reply, she checked online. "It says here that domestic cats take one year to grow from kitten to cat," she told Pipsqueak. Her voice shook.

*Maybe I'm still asleep and this is a dream,* she thought.

*Maybe I hit my head and lost my memory for a year. Or fell into a coma and am just waking up a year later . . .* Zoe took a deep breath and told herself firmly to calm down. She was overreacting. There had to be a rational explanation for this.

"I think . . . I think something's wrong. Not you. You aren't wrong. But something could be wrong *with* you." She swallowed a lump in her throat. She didn't want anything to be wrong with Pipsqueak.

Pausing her bath, Pipsqueak rubbed against Zoe again.

Zoe stroked the cat's neck. Her fur felt the same. Just as soft as it was before. Pipsqueak began to purr.

Zoe's phone binged. Harrison. "Photoshop?"

*Seriously, Harrison?*

She wanted to text him back a rude emoji. Her phone didn't have any. She texted a turtle and a thinking-face emoji instead.

He texted back: "Reptile head?"

"Slow brain," she corrected. "Idiot."

He sent her a bunny.

"Be serious," she typed. There had to be an explanation. Maybe a medical one. "Could cat be sick?" Weren't there diseases that caused rapid growth? *Please don't be sick.* Even after just two days, Zoe already loved her—the softness of her fur, the special *mew* when she saw Zoe that seemed to be just for her, the twitch of her no-longer-tiny nose when she sniffed anything new. Zoe loved the way Pipsqueak climbed onto her bed in the middle of the night to sleep next to her head and how she'd nuzzle her by headbutting her and rubbing those furry cheeks against her face.

Harrison didn't reply for a while, and Zoe watched Pipsqueak settle back down and resume her cleaning routine, moving from chewing her toes to licking her tail. Hair stuck together in the wake of her tongue as she covered every inch. She didn't look sick, and she wasn't acting sick. She was just . . . larger than yesterday.

Much larger.

*Maybe this is normal? Or not normal, but . . . not bad?* Maybe she'd be okay, so long as Zoe got her help. If Pipsqueak were sick, there could be a medicine for her to take. This might not be panic-worthy.

At last the phone binged again. "Too much growth hormone? Happens in humans. Also really bad SF movies. Like *Attack of the Killer Giant Kitten*."

She looked up "too much growth hormone." It had to do with

the pituitary gland, she read, which produced hormones. A certain kind of tumor in the pituitary gland could cause excessive growth.

"Going to vet. Want to come?" Zoe typed. "Also, not real movie."

He texted back, "Yes." And "Should be."

She'd known he'd say yes. He could never turn down a chance to find answers to an unanswered question. She also knew he was trying to cheer her up, but it wasn't working. What if Pipsqueak had a tumor that had caused this?

To Pipsqueak she said, "Stay. I'll be right back."

She hurried to the bathroom, showered in record time, and came back to her room wrapped in a towel.

Pipsqueak wasn't there.

"Uh-oh." She'd told Mom she would keep the kitten out from underfoot. She shouldn't be roaming outside Zoe's bedroom. *Especially if this is* Attack of the Killer Giant Kitten, she thought, and then pushed the ridiculous notion aside, tossed on some mostly clean clothes, and hurried out to hunt for Pipsqueak.

She checked the bedrooms—all empty. Her parents and Alex were awake, of course, since they were all annoying early birds and all had work today. Dad would have already left. Peering into Alex's room, she imagined it stripped of his posters, his books, his toys. Of course he wouldn't take all of it. Just a couple of suitcases at most. *He'll leave behind whatever he outgrew. His Voltron lions. His Transformers. His high school baseball trophies . . .*

*Me.*

Backing out of his room, she headed downstairs. She heard her brother's voice from the kitchen.

"Alex, have you seen Pipsqueak?" she asked as she rounded the corner and saw her mother lifting her beloved Christmas cactus, a droopy plant that was supposed to bloom once a year but never did. Alex was holding a trash bag open under it with one hand and brandishing a plastic fork like a weapon with the other.

"Happy actual birthday, Zoe!" Alex said cheerfully.

"What—" she began to ask.

Using the fork, Alex flicked a brown mass out of the dirt around the cactus and caught it in the trash bag. Mom glared at Zoe. "You need to teach your kitten to use a litter box," she said, her voice clipped. "Not my plants."

*Oh no,* Zoe thought. "I'm sorry. I—" *Please don't make me give her away! Not now. Not when there might be something wrong with her—*

"This is your warning. After this, I don't want to see a single hair of that kitten's tail where it doesn't belong, much less a pile of poop in my favorite plant."

Alex peered into the trash bag. "I don't understand how one little kitten could produce so much poop. It's like the poop miracle. Or anti-miracle."

"Sorry," Zoe said weakly. *I'll make sure she stays out of Mom's way.*

*As soon as I find her again . . .* She glanced around the kitchen, looking for Pipsqueak. She hoped the cat wasn't pooping somewhere else.

"Sorry. I'll get her out of the house. I need to take her to the vet anyway. To have her checked out. Because I want to make sure she's healthy. She's, uh, a growing cat."

"If you can't take care of her yourself, you can't keep her," Mom said. "That was the deal, young lady. You're twelve today. You're old enough to be responsible."

Any thought she had that she might tell her parents about Pipsqueak's quick growth vanished. She didn't want to give them any excuse to take Pipsqueak away. She looked at the Christmas cactus. *Any additional excuse,* she amended.

*I can take care of her myself. She's mine, and I can do this.*

"Can, um, one of you give me a ride to the vet?" As soon as the words were out of her mouth, she knew the answer. Her parents both had work, and Alex would be off at his summer job, an internship with the local newspaper. Mostly fetching coffee. "Sorry. Never mind. My cat. My responsibility."

"I'll be in and out today," Mom said. "I have some meetings at the mayor's office. Go to Surita if you need anything. She's in charge when your father and I aren't home. Do you have any library programs this afternoon?"

Zoe had dodged being sent to camp by promising to attend as many free programs at the library as possible. Mom and Dad had said she could have a relaxing summer if she didn't let her brain rot. "Not today."

"Good. Then use today to take care of your new pet."

Zoe backed out of the kitchen. "Absolutely!"

Resuming her search, she found Pipsqueak sprawled in a patch of sunlight on one of the living room windowsills. She'd knocked over two picture frames to make room. Zoe picked them up, checked to make sure they weren't broken, and then studied Pipsqueak. The cat stretched across the sill, filling it entirely and clearly not feeling the slightest bit guilty. Seeing Zoe, Pipsqueak began to purr, but Zoe felt a mix of worry and fear. *Maybe there's a simple explanation. Maybe she's fine, just fast-growing.*

*Or maybe something is terribly wrong with her.*

It wasn't hard to look up a local vet and make an appointment for that morning. It was harder to figure out how to get there. Her parents and Alex weren't options. Harrison's parents were off at work. That left Surita. *Mom did say to ask Surita if I needed anything.*

"It's not like we can just walk there," Zoe said to Pipsqueak. "It's too far for that."

After texting Harrison the plan, she found a box that seemed the right size for a full-grown cat, cushioned the bottom of it with a towel, and poked plenty of air holes in the top.

She wondered how to get the cat into a box. Finished with napping, Pipsqueak was happily careening around Zoe's bedroom: from the windowsill to her desk to the bed to the dresser and back to the windowsill.

While Zoe looked up "cats in boxes" on her phone, Pipsqueak jumped off the windowsill and into the box. She curled up inside, kneading the cardboard with her claws.

"Okay, that was easy," Zoe said.

"Mew!" Pipsqueak said, giving Zoe her you're-my-hero look, which made Zoe's heart melt.

She glanced back at her phone and saw there were more than two hundred million hits on "cats in boxes." Smiling despite all her worry, she took a photo of Pipsqueak in her box, closed the lid, and carried her over to Harrison's house.

When she got there, Harrison was attempting to bribe his cousin to drive them. So far, he'd offered to do her chores for two days. Harrison's parents believed in chores for everyone, including (and sometimes especially, depending on how messy they were) guests. They'd even given chores to Zoe. "Family helps family" was their motto, and the Acharyas were loose in their definition of *family*.

"I'm fine being your babysitter," Surita was saying. "But I'm not your taxi driver."

Zoe set the box with Pipsqueak in it down on the kitchen table. The box shifted as Pipsqueak moved around.

Surita stopped talking to Harrison, raised her eyebrows, and asked, "What's in the box?" She answered herself: "Pain."

Zoe and Harrison exchanged glances. Harrison shrugged.

"Seriously? It's from *Dune,*" Surita said, exasperated. "A classic. The worms! The spice! Could there be a connection? Never mind. Isn't that box overkill for a kitten?"

"It's not a kitten," Zoe said.

"Oh?" Surita said. "You're finally admitting it's a chipmunk?"

"Please . . . we need a ride to the vet."

Surita sighed heavily, as if they were asking her to donate a kidney, not just take a break from sitting around and playing on her phone. She loved her obscure SF references, but at least it gave Zoe an idea for how to tempt her to drive.

"The vet is across the street from Eastbury Town Comics," Zoe wheedled.

That worked. Surita agreed to drive them.

Sitting in the back seat, Zoe held the box on her lap. As soon as the car started moving, Pipsqueak started meowing. She had a deeper, louder meow than she had had as a kitten—which was, weirdly, yesterday. Zoe missed the tiny *mews*. This meow was heartbreaking. It tugged at Zoe, making her want to open the box and hug Pipsqueak until she felt better. Zoe hugged the box to her chest instead. "Shh, it'll be okay." The box shifted in her lap, as if Pipsqueak were pacing in circles inside it.

At last they reached the vet, and she and Harrison piled out.

"Text me when you're done," Surita told them. Waving, she drove to the comic book store across the street, leaving Zoe and Harrison in the vet parking lot.

Harrison headed for the door, but Zoe hesitated.

"Come on," Harrison said. "The vet will know what's going on with her."

Zoe was more nervous than she'd ever been going to a doctor for herself, even more nervous than when she knew the nurse would do one of those strep throat tests that always made her gag. *Please, please, don't be sick.* Or, if Pipsqueak was sick, Zoe hoped there was a way to fix whatever was wrong. "It'll be okay," she said to the cat.

No longer in the car, Pipsqueak had settled down in the box. Feeling as if that were a sign that the cat trusted her to do the right thing, Zoe followed Harrison inside.

Other animals were in the waiting room with their anxious owners. A woman with hair as poofed as her poodle was paying for medication, and a mustached man with a parrot was giving detailed instructions for how to care for the bird while he was on vacation. This vet boarded animals as well as examined them. Zoe could hear, muffled through the walls, the squawks, squeaks, meows, and barks of various unseen pets.

The poodle barked at Pipsqueak's box.

"Mew!" Pipsqueak cried.

When it was Zoe's turn, the smiling assistant at the front took Zoe's name and address info, recording it all in her computer, then led them into one of the examination rooms. It had a silver metal table with a scale on it, like the kind in the fish market section of the supermarket.

"You should buy a cat carrier," the assistant told them, still with a smile on her face. "Much easier to carry, especially as your darling grows. Now, let's see this beauty."

Zoe put the box on the table and opened it. She peered in. Did Pipsqueak look even bigger after the car ride? Maybe. It was hard to tell with all the fur.

The assistant clucked her tongue. "Ah, what a pretty girl you are. Come on, pretty girl." To Zoe, she said, "Does she have a history of biting?"

"I've only had her three days," Zoe said. "But she hasn't bitten me." She felt as if she should defend Pipsqueak, explain how she hadn't been shy once she'd gotten over her initial fear, that she'd cuddled up to Zoe right from the start, that she was alert and curious and sweet and fun.

Pipsqueak's fur was fluffed, the way it was when she first saw Fibonacci, and her tail was extra bushy. The assistant made soothing noises as she lifted her out, one hand under her stomach and one holding her by the scruff of her neck. Pipsqueak looked plaintively at Zoe and then hissed at the vet's assistant.

"I don't think she likes being held like that," Zoe said. Pipsqueak's pupils were so big, they pushed her irises into thin slivers, and she strained to reach Zoe, but the assistant's grip was tight. Zoe began to regret bringing her here. She hadn't meant to scare her. *It's for her own good,* she reminded herself.

"This type of hold is calming to them, similar to the way their mothers used to carry them." The assistant lowered her onto the scale. "Thirteen point one pounds. Heavy, but not unhealthy for her large bone structure. The vet will be in to see her soon." She lifted Pipsqueak and handed her to Zoe.

Even though Zoe knew Pipsqueak wasn't kitten-size anymore, she forgot to brace herself for the cat's new weight. Pipsqueak filled Zoe's arms, and Zoe took a step back, steadying herself and trying to look like she knew how to hold a grown cat. It felt a lot different from cupping a kitten in the palm of her hand. Pipsqueak's legs sprawled out in all directions, and her fur tickled Zoe's nose. She dug her claws into Zoe's shirt, clinging as if she never wanted to let go.

"Got her?" the assistant asked as she opened the door.

"Oh yeah," Zoe said. "I'm fine."

From outside, a cat meowed.

Ears flicking forward, Pipsqueak immediately squirmed out of Zoe's arms, leaped to the floor, and darted between the assistant's legs. Zoe chased after her. "Pipsqueak, come back!"

The back room of the veterinarian's office was a junction of corridors: one led to a bank of cages partially filled with an assortment of dogs; another had a row of cat cages; and a third had a stack of cages for hamsters, snakes, birds, and other pets. Pipsqueak was climbing across the top of the cages that held rodents.

Still smiling pleasantly, the assistant shooed Zoe back into the exam room. "No worries. We have experience with this. Please stay in the examination room. Only staff is allowed beyond this point."

Zoe retreated to the room, craning her neck to see Pipsqueak leaping from the top of a mouse cage to the top of a supply cabinet. The assistant closed the door, cutting off her view.

"Everything okay?" Harrison asked when Zoe came back in.

Zoe heard a crash, the sound of glass shattering, a woman swearing, and then a loud, indignant *Rrr-row!* A few minutes later the assistant returned with Pipsqueak in her arms and a woman in a doctor's coat beside her. "You have a curious one here!" the assistant said with a perkiness that sounded a bit forced.

"Sorry." Zoe felt as guilty as if she'd been the one wreaking havoc in the back rooms. She also, secretly, felt a little bit proud of Pipsqueak for being clever enough to evade two animal experts, at least for a few seconds. Whatever was wrong with her hadn't affected her cleverness or her speed. "Do I need to pay for damages?"

Just as cheerful-looking as the assistant, the vet laughed. She had a warm chuckle, like a benevolent grandmother. "Most would say paying for the check-up is damage enough."

Harrison laughed, though it was more a dutiful recognizing-an-adult-made-a-joke kind of laugh than a real one. Zoe was too anxious to even fake it.

The assistant held Pipsqueak down on the metal table while the vet examined her, feeling along the cat's belly, behind her ears, and checking beneath her tail. Pipsqueak was quivering, her eyes fixed on Zoe, and Zoe wanted to pick her up and run home. *I'm sorry,* she thought at the cat.

"Good musculature," the vet commented. "Healthy coat."

*So far, so good,* Zoe thought. *Maybe she's okay?* She allowed herself to hope that she'd overreacted. "She's been growing very fast," Zoe ventured.

The vet chuckled again. "I bet your parents say the same about you."

Zoe instinctively slouched her shoulders as Harrison murmured, "Yeah, it's not *exactly* the same."

Using an instrument, the vet peered into Pipsqueak's ears, then pried her mouth open to peer into her throat. She listened to Pipsqueak's heart.

So far the vet hadn't seemed to notice anything unusual. That was good, right? Zoe wanted her to be healthy. "She really has been growing fast," Zoe said. "We were thinking there could be something wrong with her pituitary gland." She pronounced it carefully, hoping she was saying it correctly. She had a vague memory of hearing it mentioned in school, somewhere between talk of mitochondria and chlorophyll. "She was a kitten yesterday."

The vet took on a disapproving look. "That isn't possible."

"I . . . But . . . I mean . . ." She hadn't thought about what to do or say if the vet didn't believe her. This was a vet! A doctor! She'd gone to school! There were diplomas on the wall and everything. She should be able to diagnose whatever was wrong with Pipsqueak.

"It's true!" Harrison said. "She has pictures."

*Great idea!* Zoe pulled out her phone and scrolled through the photos. "This was yesterday. And see, the day before. That's compared to my hand."

"Very funny," the vet said, though she wasn't laughing, and her smile was strained.

"It's not a joke," Harrison said.

"These were obviously taken a while ago. Cats don't grow that quickly." She returned to checking Pipsqueak.

"But the pituitary gland . . ." Zoe tried again.

"There are no documented cases of gigantism in cats. In rare cases, cats *can* have problems with their pituitary gland, but it causes feline acromegaly, most commonly in male cats over age eight. Symptoms include a broader face, poor coat, weight gain—"

"She's definitely had weight gain!" Zoe said, waving her phone in the air. "Look!"

"Acromegaly does not cause size increase like you're describing." The vet gestured at Zoe's photo. "I don't know if you two made a bet or if you just think you're funny, but an animal's health is not a laughing matter."

"We're telling the truth!" Zoe cried. "Please, I just want to know if she's okay."

"In that case, you should be relieved to hear that you have a healthy three-year-old cat. If you have any questions about her care—"

"She isn't even three weeks old!" If Pipsqueak was healthy, why had she grown so much faster than normal kittens? There had to be an explanation!

The vet pressed her lips together. The assistant's smile, which had seemed permanently affixed to her face, was wiped away. "We recommend an annual shot for rabies, distemper, and feline leukemia," the vet said. Before Zoe or Harrison could say anything, the assistant jabbed Pipsqueak in the hind leg with a needle and then deposited her back in the box. "She'll need a booster in three to four weeks. You should also consider having her spayed, if you don't want kittens. Highly recommend, especially if you intend for her to spend any time outside. Please schedule an appointment for both, and no more practical jokes."

She and the assistant swept out of the room.

"Mew," Pipsqueak said plaintively.

One of the dogs from the back room howled.

They closed the box and carried her out and Zoe used her birthday money to pay for the visit as well as a few cans of overly expensive cat food (as the vet's receptionist reminded her, you weren't supposed to feed milk to a full-grown cat unless you wanted to risk digestive issues), a bag of dry food, litter, and a litter box. Harrison texted Surita, and they met her in the parking lot. Surita was carrying a plastic bag that was fat with comic books. She dodged a man trying to drag his dog—a very enthusiastic terrier who was straining at his leash, trying to reach Zoe and Harrison—to his SUV. "Come on, it's not playtime," the man was saying.

Surita gave them a wide berth. When she reached Zoe and Harrison, she glanced back at the dog, which was still desperate to play. "Looks like you've made a new friend."

"Cute puppy," Harrison said.

"Don't get any ideas," Surita said. "Aunt Rachel and Uncle Rizwan aren't going to want another dog."

Harrison held up his hands in surrender. "It's not me you have to worry about. Zoe's the one who collects animals like other people collect Pokémon."

"So what did the vet say about your little rodent?" Surita asked.

"She's healthy," Zoe said.

She told herself that was good news.

Except she still didn't know why Pipsqueak had grown so fast.

# CHAPTER 4

**By the next day,** Pipsqueak was as big as a medium-size dog, and Zoe was officially freaked out. *This isn't possible,* she thought.

Except that it *was* possible, because the evidence was sleeping on her bed.

Rushing to her computer, she typed quickly, her hands shaking. *Maybe this has happened to another cat. Maybe someone somewhere can tell me what to do!* She started with researching pituitary gland diseases, but it looked as if the vet was right—they didn't affect cats the same way they did humans. So she switched to looking for fast-growing animals. After scrolling through photos of twenty-pound Flemish Giant rabbits, she visited the *Guinness World Records* website. She learned that a cat named Merlin from the UK had the world's loudest purr (67.8 decibels), a cat named Alley performed the longest jump (six feet), and a cat named Blackie was the world's richest cat (after inheriting $12.5 million from his late doting owner). Stewie, a gray tabby Maine Coon, held the world record for largest domestic cat at over four feet long, even larger than Pipsqueak (slightly), and the largest non-domesticated cat was a half-lion and half-tiger "liger" named Hercules from South Carolina, who measured four feet tall and nearly eleven feet long.

"Are you related to any lions?" she asked Pipsqueak. Her voice, she thought, sounded on the edge of hysterical. So far, she'd seen absolutely nothing about rapidly growing dog-size cats. *How can this be happening?*

"Mrrow?"

Zoe didn't think Pipsqueak was a liger, but she could be part Maine Coon, Savannah, Chausie, Ragdoll, Norwegian Forest, or Siberian cat—supposedly the largest domestic breeds, though the websites focused more on their final size than the speed of their growth. She didn't find anything about how quickly Stewie the four-foot Maine Coon had grown. *There has to be* something *to explain what's going on!* she thought.

Glancing over her shoulder, she saw Pipsqueak licking the fur on her back. Her tail was thumping against the pillow. Zoe wondered if the cat had picked up on her anxiousness. Zoe grabbed her phone, snapped a photo, and texted Harrison.

He texted back: "Srsly? Come over. Bring cat. Must see."

"Let's go," Zoe said to Pipsqueak. "Maybe Harrison will have an idea about what's happening to you." She scooped the cat into her arms and staggered backward. Pipsqueak weighed as much as Zoe's school backpack.

She readjusted, trying to find a comfortable way to hold her.

Pipsqueak clamped her claws into Zoe's shoulder. "Ow," Zoe said, but she didn't try to dislodge her. There was something a little frantic about how the cat was clinging to Zoe.

*Maybe she's scared too.*

"Don't worry," Zoe said out loud. "I'll take care of you."

*But what's wrong with her?*

The vet had said she was healthy, but that was *before* she'd grown again.

"Okay. We can do this. Whatever's going on, we'll figure it out." She navigated her way down the stairs and called through the closed door of Mom's office, "Going to Harrison's!"

"Have fun! And don't eat all their snacks!" Mom called back.

From the other side of the house, Alex chimed in, "Eat *most* of their snacks and then steal the rest for me!"

"Sure!" Zoe shouted.

"Check with Surita if you need anything," Mom called. "Alex and I will be leaving shortly. Dad is already at work. Your kitten isn't going to make a mess if you leave her unattended, is she?"

"I'm taking her with me," Zoe said. "She . . . uh . . . wants to play with Harrison's dog. They get along great!"

"Good! Glad she's making friends."

Zoe lugged Pipsqueak out the kitchen door and lumbered across the yard to squeeze through the gate between the houses. She let herself in through the Acharyas' back door and lowered Pipsqueak to the floor.

"Harrison?" she called. "I'm here!"

She heard a boy's voice from the den—"Dude, you're kicking me out for a girl?"—and guessed that Harrison had had a friend spend the night.

"A girl and her cat," Harrison corrected.

"But we were in the middle of a level! Wait—you aren't, like, kissing her, are you? Is she your girlfriend? Ooh, Harrison has a *girlfriend!*"

"If you mean Zoe, no, she's not my girlfriend. If you mean her cat . . . we're just dating."

"Seriously. You're ditching me for Zoe the Giraffe?"

Zoe tensed. She couldn't stand the thought of Harrison's other friends talking him out of being friends with her. Especially not now, when she couldn't talk about Pipsqueak with anyone else. She remembered a conversation with her mom, an uncomfortable one where Mom went on and on about how boys and girls change as they get older. She'd talked a lot about changing bodies, which had been bad enough, but she'd also said that sometimes their friendships changed too. Sometimes boys and girls thought they couldn't be friends anymore, the way they were when they were little kids. That's wrong and stupid, Mom had said, of course boys and girls can be friends, but sometimes people have to do some growing up before they realize that. Zoe had sworn she'd never become the kind of person who thought like that, but she knew she couldn't control what other people did. *I don't need to worry about this now, not when I'm already worried about Pipsqueak. Come on, Harrison, don't do this to me. Don't become wrong and stupid.*

Pipsqueak rubbed against her ankles a few times, as if comforting her.

"I'm not ditching you," Harrison said to the boy. "Your mom said she'd be here in five minutes, and that was five minutes ago. And then you're going furniture shopping, because she apparently hates you."

A horn blared from the driveway.

"See? Five minutes after five minutes ago is now."

His friend—who sounded like Dylan, or possibly Kevin, from school—groaned. Zoe listened as Harrison herded him out the door. The front door opened and then shut. She heard Harrison's footsteps as he booked it back toward the kitchen—

And then she heard a hiss, followed by a howl and a crash.

She whipped around and saw Pipsqueak wasn't in the kitchen anymore. *Uh-oh.* Following the sounds of hissing and whimpering, she hurried into the living room, bumping into Harrison in the doorway. He'd also run toward the sound.

Pipsqueak was on the floor by the couch, hissing.

Harrison's Labrador was cowering on top of the bookshelf. Several picture frames, books, and knickknacks lay on the carpet in his wake.

"Um, that's . . ." Harrison pointed at Fibonacci. "How—" He

swallowed hard. "So what do we do?" His voice sounded a little shrill.

"Maybe a ladder?" Zoe wasn't exactly sure how that would work, carrying the dog down. If Fibonacci could climb down the ladder himself . . . "Can dogs climb ladders?"

"Cows can't," Harrison said, his voice almost a squeak. "Their knees are backward."

Lashing her tail, Pipsqueak paced at the base of the bookshelf as if guarding it.

Fibonacci whimpered.

Harrison made a kind of croak-cough, and Zoe glanced at him. Although his face was screwed up with an effort not to, he burst out laughing, doubled over with his hands on his knees. She felt a giggle bubble up, and then she was laughing too.

After a few minutes Harrison wiped his eyes. "Okay, that was the best. Never saw a cat tree a dog. So . . . how do we figure out what's going on with your cat? Should we go back to the vet?"

Suddenly Zoe didn't feel like laughing anymore. She shook her head. "And fork over more money so she can call us liars for a second time?" She never wanted to see that vet again. "Besides, the vet has no idea what's causing this. She'll just say it isn't possible."

"It's *not* possible," Harrison informed her.

"Stewie, a Maine Coon, is over four feet long. *Guinness World Records*. And there's a liger that's nearly eleven." But even as she said it, she knew this wasn't the same. There hadn't been anything online about any fast-growing cat like Pipsqueak. She was, as far as Zoe could tell, unique.

"Liger?"

"Half lion and half tiger."

Harrison raised both his eyebrows as if he didn't believe her. "Which half? Front half lion and back half tiger?"

Zoe gave him a withering glare. "Lion dad and tiger mom."

"How do you know it's not a lion mom and a tiger dad?"

"That's a tigon," Zoe said confidently. "It's smaller."

"Seriously?"

"Would the Internet ever lie? There's also a type of bunny called the Flemish Giant rabbit. The largest one on record weighs fifty-five pounds. It's named Ralph."

Harrison whistled. "That's awesome. And you know what? So is your cat. I know you're worried—your forehead is doing that kind of scrunching thing it does when you're worrying—but look at her! You have an extraordinary cat!"

Zoe opened her mouth to say she had good reason to worry and her forehead should be scrunched, but then she stopped. *He's right,* she thought. *She* is *awesome.* Zoe had been so freaked out that this was happening that she hadn't let herself think about how amazing it was.

Amazing, yes, but also unnatural and a little scary. "But *why* is she extraordinary?" Zoe asked.

Both of them stared at Pipsqueak.

And then the cat spoke. Out loud and unmistakably clear, in a voice that sounded a bit like a running motor. "Stop staring at me. I don't know why this is happening either."

After a full minute of stunned silence, Zoe stuttered, "D-d-did you talk?"

"Obviously, yes, I talked. I talk. Talky, talky, talky— Whoa, wait . . ." Pipsqueak's ears perked forward. "You can understand me? Do you speak Cat?"

Harrison's mouth was flopped open. He managed only, "Unghhh . . ."

"I don't think I speak Cat." Zoe could not stop staring at Pipsqueak, who was staring back at her, equally shocked. "Harrison, can you speak Cat?"

"Nnnungh . . ." He pointed at Pipsqueak with a shaking finger.

*He hears her too,* Zoe thought. *It's not just me. She's talking!* Zoe dropped to her knees next to Pipsqueak. *Wow!* "You're speaking English."

"I'm a cat. Cats can't speak English."

Harrison let out a whoop, as if he were at a football game and Pipsqueak had just scored. "Exactly what I was going to say! Took the words right out of my mouth! Oh, no, wait, even better: cat got my tongue!"

Pipsqueak shot him a glare. "I do not." Then she switched back to Zoe. "If you're not speaking Cat and I'm not speaking Human, then how are we talking?"

"We can't be!" Harrison cheered.

*He's losing it,* Zoe thought. "Harrison, deep breath. Calm down." It would be best if they all stayed calm. Then they could figure out what was going on, if this was some kind of trick . . .

Harrison was not staying calm. He was jumping from foot to foot. "We can't be—because she's a cat!" He said it triumphantly, as if it were proof that this was some kind of illusion.

"We established that already, dog boy," Pipsqueak said.

"Cats can't talk!"

"Again, I can," Pipsqueak said. "Obviously, because I am. Try to keep up." She was fluffed all the way to the tip of her tail, which she was swatting back and forth, agitated. "Why is this happening to me, Zoe?" Her voice was small and kittenlike. "Why am I growing so fast? Why am I talking with humans?"

*She is scared,* Zoe realized. *Just as scared as I am. She doesn't know why this is happening either.* Reaching out, Zoe stroked the back of Pipsqueak's neck. The cat felt tense, and Zoe wished she knew how to make it all better. "I don't know, but we'll figure it out. It'll be okay." *Somehow,* she thought.

Pipsqueak let out a terse "Mew."

"Gotta be magic!" Harrison crowed. And Zoe suddenly realized that Harrison wasn't acting this way because he was scared. He wasn't scared at all; he was excited. "Or aliens. She could be a space cat!"

How could he be excited? This was serious! "You aren't helping," Zoe said.

"Radiation? Government experiment? You found her lost, right? Maybe she escaped from a lab where scientists were creating super cats!"

Zoe supposed that wasn't impossible. "It could be some kind of mutation." Maybe her kitten had been exposed an unstable chemical. Or an ancient mythical stone/amulet/knickknack. TV shows always had an explanation like that. "Maybe she was near a supernatural crystal that made her change."

"Yeah, and next she'll develop laser beams for eyes. *Pew-pew-pew!*" Harrison mimed lasers shooting out of his eyes. "Don't you get it? If there's no ordinary explanation, then there has to be an extraordinary one! And that means amazing things are possible!"

Zoe wasn't sure the ability to talk led directly to laser beams, but this time, she couldn't help grinning. Harrison's enthusiasm was contagious. "So you think she's a superhero cat?"

"Exactly! This is amazing! Now if we can just figure out what caused her amazingness . . . Was she bitten by a radioactive spider or born this way? Gamma radiation? Genetic manipulation?"

Zoe looked at Pipsqueak again, trying to see her the way Harrison saw her. *Maybe he's right,* she thought. *Maybe she's something to marvel at, not worry about.* The possibilities were endless once you gave up worrying about the limits of reality. "Do you think she'll join the X-Men or Magneto?"

"Definitely Magneto," Harrison said. "She's a cat. Professor X is like the dog of mutants—totally friendly to everybody. Magneto wants to go his own way, thinks he's superior to humans, and eats canaries."

"Does not."

"He killed the Black Canary."

She spotted the gleam in Harrison's eyes. "Hah! You're just trying to bait me. That's an entirely different comic universe. Black Canary is DC; Magneto is Marvel."

Behind them, they heard Harrison's cousin Surita say, "I like your friend, Harrison. She's got her facts straight."

At the sound of her voice, Zoe, Harrison, and Pipsqueak all jumped. Quickly Zoe grabbed a blanket from the back of the couch and tossed it over the cat.

Zoe held her breath, waiting for questions or at least a comment. But Surita was reading on her phone as she strolled through the living room to the stairs. She hadn't seen Pipsqueak. Zoe and Harrison exchanged glances. Harrison's lips were vibrating, as if he were about to burst out laughing again. Zoe didn't think there was anything funny about this.

Before Surita reached the stairs, Zoe dared ask a question.

"Surita . . . what would you do if you discovered a miracle? One of your unexplained mysteries? Like if you found Bigfoot in your backyard."

"I'd help him hide," Surita said in a duh-stupid-question voice. "Unlike those idiots outside the Eastbury House of Pizza. Not that anyone believes them."

Pipsqueak flicked her tail, and Zoe bent to adjust the blanket, subtly.

"What idiots?" Harrison asked.

Surita waved her phone at them. "A bunch of kids are saying they saw a flying poodle. Or maybe a sheep. One of them posted a video, but it's fuzzy and far away. Everyone's saying it's fake. And obviously it is. Nothing that cool ever happens in Eastbury."

Zoe and Harrison exchanged glances again.

*A flying poodle?*

"If it did, though," Surita continued, "they should have kept it secret."

"But if you saw a flying poodle or, for example, a giant alien cat," Harrison said, "wouldn't you want to tell the world about it? If only to reassure yourself that you weren't hallucinating?"

"Have you seriously never seen a single movie or read a single book?" Surita said, waving her phone in the air for emphasis. "Do you know what happens whenever people find out about the alien eating candy in the closet or the kid with telekinesis who can also walk through walls? Panic. Destruction. War. Plus a tragic, heart-wrenching moment where the 'lucky' kid who found the miracle has to run from government psychos who only want to dissect the nice giant gorilla, and then King Kong or the alien or the fairy or whatever dies or leaves. End result: every time, the kid and the creature have to say goodbye and never see each other again." She shook her head. "Nah, I'd totally keep it secret. No question. Averting horrific tragedy and heartbreak is *always* the right choice."

She went back to scrolling through her phone, completely oblivious to the fact that Zoe was staring at her in horror. Zoe did not want government psychos, or tragic, heart-wrenching moments, or any of that!

They listened to her footsteps as Surita tromped upstairs.

Only when they heard the door shut to the guest room did they breathe again. Zoe pulled the blanket off Pipsqueak, who rolled onto her back and seized it with her claws. Zoe tugged, and the cat pulled harder.

"Okay, so we keep Pipsqueak a secret?" Harrison asked. "Even though she's the most incredible cat ever?"

"Yes, we absolutely keep her a secret!" Zoe gave up on the blanket. Pipsqueak kicked it with her back paws. They'd already tried to tell the vet, but she hadn't wanted to listen. Of course, Pipsqueak hadn't grown so much then. Or talked. "Right, Pipsqueak? What do you think?" She'd never asked the opinion of a cat before, but it felt right. This was Pipsqueak's future they were talking about. *She should have a say in what we do,* Zoe thought.

Pipsqueak quit playing with the blanket. "The girl who doesn't like kittens said they have to say goodbye every time. I don't want to say goodbye to you. Keep me secret."

Harrison sighed dramatically. "Fine. So what are we supposed to do?"

"You could do something about *that.*" Pipsqueak pointed her nose toward Fibonacci, who still cowered on top of the bookshelf.

All three of them looked up at the dog, who whimpered.

"Oops," Zoe said.

# CHAPTER 5

**EVENTUALLY THEY WERE ABLE TO COAX** Fibonacci down from the bookshelf, knocking off only a few more books. And a picture frame. And two snow globes. He cowered in the corner for the rest of the afternoon while Zoe and Harrison switched between being amazed and being freaked out—and came to zero conclusions about why this was happening and what to do next.

"Zoe?" Surita's voice drifted down from upstairs. "It's five thirty. Your parents are going to want you home for dinner. Probably."

"Okay! Thanks!" Zoe called back. To Pipsqueak, she said, "We have to get you hidden in my bedroom before my family gets home from work."

"And feed me dinner? Please?" Pipsqueak jumped off the couch, where she had been resting, and landed with a solid thump. She trotted toward the kitchen. Zoe followed her, and Harrison followed them. Glancing back, Zoe saw Fibonacci poke his nose around the corner of the couch.

"I'll keep looking online," Harrison said. "See if I can find any clues to all this. Promise you'll text me if she grows more?"

"Maybe she's done growing," Zoe said hopefully. She asked Pipsqueak, "Do you feel done?"

Pipsqueak nosed the back door open. "I feel hungry."

Zoe wondered if that was a bad sign.

"She needs to eat," Harrison said. "She's a growing cat."

"Very funny," Zoe said.

She checked in all directions to make sure no one was watching, and then she scurried across Harrison's yard and hers. Quickly Zoe opened her back door and let Pipsqueak inside. The cat bounded for the refrigerator. "More milk?" she asked, adding a plaintive meow.

"You heard the vet's receptionist," Zoe scolded her. "You're not supposed to have milk if you're not a kitten. And since you're not kitten-size . . ."

"The vet said I'm impossible, and she called you a liar," Pipsqueak said, curling around Zoe's legs and looking up at her with those hero-worship eyes. "I don't think we should listen to anyone at the vet's."

Zoe was tempted to agree, but she was also trying to be responsible. "Just because she doesn't know about supernatural cats doesn't mean she's wrong about your stomach. You don't want to vomit."

"I don't want vomit," Pipsqueak agreed. "I want milk. Please!"

Zoe went for the bag of dry food. "How about some nice kibble?"

"Please, please, mew?" Pipsqueak said plaintively. She rubbed her side against Zoe's leg. "Please, Zoe."

Sighing, Zoe got the milk out of the fridge and filled a bowl on the floor. Pipsqueak immediately began lapping it up. "You are"—Pipsqueak said between licks—"the best, kindest, smartest, nicest"—lick, lick—"human"—lick—"ever." Lick. "Uh-oh."

"What do you mean 'uh-oh'?"

Zoe heard a car pull into the driveway and hurried to the window. Mom was home. She had to get Pipsqueak out of sight. Otherwise Zoe would have a whole lot of explaining to do, and zero explanations. "Pipsqueak—"

She turned around just as the cat threw up on the kitchen floor.

"Sorry," Pipsqueak said miserably.

"You okay?"

"I didn't want to outgrow drinking milk."

The cat seemed okay now that the milk was out of her and pooling across the linoleum. "Come on. I'll bring you food you can digest." She herded Pipsqueak up to her bedroom. "Stay here and stay quiet, okay?"

Shutting the door, Zoe hurried back down to the kitchen and grabbed a wad of paper towels. She was soaking up the milk as Mom walked through the door. "Hi, Mom! Just spilled milk! Sorry. Cleaning it up. Nothing to worry about here!" Zoe winced at herself. *That sounded far too suspicious,* she thought.

"At least you're cleaning it up yourself. Spray it with Lysol, please," Mom said as she dropped her purse on the table, then peered into the fridge. "Why didn't I thaw the chicken?"

*Okay, good. She's not mad about the mess,* Zoe thought. She fetched the Lysol. *And she doesn't seem to have guessed I have a possibly alien or supernatural talking cat in my bedroom.* "We could have pizza?" Zoe suggested.

"You always say that. I swear, you'd eat pizza for every meal if I let you."

"I had cereal for breakfast," Zoe pointed out. "You can even put pineapple on the pizza, which makes it completely healthy. Because of fruit."

"How was your day? Did you have fun with your kitten and Harrison?"

"Great!" *My cat grew and started talking, and I'm really trying hard not to freak out about it, but it's* not *normal.*

"If you promise to keep an eye on her and do your best to keep her out of my plants, you can bring her out of your room. Just for a little while."

"She's asleep," Zoe said quickly.

Zoe thought she heard a noise from her bedroom: "Mrrow?"

"And hungry." Zoe grabbed the bag of cat food and a bowl. "I'll feed her. In my room, so there isn't a mess out here. And then she'll probably sleep."

"I know I wanted you to transition her to being an outside cat as soon as possible, but you might want to keep her inside a while longer. Local news is fussing over some wild animal sighting. A stray of some sort, obviously, though the little old lady they were interviewing insisted the creature was bright green. And then her husband said he wasn't green at all. He said it was a *flying* dog! I love local news. At least when it's not criticizing the mayor's office."

"I'll keep Pipsqueak safely out of sight," Zoe promised. "What kind of flying dog?" She thought of the flying poodle Surita had mentioned.

"Who knows what kind of dog? The impossible kind! Apparently, all the hubbub caused a traffic jam downtown, which is why I didn't ask your father to bring home take-out—a fact I am now regretting, since I didn't thaw the chicken."

"I'll feed my cat while you microwave the pizza?"

At that moment Alex came in the door, as if magically summoned by the word *pizza*. He dumped his backpack by the doorway. "Can we put pineapple on it?" he asked. "Makes it healthy, you know."

"See?" Zoe said.

"We should be teaching you to eat *actual* healthy food," Mom said to Alex. "So you don't eat only junk at college and then come down with scurvy. I'll be mortified if I get a call from your dean telling me my son contracted scurvy due to malnutrition. Or whatever the French translation is for *bad parenting*."

At the word *college,* Zoe's smile faded. In the confusion of everything that was happening with her cat, Zoe had completely forgotten about Alex leaving for his fancy French university at the end of the summer. It felt as if she were hearing the news all over again. Zoe managed to keep her voice light. "Only pirates get scurvy, Mom."

"That's because all they eat on pirate ships is pizza."

Alex winked at Zoe. "Excellent. New career path: piracy!" He crossed the kitchen and peered into the refrigerator. "How's the kitten?"

"So nice of everyone to ask about her," Zoe said. Her smile felt frozen, as if her cheeks had transformed into plastic. "She's asleep. And shy. I'm going to keep her in my room so she's safe from dogs."

"Hey, that reminds me—did you know there was a traffic jam downtown because someone said they saw a flying poodle?"

"First report said it was a green dog, and then it was updated to flying," Mom said. "Were they even talking about the same dog? Maybe there are multiple absurd dogs. Or no dog at all. Honestly, I don't know what is going on at the news station that this even made the broadcast. It isn't April Fools' Day."

"The radio said several people claimed they saw whatever it was. There were a whole bunch of police cars and fire trucks, everyone out looking for it. Completely overran the parking lot near that comic book store."

Zoe wondered what people had seen, then dismissed it as not her problem. She had enough problems on her own. A growing problem.

"I hope they stop causing unnecessary hysteria," Mom said.

"Imagine if they continue spouting nonsense while people try to commute to work in the morning."

Retreating as her mother and brother compared commutes, Zoe brought the cat food to her bedroom. She shut the door behind her and poured the kibble into the bowl while Pipsqueak watched her from the bed. "Family's home," Zoe whispered. "You'll need to stay in here until everyone goes to sleep." She didn't want to imagine what Mom and Alex would say if they saw Pipsqueak now. "You okay?"

"Yes, but . . . If I were a flying poodle, would you still love me?"

Clearly, Pipsqueak had been eavesdropping.

"Of course I would. Are you going to start flying?" She really had zero idea what else Pipsqueak was capable of. All of it was impossible . . . which meant that any of it was possible, as Harrison had pointed out before he launched into yet another string of not-so-plausible explanations. He was becoming obsessed with figuring out why this was happening, but Zoe was more worried about what she was supposed to do about it.

"I don't know," the cat said, "but what if I do? Or what if I grow even bigger? Or, like dog boy said, if I develop laser beams for eyes? Or sprout wings? Or extra heads?"

Zoe sat on the edge of the bed, next to her. She hadn't meant to upset Pipsqueak with all her own worrying. "Hey, I said I'd help you, and I will. Don't worry. If you grow more or develop lasers . . . Well, we'll figure out what to do together, okay?"

Pipsqueak curled around Zoe, pressing against her and looking up at her adoringly. "I'm so glad you were the one who found me. You're even better than milk. I love you, Zoe."

Zoe smiled. "I love you too. I'll be back as soon as I can."

"Come back fast." Then her voice got small. "I don't want to be alone if I'm going to change so much I cause a traffic jam."

"I won't ever leave you," Zoe promised. "You're mine, and I'm yours, for always."

They had microwave pizza for dinner, but Zoe was too distracted to enjoy it. She kept thinking about Pipsqueak waiting for her in her room. Pipsqueak reminded Zoe of all those animals she'd tried to help over the years—though helping *them* had seemed a whole lot simpler. *I hope I can do this.*

She planned to go online again after dinner and see if anyone anywhere had ever dealt with or heard of a talking animal like Pipsqueak. Or if there were any updates on the unusual animal sightings downtown. So far, no one had mentioned seeing a giant talking cat.

*But maybe there will be a clue. There could be some kind of connection between the weird sightings in town and Pipsqueak . . .* It seemed like an awfully big coincidence that someone could have seen an unusual dog around the same time that Zoe met an unusual cat.

Unfortunately, Zoe couldn't leave the table until dinner was over—family rules—and everyone seemed to be lingering over their slices. Instead of inhaling their food, they were busy planning the guest list for Alex's going-away party.

"You don't think it's a terrible idea to mix friends and family?" asked Alex.

Dad grinned at him. "Aw, are you afraid we're going to bring out baby pictures and embarrass you?"

Mom made a note. "Baby pictures. Excellent idea. We'll have a slide show. How about that one where you're in your highchair, naked, with spaghetti dumped on your head?"

Alex buried his face in his hands. "I am going to be paying so much money to therapists. So. Much. Money."

Zoe knew how he felt. Every time Mom and Dad showed anyone an old photo of her, it started the endless "Oh, how much she's grown!" talk, as if she hadn't noticed she couldn't fit into any of her favorite T-shirts.

"You're still on our health plan," Dad said supportively. "Get all the therapy you need."

"We should ask everyone attending to come with an entertaining anecdote about Alex that they can share at high volume," Mom said.

Alex groaned. "I graduated. I didn't *die*."

Dad saved him. "Anecdotes might be a bit much. Besides, you can't predict what's going to come out of Uncle Ernie's mouth."

*So true*, Zoe thought. Uncle Ernie was actually Great-Uncle

Ernie, her dad's uncle. He was infamous for jokes involving either body parts or really bad puns. Bonus points if he managed both in the same joke. Luckily, he lived in Virginia, so he didn't make it to every family party.

"Fair point," Mom conceded. "Remember last time, when he told everyone his limerick about a sewage treatment plant . . ."

All of them shuddered, then laughed. Everyone *liked* Uncle Ernie; they just didn't trust his sense of humor. Zoe wondered how he'd react to a dog-size cat.

"You can't choose your relatives," Dad said, then became serious. "Speaking of relatives, should we invite Alecia?"

There was silence around the kitchen table.

Zoe quit worrying about Pipsqueak for a minute and instead focused on Mom. Aunt Alecia was Mom's younger sister, but they hadn't spoken much lately. Zoe knew they'd had an argument, a bad one, and that was why Aunt Alecia hadn't visited in a while.

*If anyone would know about weird animals, it would be Aunt Alecia. I should have thought of her sooner!*

Aunt Alecia was what her parents liked to call "quirky." Dad said that she "marched to the beat of her own drummer." Mom often replied that she'd fired the drummer and hired a bagpipe band. She lived in New Hampshire, where she carved those wooden lawn ornaments sold by the roadside and in New England country stores: bears, turtles, totem poles. But that wasn't the quirky part. The quirky part was that she believed in aliens and elves and fairies. She was "keeping an open mind on the Loch Ness Monster" and had not ruled out the possibility of Bigfoot.

When Zoe was little, her aunt used to bring her "treasures"—carvings of animals, sometimes mythical ones, that she'd made. As Zoe got older, she loved her aunt's cheerful descriptions of creatures that didn't exist. Zoe missed her visits. She'd always been one of Zoe's favorite people. Aunt Alecia used to ask about Zoe's rescue attempts and seemed to really listen and care about what Zoe said. And she'd give great advice, such as what to do if a bird fell out of a nest or how to help a stranded fish. She knew a lot about helping animals.

Zoe thought that Aunt Alecia would believe in a talking cat.

She wondered now if Aunt Alecia had ever met one.

"I don't think that's a good idea," Mom said with a sigh. "She was angry after our last conversation, even though I apologized as much as I could have, given that I was right."

"You could invite her," Dad suggested. "As a new olive branch."

*Yes, invite her!* Zoe thought. *If she comes, I can ask her about giant cats. Maybe even introduce her to Pipsqueak.* Zoe was sure her quirky aunt would be willing to help her figure out what to do. Except that Alex's party wouldn't happen for several weeks, and that was a long time to wait.

"She disconnected her phone years ago and doesn't do email—because, she said, she doesn't want to be 'traceable.' All

I did was ask her to tone it down a little since I was going to be switching to a job in the public eye, in order to work on the mayor's new environmental initiative. Even she had to agree it's important . . ."

"You could send a letter," Dad said.

Mom stood and cleared her plate. "I don't know that this is the best time for my sister to visit. Maybe once things settle down at work . . . I want to make a difference, and I can't do that if the press is more focused on my oddball sister than on the mayor's policies. Just look at the circus over the ridiculous 'flying dog.' They love sensational stories."

Zoe noticed that she and Alex were holding themselves very still, as if that could make them invisible. This wasn't the kind of conversation they wanted to be a part of.

"It's just that you've said you regret how distant you two have become," Dad said. "I thought this could be an opportunity to change things."

"She'll never change the way she is." Mom sighed, then rubbed her eyes as if she were tired. "She brings complications that I don't have time for right now." She smiled brightly, as if trying to erase the entire conversation. "Speaking of complications . . . if this wild animal sighting situation isn't resolved soon, the mayor's office may need to address it. I'll need to be prepared with a statement." She retreated to her office. The door closed.

Zoe, Alex, and Dad sat in silence at the kitchen table. *Guess*

*Mom is done talking about that,* Zoe thought. She wondered how Mom would react to the "complication" of a giant cat and was certain the answer was "not well." Aunt Alecia, though, she'd understand . . . wouldn't she? She'd listen and try to help, or at least offer advice. Zoe wished she could contact her aunt on her own . . .

She heard a *thump* from up in her bedroom.

*Pipsqueak!*

Zoe jumped up. "I just have to check on whatever fell . . . because of . . . gravity. Excuse me."

"Was that your kitten?" Alex asked. "Want help?"

"All set. Thanks!" She fled upstairs, slipped into her room, and shut the door behind her.

Pipsqueak was perched on Zoe's desk, filling the entire surface. Her face was smushed against the window. Everything that had been on the desk, except (miraculously) for one can full of pencils, littered the floor.

"Pipsqueak, what are you—"

A bird sat on the tree outside the window.

"I don't know why, but I really, really want it," Pipsqueak said intently.

She pawed the glass, and Zoe had the sudden worry that it was going to break. Pipsqueak might not know her own strength. Certainly she hadn't been careful leaping onto the desk. Bending, Zoe began to pick up her books and papers. "I know the bird is fascinating, and all your instincts are telling you to chase it, but can you listen to me for one second? I have an aunt who knows about weird stuff . . . She's really great. You'd like her. And she believes in elves and fairies and such, so I think she'd like you. Anyway, she always used to offer me advice with my animal rescues . . . She might have ideas on how to help you. Maybe she'll know what's happening. Maybe she'll even know how to reverse this and how to help get you back to normal! It's possible. I mean, it's not any more impossible than you growing and talking in the first place. I know we said we'd keep you a secret, but do you mind if I write to her for advice? I think it's worth a try."

"If I say you can write to her, can I chase that bird? Please, please, please?"

"No."

As the bird hopped along the branch, Pipsqueak's tail lashed from side to side. "But I *really* want that bird! Please, Zoe!"

"You really wanted milk, and that wasn't a good idea." The more Zoe thought about it, the more she thought contacting Aunt Alecia *was* a good idea. "Can I trust you to stay here and not bash through the window while I get her address?"

"No?" the cat said hopefully.

"Pipsqueak?"

"Okay. Fine." She flopped down on the desk, her tail twitching.

Zoe hesitated a moment, then hurried down to Mom's office

and knocked on the door. She could hear the sounds of Alex and Dad in the kitchen, cleaning up from dinner.

"I'm working!" Mom called through the door. "Are you dying or bleeding?"

Zoe stuck her head in. "Can I look at your phone?"

Mom was scowling at her computer screen and clicking on her mouse as if it had offended her. "Why? You have your own."

She thought fast. "I want to see if yours has any embarrassing pictures of Alex. You know, for his graduation/going-away party."

Mom smiled. "Glad you're taking an interest in his party. We were worried you were going to sulk about it. You haven't been very good at hiding how you feel about his plans. You know it's a wonderful opportunity for him. As your father keeps saying, it's an adventure of a lifetime."

Zoe did *not* want to talk about this right now. "Yeah. Um, sorry?"

With another smile, Mom handed over her phone. "I'm just glad you're coming around."

"Right. Yep. I am." Clutching the phone, Zoe scooted out into the hallway and scrolled through, looking for Aunt Alecia's contact info. *There it is.* She copied the address into her own phone and then found paper, an envelope, and a stamp.

Shutting herself in her room with Pipsqueak, she sat on her bed and wrote the letter.

*Dear Aunt Alecia,*

*I have a problem with my cat that I think you might be able to help with. She's unusual. You see, she recently started growing much faster than an ordinary cat . . .*

Zoe didn't mention the talking. She didn't want to give her aunt extra reasons to doubt her, but she did write about the other animal sightings in town—the flying poodle or green dog or whatever it was. She didn't know if it was connected to what was happening to Pipsqueak or not, but it seemed important enough to mention, if only as proof that she wasn't the only one who'd seen an unusual animal. She included a plea for advice and whatever else Aunt Alecia could do, and she signed it, *Your niece, Zoe.*

Hearing a thump and a yowl, she jumped up.

Pipsqueak had tumbled off the desk, along with the can of pencils, and was shaking out her fur. The bird had flown away, and Pipsqueak looked unhurt.

"Sorry," Pipsqueak said. "I forgot I'm bigger now."

Zoe added to the letter: *Please write back soon!*

# CHAPTER 6

**ZOE SLEPT ON THE FLOOR.** She didn't fit in the bed.

Especially since Pipsqueak slept diagonally.

She woke, uncomfortable, to a knocking on her door. "Zoe?" Dad called from the hallway. "Are you awake, Zoomaroo?"

The knob began to twist.

She shot upright. "Don't come in! I'm getting dressed!"

The knob quit turning.

"Just wanted to make sure you didn't sleep through the day," Dad said. "Alex and I are off to work. Your mom is already at the office. She has a few things to do that she can't do from home, but she'll have her cell phone if there's an emergency, and she'll be back as soon as she can. And of course, Surita will be home all day. She's in charge if anything comes up. See you at dinnertime!"

"Yep, see you!" Zoe sagged in relief before glancing at Pipsqueak.

She'd grown again.

Easily the size of a full-grown African lion, Pipsqueak filled the entire bed.

*This is impossible,* Zoe thought. It was already impossible before this morning. But now . . . *it's even more impossible.* She was one hundred percent certain that no cat in the *Guinness World Records* had ever grown this large this quickly. "You grew again!" She heard the panic in her voice and tried to sound more positive: "Harrison is going to love this!" But her enthusiasm sounded fake even to her own ears. She couldn't pretend this was okay.

Pipsqueak began kneading the bed with her claws. "*You* don't love this. I could tell when you saw me. I didn't mean to grow *more!*"

"Shh. Calm down. I know you didn't. And I'm sorry—I was just surprised. We'll find a way to help you." She didn't know how she was going to restore Pipsqueak to an ordinary size, but it seemed like the right thing to say. "Everything will be fine."

"You say that a lot. I'm starting to think it's more a wish than a fact. Did you hear from your aunt? Does she know how to fix me?"

Zoe had put the letter to Aunt Alecia in the mail the night before, but it was still sitting in their mailbox. Far too soon for a reply. "It'll be a few days." She hoped her aunt had useful advice. "We'll just have to keep you out of sight until we hear from her."

That was doable while her family was busy with work, but it was going to get a lot harder once the construction workers came to work on the laundry room, a week from Monday. She hoped Aunt Alecia wrote back quickly. She had just over a week before the house would be full of strangers.

Rising up, Pipsqueak peered out the window. Her tail swished back and forth. "Can we go to dog boy's house?"

Zoe didn't think it was likely she could get a lion-size cat into Harrison's house without Harrison's family noticing. Or without giving his dog heart failure. "I don't think we should leave my room."

"What if I keep growing and outgrow this room? Or the whole house?" Pipsqueak was trembling, which made her whiskers quiver and her fur vibrate. "I just found a home! I don't want to lose it! I don't want to lose *you!*"

Climbing onto the bed with Pipsqueak, Zoe wrapped her arms around her neck. She wasn't sure what to say—she couldn't promise that the cat wouldn't keep growing. Zoe looked out the window over Pipsqueak's furry head. She saw their barbecue grill in the backyard, along with their swing set, unused for years, and the shed.

The shed was tucked into the corner of the yard, and it went unused most of the time. Alex had nicknamed it the Shed of Possibilities. It was supposed to be Dad's pottery shed, back when he toyed with taking up pottery. Then it was Mom's fix-it shed when she was in her do-it-yourself stage. When Alex was learning how to play saxophone and sounded like a dying cow, it was a music shed. Then it was a gardening shed. And now it was a store-random-stuff shed. *Maybe it can also be home to a giant cat,* Zoe thought.

"How would you feel about having your own room?" Zoe asked.

She could set it up with a bucket of kibble, a bucket of water, and a lot of blankets for a bed. Whenever no one was watching, Pipsqueak could use the backyard as a litter box, and once the construction workers started coming, she could hide whenever they were here.

"Outside? Away from you?" Pipsqueak asked.

"Outside is where the birds are." It was a brilliant idea. She'd be out of sight of Zoe's family but still close by, and she'd have plenty of room to grow. The shed had a high ceiling and wide barn doors; Dad had wanted extra room for shelves he'd never filled.

"Birds? Really? You are the best human ever. Let's go."

Together, they went outside.

While Pipsqueak sniffed at the grass, Zoe opened the shed doors. Dust billowed out. Coughing, she waved it away and poked her head in. Sunlight streamed through the high window, causing the bits of dust in the air to sparkle. The shed was stuffed with old lawn equipment, a broken potter's wheel, and a lot of boxes—some full and many others empty.

*Perfect,* she thought.

Zoe set to work. She shoved an old lawn mower into one corner of the shed and the broken potter's wheel into another, then hauled all the empty boxes out onto the lawn to be added to the recycling later. She also discovered three full boxes of books—her parents' old textbooks and lots of paperbacks—which she put back in the shed but in a neater pile, up on a shelf.

Once she got the shed cleared out enough, she raided the laundry room in the basement for old sheets and towels. Dragging them outside, she set them up as a soft nest within the shed. "Pipsqueak?" she called.

Instead of the cat, Harrison stuck his head into the shed. "Hi. I came to warn you that we have to keep Pipsqueak hidden, but I see you're already working on a hiding place."

"She stole the bed last night. So I'm making her a new bed." She added another sheet to the stack. *Looks comfy to me,* she thought. *Pipsqueak's going to love it.* "Wait, what do you mean you came to warn me? We already agreed to keep her secret."

"Yeah, that was before there were more flying poodle sightings. They're calling it a UFP, for Unidentified Flying Poodle." He showed her his phone, scrolling through photo after photo of downtown Eastbury, swamped with tourists and their cell phones.

"You think there's really a flying dog?" A week earlier Zoe would never have believed it, but Pipsqueak was proof that impossible creatures were possible.

"It doesn't matter whether I do or not," Harrison said. "All these people believe it. But they'd be just as happy to take a selfie with a giant talking cat and then post it online for everyone to see."

That wasn't so bad. "A photo isn't terrible."

"Yeah, until it brings the scientists and the military and everyone else that Surita said we need to watch out for. It would be an Internet circus. Not to mention all the reporters and animal control people and just plain curious people who'd start pounding on your door."

Mom would hate an Internet circus. She wanted all attention on her new environmental policy, not on their family. If having a weird sister was a problem, it would be a thousand times worse having a daughter with an overlarge talking cat. "We need to stay out of sight of the tourists," Zoe said.

"Well, the shed is a brilliant idea."

Zoe grinned, pleased. She'd thought so too. "Pipsqueak, want to try it out?"

Pipsqueak didn't answer.

"I think she likes the boxes better," Harrison said.

Zoe peeked out of the shed, and sure enough, Pipsqueak had squirmed into the mountain of empty boxes and was napping. Zoe laughed. She thought of the thousands of online photos of cats in boxes. "Okay then. Redesign!"

Evicting Pipsqueak from the boxes, Zoe tossed a box to Harrison, who caught it and tossed it into the shed. She threw the next box. And the next.

"Faster!" Harrison called.

She tossed box after box until he was buried in cardboard and both of them were laughing. Together they created a box fort, piling the boxes high inside the shed in the shape of an igloo, large enough for a lion-size cat. They spread the old towels and sheets inside, making a comfy bed.

Finishing, Zoe called to Pipsqueak, "Come try it out!"

Pipsqueak trotted in, sniffed the boxes, and then crawled inside the box igloo.

"What if she doesn't like it?" Zoe whispered to Harrison, suddenly anxious again. She didn't have a backup plan for where Pipsqueak could live. If the shed didn't work . . .

The cat stuck her nose out. "It's perfect!" she declared, purring loudly.

*See, I can handle this!* Zoe thought. *Tourists or no tourists, I can take care of her and keep her safe and happy.* She'd never felt so proud of herself. It was a really nice feeling. *I did this.*

From the house, Zoe heard her mother call, "Zoe!"

"Uh-oh. Stay here," Zoe told Pipsqueak. She had hoped Mom would be stuck at the mayor's office a bit longer. Surita was a wonderfully inattentive babysitter.

Zoe scurried out of the shed with Harrison.

Hands on her hips, Mom stood in the kitchen doorway surveying the mess of gardening and pottery supplies Zoe had pulled out of the shed and strewn across the yard. "What are you doing?"

In her best perky voice Zoe said, "Harrison and I are building a box fort! That's okay, Mom, isn't it?"

Mom sighed again. "Your father and I should have insisted on camp—we shouldn't have given you veto power on that. But we thought with Alex going away, one laidback summer with just family and friends was a good idea."

"It's still a good idea," Zoe insisted. She couldn't go to camp and leave Pipsqueak, not with people on the lookout for weird animals. "You said I could spend the summer at home as long as I didn't spend all my time moping or letting my brain rot. And I'm not! Box fort!"

*Rattle, clank*—from the shed.

"Wind," Harrison said quickly, at the same time as Zoe said "Squirrels."

"I promise I'll clean everything up," Zoe said. "You don't need to worry about a thing." *Stay inside, Pipsqueak!* Smiling as innocently as she could, she leaned against the shed door.

Mom studied them both for a moment, clearly suspicious but just as clearly not sure what she was suspicious about, and then her phone beeped. Another sigh. "First you wanted a kitten, and now you're redecorating the backyard. You know, I pictured a much calmer summer."

*So did I,* Zoe thought.

"Speaking of your new kitten, where is Pipsqueak? You haven't left her unsupervised where she could get into trouble, have you? She's your responsibility."

Zoe and Harrison looked at each other. "She's at Harrison's house," Zoe said.

"Yeah, with my cousin."

"Surita loves kittens," Zoe said, hoping her mom never talked to Surita about her views on kittens, puppies, and rainbows. "She's happy to watch her. And us. She's been keeping a close eye on us. So none of us get into trouble."

"Fine," Mom said. "I don't want to find a single gardening shear on the lawn." Mom wagged her finger. "And don't injure yourself on any trowels or rakes or anything. And don't touch any poison ivy. Or play in traffic. Or with matches. Or juggle knives."

Answering her phone, Mom hurried back inside. As the kitchen door swung shut, the shed shook again. *Crash, rattle, squeak.* And then a muffled "Oops!"

Zoe and Harrison opened the shed door to see Pipsqueak standing king-of-the-mountain style on top of all the boxes, several of which were crushed beneath her. Tools had fallen off the shed walls, and the pottery wheel had tipped on its side. One box of books had spilled off the shelf.

Pipsqueak stared at them guiltily, and they stared back. "Sorry."

"It's okay," Zoe said.

"Can I read one of these books?" Pipsqueak asked.

"Sure," Zoe said automatically, then: "Do you know how to read?"

Picking up a book between her paws, Pipsqueak opened it and used a claw to turn a page. "Yes, I do!" She sounded delighted.

Zoe tried to decide what was more amazing: that her cat had grown, that she could talk, or that she could read without a single lesson. She watched Pipsqueak study the words, carefully turning pages with one extended claw. "You read," she said, "and we'll clean up."

As Pipsqueak turned the pages, Zoe began cleaning up the gardening supplies and the rest of the mess, finding new homes for things in the garage or behind the shed, and straightening the boxes.

Harrison half helped while staring at his phone. "So she can talk *and* read . . . That's new data! It should help us figure out why . . . Hey, look, there's been another sighting of the UFP. This one is behind the elementary school."

Their old elementary school wasn't far away. Zoe hoped the poodle went in some other direction soon. The last thing she needed was for some weird dog to accidentally lead people closer to Pipsqueak.

The more she thought about it, the more it seemed a huge coincidence that there could be two supernatural creatures in their little town at the same time. Could there really be some connection?

"Maybe the Unidentified Flying Poodle and Pipsqueak both escaped from a lab," Harrison said, apparently thinking the same thing Zoe was. "Pipsqueak could be a science experiment."

"Or she could be the pet of a giant cat lady," Zoe suggested, "and her owner is going to climb down the beanstalk to search for her."

"Or a superhero's sidekick."

Looking up from her book, Pipsqueak said, "I'm no one's sidekick. And I do *not* belong to a giant cat lady. I belong to you, Zoe. And you belong to me. You said so. *You're mine, and I'm yours. And I will take care of you forever and ever.*"

"I will," Zoe promised. "But until we know how to help you, you have to stay hidden. Can you do that? If you're seen, you could be taken away. At best, we'll have tourists camped out on our front lawn day and night. At worst, we'll have SWAT teams and military and—"

"Zoe, you're scaring her," Harrison said. "And me. This is why she's in the shed. It was a good idea! She'll be safe here."

*What if it's not enough?* Zoe thought. *Then what will we do?*

"I'll stay in the shed," Pipsqueak vowed. "No one will know I'm—"

All of them jumped as Zoe's mom's voice rang out again, "Zoe, time to come inside. Harrison, you should head home too."

Quickly Zoe said to Pipsqueak, "Stay hidden. And don't worry. You'll be fine here."

Retreating into her box fort, Pipsqueak stuck her head deep into one of the larger boxes. If you peeked inside the fort, the rest of her body, from the neck down, was still visible, but her face was in the box.

With one last smile at Pipsqueak, Zoe hurried out of the shed, and Harrison shut the door behind them. "Kind of would love to see the look on your mom's face if we told her we had a giant talking cat in the shed."

"But we're not going to do that, right?" Zoe said.

"Right."

"No more dithering, you two!" Mom called. "The news is reporting more sightings of that flying dog, one of them just half a mile from here. They're recommending keeping all children and pets inside until the menace—flying or not—is caught."

"Definitely no telling anyone," Zoe whispered to Harrison.

That evening, after saying good night to Mom, Dad, and Alex, Zoe waited until she heard the TV in the living room switch on, and then she climbed out of her bedroom window. She wasn't as short and scrawny as Harrison, and it took her longer to maneuver, but she made it. By the light of the kitchen, she crept across the yard to the shed.

Zoe knocked, then opened the shed door. "It's me."

Pipsqueak padded outside. "Finally. I was lonely waiting for you." She flopped on the grass, and Zoe sat next to her, close enough to plunge her arms into the cat's fur and pet her neck and cheek. It felt like hugging a very fluffy lion.

"How did you know I'd come?" Zoe wondered if she'd become telepathic.

"I didn't. But I hoped you would."

"I always will," Zoe said firmly. "Just like you said: you're my cat, and I'm your person. You can count on that."

It was a clear summer night, stars visible to the haze of the horizon, fireflies flickering around the yard, and crickets chirping. An enormous cat was purring. *You know, a typical summer night.*

A perfect *summer night,* Zoe corrected herself.

"It's nice out." She thought of the flying poodle and wondered where it was, what it was, and if it was still half a mile away, looking up at the stars too.

"Mmm. I'm still growing." Rolling onto her back, Pipsqueak kicked one paw skyward, as if playing with an invisible ball of yarn. "What if I don't ever stop?"

"You'll stop."

"You're worried I won't," Pipsqueak said. "I can tell."

There wasn't much Zoe could say to that. It was true. The shed would work only so long as Pipsqueak fit into it. If she grew to, say, larger than an elephant, they could have a problem. Zoe hoped Aunt Alecia would know what to do. "We'll find a way to stop whatever's happening to you."

They lay side by side, not touching, looking up at the stars. Zoe wondered what Pipsqueak was thinking about. Did she have any idea where she came from? Did she wonder if there were others like her?

"Do you think fireflies are tasty?" Pipsqueak asked.

*Okay, so she's not worrying* that *much.* "Yuck. No. They're bugs."

"Crickets are tasty."

"Why are you eating bugs? I feed you kibble."

"For the record, I know you're feeding me Harrison's dog food," Pipsqueak said. "I can read the label. I may go on a hunger strike in protest." She thought about it for a moment. "After breakfast tomorrow."

"You ate all the cat food from the vet, and Harrison's parents buy economy-size dog food," Zoe said. "But I'll find a way to get more cat food. How do you even know what a hunger strike is?"

"*World History: From Pyramids to Pyramid Schemes,*" the cat said. "Eleventh edition. It was on the shelf in the shed. I read it while you were inside with your family. I thought it would have a lot more cats in it. There was a cat on the cover."

"Oh." Zoe had no idea what to say to that. "Pipsqueak . . . We should start thinking about what we'll do if I can't keep you safe here." She hated to say it, but all it would take would be for Pipsqueak to step out of her shed to relieve herself or chase a butterfly at the same time as one of the construction workers glanced into the backyard. Or for Mom or Dad to decide they needed something from the shed. Or for Alex to insist on seeing her new tiny kitten. As much as she tried to convince herself that everything was fine, it could dip into VERY NOT FINE very quickly. "I've sent that letter to my aunt, but it will still be a few days until I hear back, and even then, she might not know what—"

"I don't want to talk about this right now," Pipsqueak announced. "Stop talking." She placed her paw on Zoe's face. Her claws weren't out, and the pads of her paws were as soft as pillows. It tickled a little. "Everything's fine at this moment in time, and that's enough."

Zoe laughed in spite of herself. "All right. What do you want to talk about?"

"Fireflies," Pipsqueak said. "I'm going to eat one."

"Suit yourself."

Stretching her back, Pipsqueak stood. She sniffed the air. She held herself still, and when a firefly blinked, she bounded over, snapping at it. Lying on the ground, Zoe watched her—the giant cat bouncing all around her. The cat's jaws closed over a patch of air where there was a firefly.

Its light winked out.

Then Pipsqueak spat. "Yuck."

"Told you so," Zoe said.

"Humph." Pipsqueak plopped back down on the grass. They resumed looking at the stars, and Zoe tried to identify the North Star. It was up from the Big Dipper. Squinting, she traced a line with her finger.

Maybe this couldn't last. Maybe Pipsqueak would grow too big for the shed. Maybe she'd be spotted. But none of that had happened yet. And there was the chance it wouldn't. *And like Pipsqueak said, that's enough,* Zoe thought. *She's happy.*

*And so am I.*

She had to stop worrying so much.

*This is going to work.*

# CHAPTER 7

*THIS IS NOT GOING TO WORK,* Zoe thought five days later.

She'd squirreled herself away in her room to read through Aunt Alecia's letter, which had finally arrived. So far, she'd read it twice. While her family watched TV in the living room after dinner, she read through it a third time:

*Dear Zoe,*

*Thank you for reaching out to me! You did exactly the right thing. I have helped many extraordinary creatures, and I can help your cat too. Just bring your cat to my house. I'll explain everything once you get here.*

*I know you must be worried, but keep your wits about you and everything will be fine. Your life will be back to normal before you know it.*

*Come as soon as you can.*

*And do NOT let anyone see her. That's very important—her safety depends on your secrecy.*

*Love,*

*Aunt Alecia*

On the surface, it sounded like the perfect solution: just take Pipsqueak to New Hampshire, and Aunt Alecia would help them. In fact, it was even better than Zoe had dared hope. She could help Pipsqueak! Maybe stop her from growing larger. Or even change her back to her proper size.

*But I can't go to New Hampshire.* How would she get there? It wasn't as if she could say, "Hey, Mom, Dad, can you drive me and my giant cat to New Hampshire?" No, she'd have to write back to Aunt Alecia and ask her to come here. In the meantime, Pipsqueak would be safest hidden in the shed. She was happy there. She had plenty to read, and Zoe was sure she'd be able to keep her family from discovering her before Aunt Alecia arrived.

She calculated how long it would take: two days for her letter to arrive, another for Aunt Alecia to drive down. At most three days. Less, if Aunt Alecia left as soon as she received the letter. It couldn't be more than a few hours' drive. *I can keep Pipsqueak hidden for three more days.*

Unless Aunt Alecia didn't want to come. She and Mom weren't speaking . . . *What if I send another letter, and Aunt Alecia* doesn't *come?* So far, Zoe had managed to keep Pipsqueak hidden, but there was a limit to how long the excuses of "my kitten's shy" or asleep or at Harrison's were going to work, or how long it would be before someone wanted to fetch something from the shed. Plus, construction on the new laundry room would start soon, and more people would be tromping through the house all day, throwing everything into chaos and glancing out the windows into the backyard, where Pipsqueak was hidden. And even if they miraculously weathered all that, Pipsqueak was still growing. At some point she could outgrow the shed, and then what?

Zoe heard the doorbell ring and then footsteps as someone went to answer it.

"Zoe!" Alex called. "A reporter wants to talk to you!"

*A reporter?* she wondered. *Why would a reporter want me?* She thought immediately of Pipsqueak. Surita had predicted reporters would come if they knew about her . . .

Quickly Zoe folded the letter and hid it in her dresser drawer. She hurried downstairs. Mom and Alex were standing at the door, chatting with a woman who had her phone out, her finger poised over the screen. When Zoe approached, the woman smiled politely.

"I thought she was here to talk to Mom," Alex said. "But she's here for you."

"Are you the owner of a kitten named"—the reporter consulted her phone—"Pipsqueak?"

Zoe glanced at Mom. Zoe had never had a reporter talk to her before. Her mom nodded, encouraging her to answer. "Um, yes?" Zoe said.

"And did you bring this kitten to Eastbury Veterinary for a recent checkup?"

*Oh no.* "Um . . ." She looked again at her mother.

"News 12 is following up on a lead," Mom explained. "The

owner of the 'flying poodle' claims she went to the local vet recently, so they're talking with other pet owners who visited the same day."

"*Alleged* flying poodle," the reporter said. "It was supposedly last sighted a few blocks from here. Did you see anything unusual during your visit?"

*Aside from a cat who should have been a kitten . . .* "Nothing at all."

The reporter held up her phone, displaying a photo of a poodle. "Do you remember seeing this dog?"

"No. Um . . . maybe?" She'd seen a poodle in the waiting room. Could it have been the same one? "Yes, there was a dog that looked like that. But it wasn't flying. It seemed like an ordinary poodle."

"And did anything unusual happen during your exam?"

*The vet didn't believe me about Pipsqueak.* "Nope."

The reporter made more notes. "Has your cat exhibited any abnormal behavior?" It took all of Zoe's self-restraint not to glance toward the back of the house. She shook her head. "My kitten's fine. Totally normal. No problems." She tried a smile, but it felt as fake as a doll's smile, so she stopped. Putting her hands behind her back, she twisted them nervously.

"Can I see her?"

*No!* she shouted silently.

"Ooh, does this mean our photo will be on the news?" Alex asked. "Hey, Zoomaroo, your kitten's going to be famous!"

The reporter snorted. "Only if your cat sprouted wings."

Alex laughed, and Zoe joined in halfheartedly. *I can't say yes. What can I tell her that will make her go away?* "I'm sorry, but I let her outside after dinner. She's off exploring the neighborhood somewhere. You know how cats are."

"She's not missing, is she?" The reporter perked up. Her finger twitched over her phone, ready to take a note.

"Not missing. Just out playing."

The reporter studied Zoe for a while, and Zoe did her best to look as innocent as possible. "All right. Well, thank you for your time. Please contact me if you notice anything out of the ordinary, either in your pet or any neighboring animals." She handed Zoe's mom a business card.

Alex shut the door as she left.

"Zoe, I thought I told you to keep your kitten in your room," Mom scolded. "With all the strange animal sightings, it's not safe to let her out unsupervised."

"She's safely inside . . ." Zoe's mouth felt dry, as if it were coated in chalk. "I didn't want her getting scared. She's shy around anyone but me."

"You could have said that instead of lying to that nice reporter," Mom said.

"I'm sorry. I just . . . didn't think she'd understand."

Mom hesitated, as if she were debating whether this warranted a larger lecture, but instead she asked, "Everything is okay with

Pipsqueak, isn't it? I haven't seen her since the Christmas cactus incident."

"I've been trying to keep her out of your way," Zoe said. "Really, though, she's fine. I don't know what that reporter was talking about."

"We should get costume wings and attach them to Zoe's kitten," Alex said. "I bet that's what the dog's owner did. In a few weeks it'll be revealed as a hoax, and then she'll go on all the talk shows . . ." He continued talking as he and Mom drifted back to join Dad in the living room.

Zoe tuned him out, watching through the window as the reporter got in her car and drove away. *That was close.* She tried to calm her racing heart. *But it's over. The reporter's gone. So long as no one actually finds a real flying poodle or anything, maybe all of this will die down, and the only people I'll have to worry about hiding Pipsqueak from will be my family. At least until construction starts next week . . .*

Early the next morning, Zoe's phone beeped. She'd climbed into bed late at night after stargazing again with Pipsqueak, so it felt extra early. Flopping over, she read the screen containing Harrison's text: "Check Channel 5 News," plus a link.

Rubbing her eyes as she sat up, instantly awake now, she clicked on it.

Scrolling through, she read fast: the Unidentified Flying Poodle had been caught, and it was in fact a poodle that could fly, or at least float. Now that the UFP was confirmed as real, fans of unexplained phenomena were pouring into Eastbury along with scientists from across the United States.

Zoe skimmed, looking for what happened to the poodle: it had been taken away for study at an unnamed facility in Boston. "Taken away," Zoe whispered.

Surita had been right.

As her stomach sank into her feet, Zoe read another article. This one confirmed that the poodle had been traced back to a local veterinary clinic, just as that reporter had said. "Before we brought Fluffy in," the owner was quoted, "she was an ordinary poodle. Not *ordinary*. She's pedigree! Would have been a show dog, except for her teeth. She has an overbite." After the clinic, the poodle had disappeared from her owner's backyard, with no sign of digging free or breaking through the fence, and she'd been caught drifting across Route 20 in Shrewsbury, floating after a terrified squirrel. There were rumors that the poodle had even been talking, but that was dismissed as too far-fetched, especially since there were also rumors that the poodle was bilingual (French and English), able to read, and skilled at tap dancing. It was difficult to tell what was true and what was a hoax. Zoe saw dozens of Photoshopped pictures of flying dogs, cats, and rabbits. She even saw one meme devoted to flying tacos floating through the center of Eastbury.

But if the poodle really could talk (and read), then maybe she was like Pipsqueak, only flying instead of growing.

According to the article, everyone was on the lookout for other animal anomalies. *It's not over,* Zoe thought. *It's worse.* News of the UFP had spread all over social media. There were dozens, maybe hundreds, more posts about their town and the poodle. And people were debating what it meant, what to do, and what else could be out there.

But even worse were the pictures of the poodle owner's house. People were camped out on the lawn, pressed against the window, hounding the owner whenever she stepped outside.

*If people find Pipsqueak, this will happen to us!* Zoe imagined the reporter coming back with a whole camera crew. She thought of Mom and how she'd feel about Zoe being the focus of all that . . . And of course she thought of someone taking Pipsqueak away, and that was the worst thought of all.

She bolted out of her room and out the back door.

"Zoomaroo, where are you go—" Alex called from the kitchen table.

She ran to the shed and threw the door open.

Pipsqueak squawked and dove into the box fort, attempting to hide. It didn't work. Over the past few days she'd grown too big to fit inside the fort. Half the boxes fell over with a crash, and two-thirds of her fuzzy body was visible.

Zoe sagged against the door. *She's here. No one has found her yet.* "Are you all right?"

Wiggling backward, Pipsqueak turned around—no easy task, given her size and the size of the shed. When at last she faced Zoe, she plopped down. "You surprised me!"

"Sorry." Reaching up, Zoe stroked between her ears, just as Pipsqueak had liked when she was a kitten. Now, though, Zoe used both hands instead of one finger.

Pipsqueak cuddled her shoulder. "Is everything all right?"

"All good. No worries."

"In that case, there is something I want to talk to you about. I've been in this shed a long time, and it gets lonely and boring when you're not here with me—"

From across the lawn, Zoe heard the back door open. "Zoe? Where did you go?" Alex called. "You know you're in your PJs, right? What are you doing out there?"

Scooting out of the shed, Zoe slammed the door shut behind her. *Everything is falling apart. I can't keep her hidden much longer!* If the reporters and anomaly seekers didn't find Pipsqueak, her own family would. It was just a matter of time, and thanks to the flying poodle, she had less time than she'd hoped. "Just remembered I'd left my phone in there." She waved it in the air. "Found it."

"Good," Alex said. "You know Mom and Dad won't get you another if you lose it."

"Yes. I know I have to be responsible." She crossed the lawn to the kitchen, willing herself not to glance back at the shed. She had to trust that Pipsqueak would have enough sense to stay out of sight while Alex was in the yard. *Maybe I shouldn't have told her that everything was okay when it's not.*

The grass was wet with dew, and her feet felt soaked by the time she was back inside. She wiped off the stray bits of grass that clung to her ankles.

"How's Pipsqueak?" Alex asked.

Zoe froze mid-wipe. "Why do you ask?"

"Duh, because she's your new pet, and like Mom pointed out last night, we haven't seen her in a while."

She studied his face. He didn't look as if he suspected anything. Maybe he hadn't read the news about the flying poodle being real. It occurred to her that her reaction was suspicious. *I'm not good at keeping secrets,* she thought. Especially one this big. Literally big.

"She's great," Zoe said, forcing herself to smile. "Shy. Hides from everyone except me. It would be best if you left her alone until she feels secure." She wished she could tell Alex. But he'd want to tell their parents, and they'd want to call Animal Control. Or someone official. She was certain her parents wouldn't understand she'd promised to keep Pipsqueak safe. They were more interested in keeping Zoe safe, which was nice, but she wasn't the one who would be thrown into a government lab or locked in a cage to be gawked at. *Pipsqueak trusts me to keep her safe. And my family trusts me to be responsible.*

"You know," Alex said as he poured her a bowl of cereal, "I was thinking about what Mom was saying—you know, about you going to camp. It might be a good idea. You could have your own adventure! You're ready for more independence, and maybe if you went, it could help you understand, at least a little, why I'm ready for my new adventure."

This was a horrifying conversation for so many reasons. Zoe wished she had thought to climb out her window and avoided this. "Really can't go to camp right now. I have a new kitten. Responsibilities."

"I could take care of her for you."

"You're off at work all day. So's Dad. And you know how Mom feels about animals. Pipsqueak would be lonely."

"Then you could find a pet sitter for her to stay with. Or board her at the vet if you think that would be better. Maybe not the vet with the flying poodle incident."

She had to cut this off before her parents overheard and got excited about the idea. "There's just too much to do here. Like with your party planning! I'm going to help more with that." She cringed inwardly as she said that. She'd rather poke her eye out with a barbecue fork than plan for Alex's going-away party.

He looked concerned. "You don't have to help with that if you don't want. In fact, if you go to camp, you'll miss at least some of the planning. I know this has been hard for you. That's why a distraction—"

Looking out the kitchen window behind Alex, Zoe saw the

shed door open. "Oh, I'm plenty distracted. Um, I . . . may have left my phone charger in the shed too. Excuse me." She darted out the door, waving frantically at Pipsqueak.

Pipsqueak ducked back into the shed.

As she reached the shed door, Zoe hissed, "What are you thinking? My brother's by the kitchen window! He could look outside at any moment!" She darted in and shut the door behind them.

Pipsqueak drooped, chastised. "I was worried about you. You ran off."

"Just distracting my brother," Zoe said. "We can't let him, or anyone, see you!" She realized she was shouting and probably upsetting Pipsqueak, but this was serious. Now there were people looking for her—or others like her!

"But it's hard, always hiding," Pipsqueak said. "It's sunny, and there are birds and dogs and butterflies. And you! I don't want to be stuck in here forever, away from the world and away from you!"

"I'm sorry, Pipsqueak, but we have to keep you safe!"

"I'm supposed to be your cat, and you're my person. We should be together!"

*This is the worst time for this conversation!* "I want that too, but we can't right now. Look, if you're unhappy or bored, I can get you more books. Or maybe even a TV. If I get an extension cord and run it to the shed—"

Pipsqueak laid her head down on the shed floor and covered her face with both front paws. "I just feel so . . . so . . . so . . ."

"Restless?" Zoe supplied.

"No."

"Bored?"

"No."

"Curious?"

"No."

"Then what? You can't be seen! If you're caught, you'll be paraded around and gawked at." *Like the flying poodle.* Zoe thought of the photos she'd seen plastered all over the Internet and the news. "Curious scientists will poke and prod you. People who are scared of anything strange and different could try to hurt you. Why do you want to risk being caught?"

"Because I already feel trapped!" Pipsqueak cried. "And helpless. And I don't like it. I don't know why I'm different. I don't know why I keep growing or why I can talk and read. I don't know what I'm supposed to do. Or who I'm supposed to be! And you don't know either. I can tell you're scared too, and that scares me! I don't want to hide in fear for the rest of my life. I want to be your cat. I want to do cat things. Chase birds. Lie out in the sun. Find more boxes. You keep saying everything will be okay, but you don't *do* anything to make it okay! You just pretend that everything will be fine because you want it to be fine. I don't think that's enough. I think we have to do something!"

*She can't hide forever,* Zoe thought. *She's unhappy, and it's only a matter of time before she's discovered.*

Without thinking about it first—not even to consider whether it was a good idea, a great idea, or a truly terrible idea—Zoe said, "We'll go to New Hampshire and find my aunt. She said she knows about extraordinary creatures. Like you. She said she can make everything go back to normal."

"She'll make me small again? Make me able to be your kitten again?"

"Yes! She'll help us. We just need to get to her."

# CHAPTER 8

AS SOON AS ZOE SAID IT, she knew: *This is a terrible idea!*

But it was too late to take the words back. Already they floated in the air like balloons. She wished she could pop them.

Pipsqueak perked up. "Let's go right now!"

And *that* felt like balloons popping.

Zoe opened her mouth to say she couldn't get Pipsqueak to New Hampshire. But Pipsqueak was purring so hard she sounded like a motorboat. The words *I can't* stuck in Zoe's throat.

*It'll never work!* She silently panicked. Her parents would never let her visit her aunt with a giant talking cat. They'd freak out as soon as they saw Pipsqueak, never mind any mention of Aunt Alecia. She couldn't tell them. How, though, was she supposed to just skip off to another state without them noticing she was missing?

*Harrison. Maybe he'll know what to do.*

*Certainly I don't.*

"I'll be back," she told Pipsqueak. "There are just a few things I have to do first. Please, stay here. Don't be seen. Just . . . wait for me, okay?"

"And then we'll find your aunt and she'll fix everything?" Pipsqueak asked. "We'll go together? You and me?"

"Yes."

Pipsqueak purred.

"Not right this second, though. Just . . . wait." Retreating across the lawn, Zoe felt Pipsqueak's gaze boring into her. There was absolute confidence in that gaze. Zoe had said they'd go together, so Pipsqueak didn't doubt it. *I can't disappoint her. But I can't go.*

She fled to Harrison's house, panting when she swung open his back door.

Surita was at the kitchen table, eating a bowl of cereal. "Ugh, it is too early for me to be on babysitting duty. Couldn't you at least wait until your parents are at work before coming over? And are you still wearing PJs? You know you don't actually live here, right?"

"You don't either," Zoe said, feeling her cheeks blush bright red. She'd forgotten about her PJs. They were sort of like a T-shirt and shorts, but the shirt had a picture of a sleeping llama on it and the shorts were soft plaid. Her legs felt like giraffe legs, sticking out awkwardly from her shorts. She should have taken a few seconds to dress. *Too late now.* She headed across the kitchen.

"Yeah, whatever," Surita said. "I'm just here until Sunday."

Just past the fridge, Zoe stopped—a seed of an idea was forming. "You're leaving for camp this Sunday? It's a sleepaway camp, right?"

"Yeah. I'm a counselor this year, so I even get paid, though I also have to help tiny campers find the bathroom in the middle of the night. It's a tradeoff."

"How long is a camp session?"

"One week. Check-in Sunday. Eat a lot of s'mores. Go home Friday."

"And it's in Vermont?"

"Yes." Surita narrowed her eyes. "Why are you acting so . . . intense?"

If she went to Surita's camp, she'd have almost an entire week before her parents began to worry about her. Could she get to Aunt Alecia's and back in a week? How far away was Aunt Alecia's house? Half a day's drive, maybe? *It might be possible.* "Because . . . I think I want to go to camp."

Pivoting, she ran out of the house and burst back into her own kitchen. Everyone was awake now. Mom was eyeing the toaster, and Alex had helped himself to more cereal. Dad was taking a bite of a banana.

Seeing her, Mom demanded, "Were you outside in your pajamas, young lady? Pajamas are inside clothes. Get yourself dressed."

"I want to go to camp!" Zoe said.

Mom blinked, caught off-guard. "Okay, that's new. You still need to get dressed."

Alex was beaming at her as if this was his idea—which to be fair, it somewhat was. Dad also seemed pleased. "What changed your mind?" he asked.

*Aunt Alecia said I had to bring my cat to New Hampshire, and if you think I'm at camp in Vermont, then I can sneak away to see her!* Zoe pointed at her brother. "Alex! It was his suggestion. And I couldn't stop thinking about it," Zoe gushed. "Surita is leaving this Sunday to be a counselor for a sleepaway camp in Vermont, and I'm sure she could drive me there, if I ask. Great opportunity for new experiences. Can I go?"

Mom pressed her lips together. "A sleepaway camp? It's an extreme leap from *spend time at home all summer* to *I want to go to Vermont*. What about all those library programs you said you'd do? Or how about a local camp? A few hours a day playing basketball or doing arts and crafts. I'm sure there are a few that still have room. Or at least one, if we call around—"

"I think sleepaway camp is an excellent idea," Alex chimed in. "It'll give Zoe something that's new. Something she can be excited about." He smiled at her. "She doesn't really want to spend the summer party planning for me or listening to us drone on about my fall courses. Plus she won't have to put up with the endless hammering of the workmen on the new laundry room. You said camp starts Sunday, right? Construction starts Monday. So that's perfect."

"Yeah," Zoe said. "It will be easier on me if I'm not here for any of that. You know I've been having a hard time lately, and . . . I really want to do this. Please, Mom, Dad! It's a great camp." She realized she had no idea what it was called or what campers did there. "Surita can tell you about it."

Mom was frowning, but she was wavering. Zoe could tell from the crease in her forehead. It was the same kind of crinkle Zoe got when she was thinking hard. Mom had never liked the idea of Zoe lazing around all summer, and if she went to camp, there was a whole week that Mom wouldn't have to work from home while Surita was away. "It would depend on the cost and if they have any availability on such late notice, but it is a reputable camp. Also, with Harrison's cousin there, you would know a counselor. She can help keep an eye on you."

Zoe held her breath.

"You've thought this through?" Dad asked her. "This is something you want? You've never been away from home for more than a night. You might get homesick. And Pipsqueak will miss you!"

"I'll find a pet sitter," Zoe promised. "You won't have to worry about her. I'll take care of everything."

They didn't look convinced. Dad said, "When we mentioned camp, we were thinking of something more local, as your mother said. Are you sure you want to do this?"

She wasn't sure at all, and she hadn't thought it through. There were a million details she hadn't even considered: how she was going to sneak away with Pipsqueak without anyone noticing, how she was going to keep the camp from reporting that she wasn't there, how she was going to prevent her parents from instantly realizing she'd lied, how she was going to travel with a giant cat, and, most important, whether Aunt Alecia would really be able to help them.

She hadn't specifically said she could shrink Pipsqueak, but what else could she have meant? Making Pipsqueak small again was the only way Zoe and Pipsqueak could stay together, and Zoe would try anything to make that happen.

"Camp will keep her too busy to be homesick," Alex said.

Zoe nodded vigorously.

"I'm proud of you for considering something new," Mom said. "This is unusual. You are growing up."

Springing across the kitchen, Zoe hugged her. "Thanks, Mom."

Mom patted her back. "Don't get your hopes up yet. We've barely discussed this, and there are a lot of *ifs* and *maybes* to consider. I'd be happier if you knew other kids who were going."

"I can ask Harrison," Zoe said.

After she tossed some clothes on and inhaled breakfast, Zoe met Harrison in the shed with Pipsqueak. The cat was reading another book, *The Incredible Journey,* which had two dogs and a cat on the cover. Quickly Zoe filled Harrison in on Aunt Alecia's letter, what Zoe had promised Pipsqueak, and her plan to use camp as an excuse to leave home.

"Please say you'll come," Zoe begged.

"You want me to lie to my parents, lie to Surita, sneak away from camp . . . Do you have any idea how much trouble we'd get into if we're caught?"

"A lot?" More than they'd ever been in. She was trying not to think about that.

"How do we sneak away from camp? And then sneak back? Or are you planning to sneak away from Surita during the drive? Because I think she might notice."

"I . . . haven't figured out the details yet. But Aunt Alecia says she knows about extraordinary creatures! She can help Pipsqueak!"

He read the letter again, for the fifth time.

"She'll know what to do," Zoe said. "We just have to get to her house."

Harrison looked at Pipsqueak, who filled half the shed. Using her claw, the cat turned another page in her book. "Your aunt could explain why this happened and how . . ." he said.

*Please say yes!* "Come with me," Zoe begged.

"Okay, whoa. I know you're impulsive, but seriously? This takes the cake."

"You'll get answers."

He opened his mouth and then shut it.

Zoe took the letter back and waved it at him. "She promises to explain everything. Everything!"

"But . . . Our parents will know the second we ditch summer camp. Someone will tell them. And how's Pipsqueak supposed to come with us anyway?"

*He's considering it,* Zoe thought. She could practically see the gears turning in Harrison's brain, figuring out the challenges.

"I mean, it's not like she'll fit in a suitcase," he said.

Pipsqueak didn't look up from her book. "I'm stealthy."

"She won't even fit in a car," Harrison said.

"I'm fast," Pipsqueak said.

Harrison snorted. "You're going to run alongside Surita's car all the way to summer camp? Yeah, and then the news will be filled with reports of a giant feline on the Mass Pike. You'll be filmed by one of those traffic-reporting helicopters, and everyone will be talking about the Unexplained Mystery of the Car-Size Cat. If we're going to do this, we need a plan that will actually work . . ."

*Unexplained mystery,* Zoe thought. "We tell Surita the truth."

"What?" Harrison said.

Pipsqueak looked up from her book. "She called me a rodent."

"But she'll keep you secret," Zoe said. After what Surita had said about Bigfoot, Zoe was certain of it. "She'll want to help. This is a good idea." Or at least it wasn't as terrible an idea as hiding a giant cat in a shed and thinking it was a long-term solution. And it wasn't as terrible an idea as just running off with a giant cat with no plan for handling their parents. "She can pretend to leave with us, then cover for us while we slip away on foot to New Hampshire. It's a better idea than sneaking away from camp, where there are lots of adults and counselors watching. If Surita helps us, no one at camp will even know to miss us. Honestly, without her help, I don't think we'll even last a day."

"On foot?" Harrison said. He thought about it. "Yeah, on foot. Can't fit in a car, right. Unless you're planning to steal a van or a truck and drive it yourself—which, for the record, is a *really* bad idea, especially since I've seen you play Mario Kart—we'll have to walk. To New Hampshire. Oh! Now I know why you need me."

She needed him because there was no way she was doing this alone, and he was her best friend.

He pulled out his phone and began to type. "Camp is a two-hour drive northeast. Mostly east. It's not on the way, so you're right, leaving from here makes more sense. Your aunt's house"—he typed more—"is four hours north from here by car. Fifty-five hours by foot, according to Google Maps. Seventeen hours by bike. But that's probably for professional cyclists. We'll be slower than that. And we certainly can't do it without stopping. We'll need to camp along the way for at least a night or two. And my grandma"—his voice stuck, and he swallowed—"she taught me everything I know about camping."

Zoe nodded. It wasn't Everest, but it wasn't a stroll down the lane either. Or a bike ride to the library. Or whatever. "Do you think we can do it? If Surita agrees to cover for us? My parents already said yes to summer camp. If we stay away from highways and towns . . ."

Pipsqueak had lowered her book and was watching the entire

conversation as if they were birds twittering on a tree branch. Zoe wondered if the cat had been only pretending to be calmly reading.

"We can do it," Harrison said. "Maybe. If we take our bikes. And camp. And prepare for our muscles to be really, really sore."

Zoe took a breath and asked the most important question: "*Should* we do it?"

"Absolutely!" Pipsqueak said. Her ears were laid back. "I hate being afraid all the time. I hate that *you're* afraid. I want to know what's happening to me and to stop it. I want to be able to come back into your house and curl up in your bed. I want to *fit* in your bed. I want everything to be back to normal. I don't want to stick my head in the sand, like the ostrich in *World Biology,* Volume 1, as my body keeps changing and everything gets steadily scarier!"

Zoe put her arms around Pipsqueak's neck and hugged her, burying her face in the cat's soft fur. "Okay. We'll do it. Stay here while we talk to Surita."

As she walked across the lawn to the fence between her house and Harrison's, Zoe rehearsed what she was going to say. Harrison hurried to keep pace with her, talking partly to her but mostly to himself: "Definitely need sleeping bags. If it isn't going to rain, we can skip the tent, but if there's any chance of rain . . . I'll look at the weather. We'll need canteens. Food. Trail mix. I think we can pack so it looks like we're packing for summer camp, because *camp.* Figure on two days' travel. I've never biked that much . . ."

He was still babbling when they went inside his house, but he shut up by the time they found Surita, who was playing video games in the living room.

"Surita . . ." Zoe began.

She held up a hand.

They waited while she blasted a spaceship. She paused.

"You're back," Surita said. "And you're dressed. Don't tell me. You need a ride somewhere. Well, the taxi service is off duty today. Sorry. It's one thing to keep an eye on you. It's another to be your chauffeur. I'm not being paid enough for that."

"Actually, it's about summer camp . . ." Zoe started again.

"And a giant cat that's hiding in Zoe's shed," Harrison burst out. "Zoe's aunt says she knows about unusual animals and knows how to help them, and since a massive, horse-size cat is way unusual . . . Whoa, I shouldn't have told you this way."

Surita was staring at him, halfway between confused and angry.

Zoe jumped in. "Remember when we asked what you'd do if you found Bigfoot in your backyard? Yeah, that wasn't just a random conversation. My cat . . . Well, it's better if you come see."

Surita turned back to her game. "I hate pranks. Especially ones on me."

"It's not a prank!" Harrison yelped.

"Please, Surita," Zoe begged. "Just come see. If we're pranking you, then you can say you knew it all along. But if we're not . . . Isn't it worth it to see if we're not? Real unexplained incredible thing on the other side of the fence?"

They'd almost convinced her. Surita paused the game again.

"She talks too," Harrison added.

Surita flopped back and resumed playing.

Zoe took a deep breath and stepped in front of the TV screen. "Come out this once, and we promise we'll leave you to play in peace and won't ask for any rides anywhere the rest of the summer."

"No more taxi service?" Surita said.

"Promise. Unless you want to, which you might."

Sighing, Surita tossed the controller onto the couch, then followed them outside. Zoe felt so nervous that she had to keep herself from running full tilt to the shed. She shot a look at the house to make sure all her family were safely away from the windows. The cars weren't in the driveway. Everyone must have left for work.

Zoe and Harrison led Surita to the shed.

"I feel like there should be a drumroll," Harrison said.

Zoe knocked on the shed door. "Pipsqueak, it's me! It's safe!" She opened the door . . . and the shed was empty. *What— No!* She searched it, though that took three seconds, looking inside the boxes and behind the potter's wheel.

In the doorway, Surita was tapping her foot.

Slowly turning back to face her, Zoe opened her mouth to say she didn't know where—and she saw Pipsqueak on the roof of the house. Wordless, she pointed behind Surita.

Harrison turned. So did Surita.

"Whoa," Surita said.

"So you'll help us?" Harrison asked.

Staring at the massive cat sunbathing across half the shingles, Surita nodded. "Oh, yeah."

Getting a ladder out, they all climbed onto the roof. It wasn't a bad place to hide, Zoe thought. On the back of the house, Pipsqueak wasn't visible from the road or from any of the other houses.

"She's not dangerous?" Surita whispered.

Pipsqueak opened her eyes and said, "Are *you?*"

Surita gaped at her.

"She's not," Zoe answered both of them.

"Except if you disagree with Surita on DC versus Marvel," Harrison added.

As Surita squatted on the shingles, her eyes sparkled as if she had unshed tears in them. "I knew . . . Not *this,* but I knew something like this . . . There had to be. She's beautiful."

Zoe smiled. She felt proud, as if she'd had anything to do with Pipsqueak's magnificence. "Yes, she is. The plan is to sneak away to my aunt's while our parents think we're with you at camp."

"Solid plan," Surita approved, "or at least the start of one. How far is your aunt's house?"

"One hundred fifty miles," Harrison answered.

"And you need me to drive. Got it. Few hours up, a few hours back, done in a day. Except camp will notice if we're gone for an entire day. What's your plan for that?"

"*You* are our plan for that," Zoe said. "I'm sorry, but you can't drive us."

Harrison nodded vigorously. "It's essential that you go to camp, exactly like you're supposed to, so you can cover for us."

"But . . . I want to come! Giant cat!"

"Please, Surita," Zoe begged, "if you don't help us, we won't even make it a day without someone figuring out we're gone."

"How are you even going to get to your aunt's without me? You can't drive a car. Don't tell me you're planning to ride your bikes almost all the way to the White Mountains. Bicyclists train themselves for long-distance rides. You've biked . . . what? . . . down the street? It will take you all week just to get to New Hampshire, much less come back."

"They'll ride me," Pipsqueak said.

It was Zoe's turn to stare at Pipsqueak. "We'll . . . what?"

Pipsqueak pressed her shoulder against Zoe, and Zoe had to brace herself so she didn't slide off the roof. The cat's voice sounded anxious at first but grew stronger. "You and the boy with the stupid dog will ride me to your aunt's house, and she'll fix everything so we can come home, and I can be with Zoe without fear of anyone taking me away."

"My name's Harrison," Harrison said.

"Dog boy," Pipsqueak corrected.

Zoe hadn't thought about the fact that Pipsqueak was large

enough to ride, but she certainly was. "That's better than riding bikes."

Surita's mouth was hanging open. "Better? That's *awesome*."

"Exactly how much better than bikes are we talking about?" Harrison asked, taking out his phone and typing. After a moment he said, "Ooh, okay. Sweet."

"What?" Zoe and Surita asked.

"So there aren't any Google Maps estimates for travel by giant cat, but mountain lions routinely travel more than twenty-five miles a night to hunt. They have impressive endurance and can go many miles traveling at an average speed of ten miles per hour. The longest journey by a land mammal ever recorded was done by a mountain lion."

All three of them studied Pipsqueak.

"I'm larger than a mountain lion," Pipsqueak pointed out. "I can go faster and farther."

"Say we travel for a minimum of eight hours a day at ten miles per hour . . ." Harrison said. "It's about a hundred fifty miles. So we can be there in two days. Less if Pipsqueak can go faster and farther. This could work!"

"This *will* work, so long as you help us," Zoe said to Surita. "Please say you'll do it! Be our alibi! You have to drive us away from home, pretend you're taking us to camp, and then tell camp we aren't coming. We'll text and call home and say camp is great, and you can check in with our families too, make sure they're not getting suspicious—"

"Yeah, otherwise . . . Zoe's right—we won't make it more than a day without you," Harrison put in, "whether we're riding a giant cat or not."

"Two days there and two days back . . . You can handle that," Surita said slowly. "Grandma taught you how to camp. You have sleeping bags. You can bring food and water. I can buy more cat food."

"Is that a yes?" Pipsqueak asked. "You'll help us?"

"Give me your phones." Eyes glued on Pipsqueak, Surita held out her hands without answering the cat's question. Zoe and Harrison gave her their phones, unlocked. "First thing we need to do is hack your phones. If your parents use one of those find-your-phone apps to check up on you, they'll know instantly that you aren't at summer camp."

Zoe hadn't thought of that.

As Surita tapped on the phones, she continued talking. "Next, you'll need a plan for what to say when you call home. Or at least you need to prepare a series of believable texts. You can plan to text them about swimming in the lake or how you've learned how to canoe or what camp songs you've learned. 'Greasy Grimy Gopher Guts' is a classic—with lots of variations. Speaking of variations, campers come from all over, so you should tell them you have a bunkmate who says *pop* instead of *soda* and *water fountain* instead of *bubbler*. You want a few key specific details. Don't try to get too elaborate, or they'll never believe you. Short texts. Be witty if you can. Call sometimes, for variety and believability. But not too often, because it's too easy to be caught off-guard on the phone."

"Wow—it sounds like you've already thought this all through," Zoe said.

Glancing at her, Surita blushed. "I like to imagine what I'd do in different scenarios. You know, to pass the time. This is the discover-you-have-a-superpower-and-have-to-go-save-the-world-but-it's-a-secret scenario. Classic, really. Pretty much every superhero hides their power from their family. Even Buffy, who had a great mom, snuck out of her bedroom window for the first two seasons."

"Who's Buffy?" Harrison asked.

Surita stopped typing and stared at Harrison. "Buffy the Vampire Slayer? TV show from the nineties? Only one of the most iconic female-power characters of all time? She practically started the urban fantasy genre. Okay, you have to start with episodes one and two of season one for the intro; then you can skip to—"

"Can we talk about Buffy later?" Zoe interrupted. "After we save my giant cat?"

"Right, sorry." Surita gazed again at Pipsqueak for a moment, then took a deep breath. "Okay. You both need to convince your parents. Harrison, I can help with yours. The camp won't be a problem—they're always happy to squeeze in more campers. I've never seen it full. But there will be the issue of the camp calling your parents to report when you're a no-show."

"Can't you tell them we're not coming? You know, when you get there—say there was a last-minute change of plans and we're really sorry," Zoe said.

"Yeah," Harrison chimed in. "We leave with you, so everyone sees us drive away. Pipsqueak meets up with us around the corner, and then you continue on to camp, make excuses for us, and we go to Zoe's aunt."

"Will you do it?" Pipsqueak asked. "Will you help us?"

Pulling herself together, Surita nodded. "Yes, I'll cover for you. And I'll fix your phones. You'll still be able to use your GPS, so you won't be mapless, but to your parents it'll look like your phones are where mine is." Her fingers flew over their phones, performing whatever phone-hacking magic she knew. "You'd better keep me updated, though. And when you're back, I want to know everything. No secrets. At least from me. As for everyone else . . . as Gandalf would say, keep her secret, keep her safe."

Both of them agreed.

*Keep her secret, keep her safe,* Zoe thought. *For one hundred fifty miles.* That was so very, very far. But with Pipsqueak, Harrison, and Surita . . . it actually felt possible. *We can do it! We have to try!*

# CHAPTER 9

**THANKS TO BOTH SURITA AND ALEX,** it worked. While Surita prepared their cover story, Alex did all the arguing for Zoe. He was convinced that if she went to camp for a week and had adventures, she'd understand better why he was going to Paris, and then the rest of the summer would be filled with joy and sunshine and butterflies rather than sadness and storm clouds. Or something along those lines. He even used Pipsqueak as part of his argument. After Zoe told him she'd found a cat sitter, Alex informed their parents that she had handled arrangements for her new pet all on her own, showing her maturity. But Zoe didn't eavesdrop on all their conversations—she was too busy trying to pack for one trip while pretending to be packing for another.

Harrison kept texting:

"Packing flashlights."

Then: "Extra batteries."

Then: "Extra underwear. Grandma always said pack two more than need, in case fall in mud pit. Or tar pit with mammoth."

Then: "Packing tent."

Then: "No rain. No tent."

Then: "Maybe tent? In case weather wrong?"

She finally texted back. "Only what you can carry. If no rain, no tent. Don't tell me about your underwear. Kthxbye."

He quit texting.

In the end, she packed a few changes of clothes plus extra underwear, her toothbrush and toothpaste, her hairbrush, her phone charger, a sleeping bag, and as many snacks and as much cat food (purchased by Surita) as she could fit. She also packed all of her birthday money that she hadn't already spent on cat food and the vet. It wasn't much. She hoped Harrison had more. If the trip took longer than they'd planned, they'd have to buy at least some food on the way. Carrying enough cat food for a giant cat . . . it filled the bulk of her backpack.

Encouraged by Alex, her parents filled out the registration forms for camp, and Harrison prodded his to do the same. Harrison's parents were delighted he was showing an interest in a camp that didn't involve video games.

By late Sunday afternoon, they were ready to go. Harrison's parents had already said their goodbyes, smothering Harrison in hugs and kisses until he turned as red as a beet. Now it was Zoe's family's turn. Alex was helping them load everything into the trunk of Surita's car. It was a two-hour drive to camp, which meant they'd arrive by dinnertime—if they were actually going to camp.

"You packed your toothbrush?" Mom asked.

"Yes. And toothpaste."

"I have extra," Harrison volunteered.

Harrison had overpacked, of course. Zoe was certain he'd packed at least three times, subtracting then adding items as he went. She didn't want to see what was in his backpack. *He probably brought twenty-seven must-have essential camping supplies and six weeks' worth of underwear,* she thought. But that was his business. So long as he carried a bag of cat food too.

"You'll miss us, right?" Dad asked.

"She's supposed to be going on an adventure," Alex scolded.

"I'll miss you all every day," Zoe said. *At least that's not a lie.* She wished she dared tell her family the truth about her "adventure," but it was too risky. Aunt Alecia had said to let no one see Pipsqueak, and Zoe didn't want to take any chances. It was her responsibility to keep her cat safe. Studying her mother and brother, though, she wondered if she was making a mistake.

"Second thoughts?" Alex asked.

*And third,* she thought. *And fourth.* "None." She hugged them all and then said, "Just forgot one thing. I'll be right back." This was the plan: she'd tell Pipsqueak it was time, the cat would slip out of the backyard and meet them behind the neighbor's garage one street over. From there, they just had to make it to their old elementary school. Surita had checked: due to a weekend sports camp, the school would be open. So long as they arrived after camp ended but before the janitors locked up for the night, they'd be able to hide inside until it was dark enough to sneak out of town. A simple plan, so it should work.

She jogged inside, through the house, and out into the backyard. From the shed, she heard a faint yowling noise that sounded like a cat being squeezed. *Pipsqueak!* Zoe broke into a run and threw the shed door open.

"Pipsqueak, are you okay—"

The sound broke off and there was a rustle of boxes as Pipsqueak tried to dive behind them and instead knocked them all over. She poked her head up. "You scared me again!"

"I heard a noise. I thought you were hurt!"

"I was singing," Pipsqueak said.

"Oh. Okay. Great." Her heartbeat began to return to normal. Zoe wiped her sweating palms on her shorts. "Well, we're just about ready to leave—"

"It was opera."

"Sorry?"

"I was singing opera," Pipsqueak explained. "An aria from *The Magic Flute* by Wolfgang Amadeus Mozart. I read about it."

"Very nice." Zoe pushed on. "I wanted to make sure you— Wait, how do you know what opera sounds like if you've only read about it and haven't heard it?"

"I have an excellent imagination."

That was rather awesome, though her timing for a concert

wasn't great. "I'm sure you do. Harrison and I are about to leave with Surita. Everyone's in the driveway, exactly as planned. You know where you have to go?"

Pipsqueak kneaded the floor of the shed. *She's nervous,* Zoe realized. *That's what this is about.*

"How about a new plan?" Pipsqueak suggested brightly. "After you and the dog boy drive around with the girl who called me a rodent, you come back here and we chase fireflies."

"Yeah, but that's not what we agreed to do." *She can't be backing out.* Besides, there wasn't a way to make it un-happen. And staying wasn't an option, not with the risk of her family spotting Pipsqueak. Or a neighbor. Or an unexplained-phenomenon-seeking tourist. Or a reporter. Or one of the construction workers, who were coming to work on the new laundry room in the morning. Zoe kept her voice light so Pipsqueak wouldn't guess she was freaking out inside. This trip was going to be hard enough even with Pipsqueak fully onboard. "Besides, I thought you said fireflies taste bad."

"We won't eat them," Pipsqueak said eagerly. "We'll pounce on them, then let them go so we can chase them some more. Come on, Zoe—all I want is for us to be together, here. So how about we skip the part where we leave and just be together at home?"

Zoe closed her eyes briefly, counted to ten, and then said as calmly as she could, "I know the unknown is scary. But you were the one who said you wanted to do something."

Pipsqueak let out a sad whimper. "What if your aunt can't help?

What if she doesn't like me? What if there's nothing anyone can do to stop this, and I keep getting bigger and bigger until I'm the size of a house?"

"She said she's met other animals like you and she knows what to do," Zoe reminded her. "I'm sure she can make everything go back to the way it was. Don't you want that?"

"Of course I do."

"Then let's find out," Zoe said gently. "Together. And let her try to help you. Please, Pipsqueak. We both want the same thing: to be together, without having to be afraid anymore. This is the best way to make that happen."

The cat nodded.

"We'll meet you one street over, and then we'll hide in our old school until dark. It'll be safe." Zoe hugged the cat's neck, and Pipsqueak nuzzled her, then began cleaning her fur.

Zoe heard her mother calling from the driveway. It was time to go. "See you in five minutes, okay?" She hurried back to where Surita, Harrison, and her family were waiting.

Surita and Harrison were watching her closely, trying not to look nervous and failing utterly. Harrison was bouncing from foot to foot, and Surita was twisting a clump of purple and black hair around her fingers.

*"Finally!"* Surita puffed. "We need to get on the road if we're going to get to camp before they stop serving dinner. First night is cheeseburgers. You miss cheeseburgers, and you get sloppy

joes. No one wants camp sloppy joes. You could end up eating squirrel."

"Everything, um, okay?" Harrison asked Zoe.

"Sure!" Zoe said, hoping that was true. She hugged her parents and Alex again. She reassured them that she'd packed all her stuff, that she'd text them often, and that Pipsqueak was happy with her cat sitter (a friend of Surita's, they'd claimed). And then at last they were in the car.

"Text us tonight when you arrive," Mom instructed.

Zoe promised she would.

Surita pulled out of the driveway. Zoe and Harrison waved, and Zoe's family waved back. It was such a bizarre moment. Zoe hadn't prepared herself for waving goodbye as she drove away; she'd been too busy worrying about what it would feel like to be the one left behind while *Alex* drove off. But this would be the longest she'd ever been away from her family. Twisting in her seat, she continued to wave.

Halfway down the street, Surita said, "Are you seriously going to keep waving until they're out of sight?"

"I'll wave as long as they wave."

"That could get us caught in an endless loop," Harrison observed.

She knew it was silly, but it made her feel better—as if they were coming with her in some way. *Maybe I should have told them. Or asked for help.* It was possible they would have reacted the way Surita did . . . *Except they wouldn't.* Her parents would do what they thought was best for Zoe and Alex, and she couldn't guarantee that would be what was best for Zoe and Pipsqueak.

She quit waving after they turned the corner. A minute later, they were at the designated meeting spot: near the neighbor's garage. Surita had confirmed the owners were on vacation, and the building was shielded from view by several bushy evergreens. They parked and waited for Pipsqueak to appear.

She didn't.

*She'll come,* Zoe thought. *She wants this.*

Still . . . It wasn't until Zoe really began to worry, Surita began to tap the steering wheel, and Harrison began to gnaw on his fingernails like a chipmunk on a nut that Pipsqueak strolled out of the trees. The branches bent around her, then snapped back. A few startled birds took flight, and she crouched down, eyes upward, before relaxing and sauntering on.

"That is just too much cat," Surita said.

All three of them got out of the car . . . but before Pipsqueak reached them, she spotted a squirrel racing up a pine tree and chased after it, climbing the tree. It was a thin, brittle pine with sparse branches, and as the cat climbed higher, the tree began to tip.

"Stay back," Zoe warned.

"She'll stop before it—" Surita began with confidence.

And then the pine tree snapped. Pipsqueak rode it down with a yowl, and the squirrel zoomed off. All of them waited to hear shouts, but with the neighbors on vacation and Zoe's and Harrison's houses too far away, no one came to investigate.

Shaking out her fur, Pipsqueak said, "Oops."

"You've *got* to keep a lower profile," Surita said. "Seriously. If you aren't careful, you'll all be arrested, taken to Area 51 for questioning, and never seen again because you've had to give up your identities to work for a secret government agency that seeks out the mystical impossibilities of the world . . . On second thought, that sounds incredible."

"Unless the reason we're never seen again is that we know too much," Harrison said, "and we have to spend the rest of our days in isolation, with only the Loch Ness Monster for company."

"That would be bad," Surita agreed. "I've heard Nessie isn't much of a talker." Her eyes got even wider. "Do you think Nessie could really exist? If there's a giant cat . . . It could all be real. Vampires. Werewolves. Yeti."

"Transformers," Harrison supplied helpfully. "Teenage Mutant Ninja Turtles—"

"Guys," Zoe cut in. "Focus."

Both of them apologized.

Pipsqueak lay down beside the garage, and Zoe climbed her fur and swung her leg over the cat's back. It was a little tricky with her backpack stuffed full of camping supplies and cat food, but she managed. She leaned forward toward the cat's neck, and her arms sank into fur elbow-deep. Harrison climbed up behind her, and then Pipsqueak stood. Zoe clung to the fur.

It was not at all like the pony rides she'd begged her parents for when she was smaller. For one thing, Pipsqueak was wider. Zoe felt as if she were trying to do a split. For another, fur was vastly different from a leather saddle. Fur was amazingly soft. It also smelled like a mix of cat food and litter rather than horse sweat and leather. *Oh, wow, this is awesome!*

"If I absolutely promise never to sell or even show it to anyone, can I take a photo?" Surita asked. "I want my future self to believe it's real."

"I think it's better if you don't, for all the reasons you said to keep her secret," Zoe said, though she wished she had a picture of this too. *I'm riding a cat!*

"And you're sure I can't come with you? I mean, I know I can't. I'm your cover at camp. I've an important job to do, blah blah blah, but . . . ugh, it's not fair. I've spent my entire life wanting a magic moment, and you get one instead of me. You never even wanted this, either of you!"

*She's right,* Zoe thought. She'd never wanted an adventure, and Harrison might talk about Everest a lot, but in reality, he liked video game adventures where you could respawn after a mistake. *I wanted a quiet summer, with no packing for college or renovating a laundry room or anything different at all.*

But she'd chosen to rescue a lost kitten, chosen to keep it, and chosen to protect it.

Pipsqueak twisted her head toward Surita and then laid a paw, claws in, on her back. She began to clean Surita's face with her broad, sandpaper tongue. Surita shrieked and leaped backward. "What are you doing?"

"You were upset, and it was ruffling your fur," Pipsqueak said. "I fixed you."

"Oh, uh, cool. Thanks," Surita said, wiping her cheek. "You need to go now. Be careful! Don't let anyone see you! Don't let anyone catch you! And don't let anyone stop you! Keep her secret, keep her safe!"

With Zoe and Harrison clinging to her back, Pipsqueak trotted toward the road, across it, and into the thick patch of bushes and trees on the opposite side. Holding on tight, Zoe forgot to wave.

# CHAPTER 10

**The problem with riding** a giant cat through a neighborhood was . . . *Okay,* Zoe thought, *there are a* lot *of problems with riding a giant cat through a neighborhood!*

They stuck to backyards, on the theory that staying away from the street was smart, but backyards were full of distractions. Fences to hop over. Barbecue grills to sniff. Pets to accidentally terrify. Ten minutes into their journey they came to a house with an aboveground swimming pool. Tiptoeing up to the pool, Pipsqueak peered into the water. She smacked at it with her paw, and a few drops splashed out. "Ooooh!"

"Pipsqueak—" Zoe began, "why are you—"

Scooting away from the drops, Pipsqueak sat down.

Zoe and Harrison slid down the slope of her back, calling, "Pipsqueak!" They grabbed at her fur until she stood again, and then they crawled up to her neck.

"It's liquid," Pipsqueak explained.

"Yes, we know," Harrison said. "It's a pool. I thought cats didn't like water."

"I'm not going to doggie-paddle around, if that's what you're asking, but it's fun to splash. And I've never seen so much of it!"

She had always loved splashing milk, starting from the day Zoe had met her. *She's still that tiny kitten inside,* Zoe thought. She watched for a second as Pipsqueak swatted delightedly at the surface of the pool. "We need to keep going. There could be people around."

Pipsqueak let out a *murp*-like meow. "Oh! Sorry!"

The second distraction occurred at the end of the block, when they had to cross the street. They crouched behind a detached garage and waited for a moment when no cars were passing. Looking both ways, they urged Pipsqueak forward.

They got about halfway across when she stopped.

"What's wrong?" Zoe asked.

Pipsqueak stared at the blinking yellow traffic light. She was saying something, but Zoe couldn't make out what it was. Crawling forward onto Pipsqueak's neck, Zoe tried to hear . . .

Pipsqueak was murmuring, "Bright, dark, bright, dark . . ."

*This is definitely not like a pony ride,* Zoe thought. "Pipsqueak, if you cross the street, I promise that when we get back home, I'll borrow Mom's laser pointer and shine it around for you to chase. Red, shiny dot. You'll love it."

Pipsqueak's ears twitched.

"Just cross the street. Please. Before a car comes!"

"At this rate," Harrison said, "this is going to be the shortest journey in all of adventuring."

Pipsqueak heard that, and she ran forward across the street and up a driveway to dive behind a mass of greenery. Her ears poked up through the branches.

A car drove by on the street behind them, but it didn't stop.

Zoe exhaled in relief.

"Sorry," Pipsqueak said again. "I just have never seen anything like that before. Can we go back and play with the blinking light again? The car is gone."

"This is never going to work," Harrison said.

"All we have to do is reach the school," Zoe said. "It's not far. Lie low for a couple hours, and then we can really begin." Urging Pipsqueak forward, they trotted through the few remaining yards, crossed one more street, and emerged near the school.

Their old elementary school was a squat brick building with a gym on one end and a cafeteria on the other. A few of the classrooms were used for summer activities, but that was just during the week. Only one car sat in the parking lot.

"Funny how much smaller it looks now," Harrison said.

"You are only two inches taller than you were in fifth grade," Zoe said. "How much smaller can it possibly look?"

"Fine. Never mind."

Though she wasn't going to admit it out loud, Zoe thought it *did* seem smaller and emptier without all the arts-and-crafts projects filling the windows the way they did during the school year.

A toddler and his mother were on the playground, using the swings, so Zoe, Harrison, and Pipsqueak crept behind the bushes, past the playground, to the gym. Harrison slid off the cat's back and opened one of the double doors. As Surita had predicted, it was unlocked. "All clear," he whispered.

Glancing around to make sure the woman and her kid hadn't seen them, Zoe slipped inside.

Pipsqueak pushed her head through sideways, and Zoe and Harrison quickly yanked open the second door. Pipsqueak sauntered in as if she hadn't almost gotten stuck. She licked her fur, flattening it again.

The gym was dark, lit only by narrow windows near the ceiling, on a level with the top of Zoe's nemesis, the climbing rope. The basketball nets looked even taller in the shadows. It was eerily quiet, and Zoe realized she'd never heard the school completely silent. There were always kids talking and laughing somewhere, and you could always hear the squeak of sneakers on the hallway floors.

"Okay, we're here," Zoe said as Pipsqueak ducked under a basketball net. "Now we just have to keep out of sight until dark, when we can travel without being seen. Or at least travel without being so easy to see." Once they made it out of town, they'd be able to hide in the clumps of trees that lined nearly every New England road.

They would follow the roads to keep from getting lost. So long as they stayed out of the beams of car headlights and skirted around any towns, they should be fine. *I hope,* she thought.

Pipsqueak began trotting toward the hallway.

Zoe and Harrison hurried after her. "Where are you going?"

"If we're safe, I want to explore!" Pipsqueak said. "Is there any food here?"

"We used to eat in the cafeteria," Zoe said. "Up ahead." She pointed toward the wall of windows at the end of the corridor. "But you have to be careful that no one sees you—"

Filling half the width of the hallway with her fluff, Pipsqueak loped toward the cafeteria. Flyers on the walls rustled in her wake.

"You know it'll be empty," Harrison predicted.

"Maybe. Maybe not," Zoe said. Surita had *thought* it was safe, but what if a janitor were here already, preparing to close the school for the night?

"Certainly will be empty of cat food."

"Shepherd's pie looks like cat food. Also Salisbury steak."

Harrison shuddered. "I wouldn't feed Salisbury steak to my dog."

Pipsqueak's giant paws were silent on the hall floor. Zoe's and Harrison's shoes squealed on it, sounding like mice. Glancing back, Pipsqueak shot them a look, and they tried to walk more carefully.

By the time Zoe and Harrison caught up to her outside the door to the cafeteria, Pipsqueak was grooming herself. Her tail swished from side to side, whacking against the walls. "It smells funny in there," she complained.

"Of course it does," Zoe said. "It's a school cafeteria." She took a step inside and then reeled back. It smelled as if someone had rinsed the room in lemon juice and cleaning supplies. The janitors had been very thorough in ensuring that there was no trace of left-over food or kindergartner germs, as if they'd tried to erase even the memory of everything that had happened here by dousing it with antiseptic. "Sorry, Pipsqueak."

On the plus side, at least there weren't any people.

"Not hungry anymore. Are there any boxes to play in?" Pipsqueak stretched up against a bulletin board next to the cafeteria door, scratching it. Her claws cut long slices through the construction paper decorations. "What is this place?"

"It was our school," Zoe said.

"Yeah, try not to destroy it?" Harrison suggested.

Pipsqueak retracted her claws. "Oops. Sorry."

"It's okay," Harrison said. "I don't think anyone is going to see that and automatically think, *Must have been a giant cat.* But less damage is better."

"We learned how to read and add and stuff here," Zoe said. "And we played a lot. Mostly played. This is where we met." She pointed down the hallway toward the kindergarten rooms. "I didn't have any green crayons, and Harrison had every color invented, each crayon labeled with his name."

"I believe in being prepared," he said. "Also my dad let me use his label maker."

"I wish I could go to school," Pipsqueak said. "I think I would like it."

"Cats don't go to school," Harrison said. "No matter what size they are."

"Unfair."

Pipsqueak started exploring again, and they followed. They passed Zoe's second-grade classroom, and she peered in through the window. Harrison really was right—things did look smaller. The desks were half the size of the ones at the middle school. Zoe had forgotten she once fit into those tiny desks.

"What's that?" Pipsqueak asked, squeezing her face next to Zoe.

Zoe saw something move inside the classroom. "I saw it too." Opening the door, she stepped inside. Everything was quiet except for a soft scratching sound.

On the windowsill was a hamster cage.

Tilting her head sideways and wriggling her body like a snake, Pipsqueak squeezed her way through the classroom door. Her fur poofed out as she pushed through. "Oh, is that . . ." Her voice dropped to a reverent hush. "My first real, live mouse."

Zoe crossed to it. The poor little thing was huddled in the corner of its cage, next to a water dispenser. "Do you think the teacher forgot about it for the summer?" Zoe asked.

"That would be horrible," Harrison said.

"Or delightful. For me." Creeping between the desks—and knocking several of them aside—Pipsqueak tiptoed up to the cage and peered in. The mouse froze, its eyes widening.

"You're scaring it," Harrison told Pipsqueak.

Pipsqueak didn't move. "I want to chase it, catch it in my mouth, spit it out, and then chase it again. Please, Zoe. Please, please!"

"Absolutely not. Can't you see it's terrified?" She shooed the cat back, and Pipsqueak retreated a few steps, knocking over another chair. "It's alone, trapped inside a cage, with a giant cat staring at it."

Pipsqueak retreated the rest of the way out of the classroom door, and Zoe turned back to the little mouse. Even without the cat nearby, it still looked miserable. "I wish we could set it free."

"You can't let it out just because you think it's lonely or something," Harrison told her. "It'll starve. Or get eaten. At least in there it has its food bowl. Someone's clearly feeding it."

Zoe found a bag of mouse food next to the early-reader books, and she opened the cage and refilled the bowl. The mouse stretched out its neck and sniffed. Gently, Zoe stroked its head between its ears. "You'll be okay, buddy."

Feeling guilty for leaving it, but not knowing what else to do, Zoe headed back across the classroom. She spotted the teacher's name on her desk, Ms. Marsdell. Once Zoe was home again, she could have her parents call and make sure the class pet was okay. *Just in case. I don't like that it's here by itself.*

"Maybe we should give it fresh water too before we leave," Zoe said.

"I'll do it," Harrison volunteered. He trotted back to the cage as Zoe typed the teacher's name into her phone for later.

"Uh, Zoe?" Harrison's voice cracked. "That was a *mouse* in the cage, right?"

"Yeah. Why?" She glanced back to see Harrison staring into the cage.

"Then why does it have wings?"

"What? It doesn't—" She hurried to his side. The mouse was still huddled in the corner, but now it had brilliant blue butterfly wings on its back, popping up from its white fur. "Whoa."

"Yeah."

"*Wow.*"

"Uh-huh." Harrison's eyes were bugging out, not unlike they had when he first heard Pipsqueak talk.

Zoe gawked at it too. It had been an ordinary mouse just a few minutes ago! How had this happened? Why were there suddenly so many impossible creatures all at once? *What are the odds that there's a giant cat, a flying dog, and a mouse with wings in Eastbury? This can't be a coincidence.*

"Pipsqueak, come see this!" Zoe glanced over her shoulder toward the door, expecting Pipsqueak to stick her head back inside, but the cat didn't reappear. "Pipsqueak?"

"Zoe," Harrison said. "Mouse with wings! And it's not a bat! What do we do?"

"I don't know. I've never seen a mouse sprout wings." She called again: "Pipsqueak? You have to come see this!" *Why isn't Pipsqueak answering me?*

"Do you think your aunt has?" Harrison asked. "She said in her letter that she's met extraordinary creatures. I think we should tell her about this."

"I think we should show her."

"What?"

"We should take the mouse with us." They couldn't just leave it like this. They had no way of knowing who would find it. She thought of the mess online when the flying poodle was found. This poor mouse didn't deserve to be the center of that kind of attention.

"Can't take the whole cage. It's too big to carry." She scanned the room and spotted a shoebox diorama with the solar system inside. Dumping out the Styrofoam planets, she stabbed holes in the lid with a pair of scissors, scooped the winged mouse out of its cage, and lowered it gently into the shoebox.

Harrison grabbed the bag of mouse food and shoved it into his backpack. "Does it even eat this anymore, or will it want to eat worms? Is it a bird or a rodent? A bir-dent? A rod-ird? Wait—they're insect wings, so it should be rod-ect."

"No need to classify it right now," Zoe told him. Holding the shoebox and her backpack, she headed out of the classroom, with Harrison behind her.

The sooner they could get to Aunt Alecia, the better.

But first . . . where was Pipsqueak?

The hallway was empty.

Running through the halls, they checked the classrooms, the cafeteria, the library, and the gym. Zoe was trying not to worry. And she was failing. What if Pipsqueak had been seen by a stray janitor or a teacher getting something from his classroom?

"Where is she?" *I was supposed to keep her safe!* They hadn't been gone from home for even a night, and already Zoe had lost her. "She was just with us. Where did she go?"

Harrison pointed to the open gym doors.

Sticking to the shadows, they peeked out.

Outside, the mother from the playground was talking on her phone, laughing, and not watching her toddler, who was making kissing faces at a (normal-size) gray cat with a pink collar.

Zoe spotted Pipsqueak crouched behind a clump of bushes, barely hidden. It looked as if the bushes had sprouted a halo of fur. Her whiskers stuck out on either side of the shrubbery.

Harrison was freaking out, muttering under his breath, "She's going to be seen. Caught. Taken away. Experimented on. Put in a cage. Like the mouse. Why the mouse? Why wings? Why not a big mouse? What's going on?"

"Deep breath, Harrison. I'll get her back inside. Stay here, and watch the mouse." She handed him the shoebox.

Checking the toddler's mom one more time to make sure she wasn't looking their way, Zoe darted out to join Pipsqueak. She ducked behind the bushes, squeezing against the cat's side so there would be at least some greenery in front of them.

"What are you doing?" Zoe whispered. "You could be seen!"

"That cat doesn't have to hide," Pipsqueak said mournfully. "Look. It doesn't have to be afraid of anything. No one thinks it's terrifying or wrong."

The toddler clapped his hands as the gray cat brushed against his legs. He reached out a pudgy hand and ran it over the cat's back. The cat flicked its tail and sauntered off.

"He doesn't even know how lucky he is," Pipsqueak said.

"You're not terrifying," Zoe said. Yes, Pipsqueak was as large as a horse, but they were going to fix that.

"The mouse was terrified of me. You said so. I just want to be your cat, Zoe. I want a home and my own patch of sunlight. But I've grown scarily huge."

"You aren't scary," Zoe said. "I mean, yes, you scared the mouse, but it would've been scared of any size cat. That doesn't mean you've turned into a terrifying monster. Please come back inside before—"

The toddler saw them.

"Giant kitty!" the toddler screeched, making grabby hands.

"Run!" Zoe said. And she bolted through the bushes toward the gym doors while Harrison frantically beckoned them. Bounding, Pipsqueak followed after as the mother looked over from her phone. The toddler shrieked in glee.

They dove through the gym doors. Hiding in the shadows with Harrison, they waited to hear the mother chasing after them. Or more shouts. But there was only the pitiful wailing of the child, calling for the giant kitty to come back.

*We made it,* Zoe thought. *She didn't see us.*

Zoe peeked out and saw the mother had scooped the child up and was hurrying toward the parking lot, her phone pressed to her ear.

*Or maybe she did?*

"She definitely saw us!" Harrison said.

"We have to get out of here," Zoe said, climbing onto Pipsqueak's back. Handing Zoe the shoebox, Harrison scrambled on behind her. She wondered if this was a mistake, taking the mouse with them, especially if they were about to be caught. But there wasn't time to make another choice.

"I'm sorry," Pipsqueak said miserably. "I didn't mean to be seen. I thought if I hid . . . But I've gotten too big to even hide well."

"All the more reason to go quickly!" Zoe said.

In the distance, sirens wailed.

# CHAPTER 11

**The sirens drew closer.**

"Go, go, go!" Zoe hissed to Pipsqueak.

They darted out of the school and across the soccer field. On the opposite side of the field were woods. If they could reach them before the police got there and saw the giant cat . . . "Faster!" she urged.

As the sirens wailed, Pipsqueak jumped over the fence that surrounded the school yard and plunged into the woods. She plowed between the trees, trampling the underbrush. Branches smacked into Zoe's arms, and she ducked low, clutching the shoebox to her chest, protecting it as best she could.

Behind them, the sirens stopped.

Pipsqueak finally slowed.

"Did we lose them?" Harrison asked.

"I think they reached the school," Zoe said. "They probably got out to talk to the woman who called them." Her heart was pounding so hard it nearly hurt. "With luck, they won't believe what she saw."

"She was afraid of me," Pipsqueak said. "Because I'm scarily huge."

"Because she didn't know how sweet and adorable you are under all the fuzz," Zoe said. "And you were near her kid. She wants to protect him like I want to protect you. Even if he doesn't really need protecting. He was excited when he saw you."

Pipsqueak's ears perked forward. "You're right. He wasn't scared of me."

"I swear he cheered when you ran," Harrison said. "It *was* pretty awesome how you were able to run us out of there so fast. You couldn't have done that if you were your old size."

"That's true too," Pipsqueak said.

The woods weren't very deep. Already Zoe could see the outline of houses through the trees. Maybe it was shadowy enough in between the trees to hide them.

Still no more sirens. *We did it! We escaped!*

Zoe felt jittery, as if butterflies were dancing on her skin. She'd never felt so nervous and excited, tingling inside and out. "This is it! We're going north, to Aunt Alecia's!"

"Actually . . ." Harrison pointed toward the dark pink and blue-gray clouds that framed the setting sun. "We're going south."

"Hmm, oh, sorry." Sounding embarrassed, Pipsqueak switched directions, knocking over bushes as she turned one hundred and eighty degrees. "There was a bird . . . Never mind. Now we're going north."

*And we're off,* Zoe thought.

A few cars were on the street, and there weren't as many places to hide as there had been between her house and the school. "Keep to the backyards," Zoe suggested.

It was inching closer to evening. More people were home, watching TV or starting to prepare dinner—Zoe could see them through their windows. She hoped no one looked out into their yard to see the shadow of a giant cat being ridden by two kids, or if they did, she hoped they convinced themselves that their eyes were playing tricks on them. Pipsqueak traveled quickly from yard to yard, stepping over fences and trampling flower gardens.

A dog barked, then whimpered.

"We're going to be seen," Harrison said. "We should have waited longer."

Zoe refrained from pointing out that they hadn't had much choice.

Pipsqueak slowed. They heard the buzz of a TV inside the nearest house, and laughter above the buzz. Zoe eyed the house's roof, an idea forming. The day they'd introduced Surita to Pipsqueak, the cat had been on the roof, not visible, the slant hiding her from the street. "Can you get to the top of the house?"

"Sure," Pipsqueak said as Harrison cried, "What are you—"

Pipsqueak crouched, then launched herself onto the roof, landing lightly.

In a shrill voice Harrison asked, "Why did we do that?"

Zoe looked at the roof of the next house. According to the *Guinness World Records,* a cat named Alley had the longest jump: six feet. But the average cat was just a foot or two long. Pipsqueak was about twelve feet long. *So her jump should be . . . six times twelve . . . seventy-two feet.* "How far can you jump?"

"Oh no," Harrison said. "Tell me you aren't thinking what I think you're thinking. Because if you are, it's a terrible idea."

It was a great idea! How often did people look at their roofs? Rarely if ever. Plus it would be faster. *If it works and we don't splatter on anyone's yard.* She tucked the shoebox with the mouse into her backpack to keep it safe.

Crouching, Pipsqueak wiggled her hind legs, as if revving up. Leaning forward against Pipsqueak's neck, Zoe held on to clumps of fur. Harrison hung on to Zoe.

Pipsqueak launched herself.

Zoe felt as if she were flying. Her bones felt light, though her stomach felt as if it had been left behind. She laughed out loud.

They landed softly and cleanly on the next roof.

"That was amazing!" Zoe said.

Harrison let out a small moan.

"You can't tell me that wasn't amazing," Zoe said to him.

"Kind of? I don't—"

Pipsqueak ran across the roof and leaped to the next one. Zoe loved the way it felt when they lifted off, as if they were aiming for the moon. She loved how it felt when they soared through the air, as if they'd never land. And she loved how it felt when they landed, her face flying forward into soft fur, flush with success.

They leaped across the town until the houses were too far apart, the way they'd been near Zoe's neighborhood, and then they reverted to running through backyards. But in the spots where the houses were far apart, the yards were also bigger and deeper. So it worked.

*I never knew I'd love this,* Zoe thought.

"This is fun!" Pipsqueak said.

"Most fun ever," Zoe agreed.

"If I hadn't grown huge, we couldn't have done this," Pipsqueak said. "I still want to be small again, though. I want to be able to go home."

"That's why we're going north."

They ran on and on, sometimes leaping over roofs, sometimes through yards. Every now and then they'd have to cross a street. They did it fast, and Zoe hoped they looked like a blur to anyone who happened to see.

Soon they were beyond Eastbury. Harrison consulted the map on his phone, calling out directions to Pipsqueak until the only instruction left to give her was "keep going." They ran parallel to the roads, keeping far enough away to stay out of reach of the car headlights, but close enough to not get lost.

Zoe checked on the mouse in the shoebox. It was cowering in a corner, its wings wrapped tightly around its body. She wondered if they'd made the right choice to bring the mouse. After all, it had been safe in its cage, even if it hadn't looked happy. But it was too late now for second thoughts. *And besides, as soon as anyone spotted a winged mouse, all the tourists and reporters and everyone would have descended upon it!* They'd spared the mouse that, at least.

An hour and a half after they fled the school, their phones binged with a text from Surita saying she'd made it to Vermont. They each sent texts to their parents, saying they'd arrived at camp and everything was great.

And they kept riding.

After a couple more hours, Zoe began to nod off. Harrison was already leaning against her back, snoring lightly in her ear. She elbowed him. "We can't sleep. Not unless we want to fall off."

"Mmm. Right. Sorry."

She nestled her cheek into Pipsqueak's fur and spread her arms around as much of the cat's neck as she could reach. "Keep talking so we don't fall asleep."

"Okay. Do you think Superman accidentally breaks toilets when he pees?"

"We're not talking about that."

Harrison laughed. "Fine. How do you think your aunt knows about giant cats?"

"As far as I know, she's always believed in impossible stuff."

"Do you think she's met one? Or maybe she *is* one. She was born a cat, grew larger, crawled into a cocoon, and burst out as a human."

"That makes even less sense than your other ideas."

"Just trying to think outside the box. Or the cocoon. What if Pipsqueak isn't really a cat but is actually a robot?"

Pipsqueak let out an offended meow before saying, "I'm not a robot!"

"You're right," Harrison said. "Robots don't grow. But what if her growth were triggered by a robot? Nanotechnology!"

"You just wanted to say *nanotechnology.*"

"Yeah, I did," Harrison admitted.

She laughed. "Any other new ideas?"

"Pipsqueak could have come from outer space. Or another dimension. Parallel dimension? Pocket dimension? Mirror dimension?"

"Or the future," Zoe suggested. "A far future where giant cats rule the world."

"I like that one," Pipsqueak said.

They kept batting ideas back and forth until at last Pipsqueak stopped.

Checking her phone, Zoe saw it was near midnight. "Where are we?"

"North?" Pipsqueak guessed.

Harrison yawned behind her, got out his phone, and said, "Okay, let me just see where . . . Yeah, there's a green patch. That means a national forest. We can camp there, off the road. Catch some sleep. Continue on tomorrow." He gave directions.

Soon they were deep among pine trees, with Pipsqueak

squeezing between the trunks. Pine needles brushed against Zoe's legs. She squinted into the darkness, trying to differentiate between the layers of shadows.

Getting out her flashlight, she clicked it on and saw branches, trunks, and bushes. "Think we're far enough from the road?"

"Probably?" Harrison guessed. "I don't hear cars."

Pipsqueak flopped down, sandwiched between several tree trunks, and Zoe and Harrison slid off her back. As Harrison retrieved his flashlight, Zoe shone hers on the trees around them and tried not to feel nervous about being alone in the woods at night. *Harrison's here,* she reminded herself. *He's camped plenty of times before. And Pipsqueak—I'm not alone.*

She heard a skittering noise from the shoebox in her backpack.

*Definitely not alone.*

Sitting on the mossy ground, Zoe opened the top of the shoebox and aimed the flashlight inside. The mouse with the blue butterfly wings froze. It twitched its nose. "Hey, hi there," Zoe said softly. "You're okay. Want some dinner?"

"What's in the box?" Pipsqueak asked.

The mouse let out a shrill *Squeak!*

"Remember the mouse from the school?" Zoe said to Pipsqueak. "It grew wings, so . . . we brought it with us." Cupping her free hand under the mouse, Zoe lifted it up. "Shh, don't be scared. We're all friends here. Right, Pipsqueak?"

"Of course," Pipsqueak said. "I'm friendly, not scary." She curled her tail around herself, the picture of harmless innocence if she'd been several times smaller.

The mouse whimpered. "Don't eat me."

Harrison darted over to them with his flashlight. "It's talking. Awesome!"

Zoe was so surprised she almost dropped the mouse. *Another talking animal?* "No one is going to eat you. I promise. We're friends."

It fluttered its wings. "You can understand me?" Rising up an inch and then plopping back down into Zoe's hands, the mouse marveled, "I can *fly?*"

"I'm Zoe, this is Harrison, and that's Pipsqueak. What's your name?"

The mouse flapped its wings, rising up and then doing a loop in the air. Harrison tracked it with his flashlight. "Wow! I really *can* fly!" it squeaked. "I'm a flying mouse!"

Zoe laughed as it landed on the mossy ground. "Yes, you are."

"Sorry, Pipsqueak," Harrison said to the cat. "You were a super-cute kitten, but this is now literally the cutest thing I've ever seen."

Pipsqueak peered over their shoulders down at the tiny winged mouse. "I can't even be offended. It's ridiculously cute."

Twisting around in a circle, the mouse admired its wings. "I am magnificent."

"Are you a boy mouse or a girl mouse?" Pipsqueak asked.

"Boy mouse," the mouse said.

"Are you even still a mouse?" Harrison asked.

The mouse seemed flummoxed by that question. "Um . . ."

"Are you hungry?" Zoe asked him. Tucking her flashlight under her arm, she scooped out a handful of the mouse food and used the top of Harrison's canteen to pour some water. She laid it next to the mouse on a patch of moss.

"First wings, then dinner! This is the best day ever." The mouse began to munch.

"So, um, we're a long way from your school."

"Good," the mouse said around a mouthful of food. "It's not nice there. Especially for a mouse. Even a flying mouse." He fluttered his wings. "They're so beautiful! I'm beautiful!"

At least the mouse seemed to be taking this well. It made Zoe feel a little better about bringing him with them. "We're going to my Aunt Alecia's. She knows about extraordinary creatures like you and Pipsqueak. I know you didn't choose to come with us, but you're welcome to stay with us. She might be able to help you."

"Why do I need help? I'm free and have wings! And dinner!" The mouse stuck his face back into the food and continued gobbling.

"She might be able to tell us why you can talk and why you have wings," Harrison said.

"I'd like to know that," the mouse said, his cheeks stuffed.

"We should be there tomorrow," Zoe told the mouse. "Or the day after." According to the GPS in their phones, they'd covered a lot of miles, but they still weren't even in New Hampshire yet. "Probably the day after."

"Hope your aunt is okay with another guest," Harrison said.

After kneading a patch of dried pine needles with her claws, Pipsqueak curled up on top of a bush, flattening it. Wrapping her tail around herself, she closed her eyes.

Finishing his dinner, the mouse half fluttered, half hopped around the clearing. Harrison followed him with his flashlight beam for a while, but then trained the light on his backpack.

"It's not supposed to rain, so I didn't bring the tent," he said to Zoe. "Just find a spot without rocks or too many sticks, and lay out your sleeping bag." He sounded more excited than nervous, which made Zoe feel better. "It's not cold, so we won't need a fire. We can curl up in Pipsqueak's fur if the temperature drops."

Following Harrison's lead, Zoe unrolled her sleeping bag. She opened her backpack, shone her flashlight in, and dug into the food she'd brought. Harrison unwrapped a square of aluminum foil from his pack. In it was a cold and limp grilled cheese sandwich. When he noticed Zoe looking at it, he said, "What? It's my favorite."

She knew that. It was virtually the only thing he'd eat. "How many did you bring?" She directed her flashlight at his backpack.

"A few," he said defensively.

She raised both her eyebrows.

"A lot?"

While the mouse flew in wobbly circles above them, Zoe and Harrison ate their dinner. Zoe ate her banana first—it was only a little brown from being jostled in her backpack—then a bag of

Cheerios. She had a bagel she planned to eat for breakfast, or whatever meal they ate next. She wished there had been a way to bring cream cheese. Or pizza. Or a hamburger.

Finishing his grilled cheese, Harrison crawled into his sleeping bag. In the dark somewhere above them, the mouse chirped, "Good night, my rescuers!"

"Good night, flying mouse," Pipsqueak said.

"Good night," Zoe and Harrison echoed.

Zoe unzipped her sleeping bag. But she didn't climb in. She aimed her flashlight at the trees. "Um, Harrison . . . So what do you do about bathrooms when you're camping?"

"Don't pee in camp," Harrison said properly. "And dig a hole if you have to go number two. I brought a trowel. It was my grandmother's."

"You brought your grandma's . . . what?"

"Poop shovel. I brought her poop shovel."

"Ah." Luckily, Zoe didn't need that right now. "That's nice? I'm sure your grandma would be proud that you brought, ah, a family heirloom."

"Take the flashlight, walk in a straight line twenty steps, and then come back twenty steps. That way, you're far enough for privacy, but you can call out if you get lost. Oh, and if you need to wipe, use a leaf. But do *not* use a poison ivy leaf."

Zoe felt as if her cheeks were burning. She talked about a lot of things with Harrison, but this was not her favorite conversation. "Okay. How do I tell what's poison ivy?"

"'Leaves of three, let it be,'" he quoted. More quietly, he said, "I think my grandmother would have liked this trip. And yes, she would be proud I brought the poop shovel."

Lighting her way with her flashlight, Zoe counted twenty steps from their camp. Behind her, she could hear Pipsqueak already snoring—a kind of purr-hum—and when she glanced back, she could see the mound of the cat's great body silhouetted by the glow from Harrison's flashlight. Aiming hers away from herself, she did what she had to do and then prepared to return.

Then she heard a rustling in the bushes nearby.

She froze.

"Pipsqueak?" she whispered.

But she could still hear Pipsqueak back with Harrison, breathing her purr-like snore.

She heard a soft rumble that sounded like a growl.

*A wolf?* she wondered.

It couldn't be. They weren't in the middle of nowhere. Yes, this whole area was marked as a national forest on the phone's map, but they were close to a highway and not far from a town. She swung her flashlight back and forth, illuminating the nearest trees.

*There aren't wolves this close to where people live,* Zoe thought. But it had sounded wolflike. Maybe? She saw a shape pad out of the darkness into the beam of her flashlight.

A dog!

What was a dog doing out here? They weren't near any houses.

As it drew closer, she saw it wasn't an ordinary dog. It was shaped like a terrier, medium-size with scruffy fur . . . but its fur was green. Not greenish, but bright green.

Zoe wondered if it was lost. She took a step forward. "It's okay, puppy . . ."

The dog tensed and opened its jaws to reveal row after row of teeth. Far too many and far too sharp. Like a shark. They gleamed with drool in the light of the flashlight.

She screamed, pivoted, and ran toward their camp. Her flashlight beam bobbed in front of her. Ahead, she saw Harrison aim his flashlight at her.

"What's wrong?" he called.

"Dog! Teeth!" She heard it chasing her, crashing through the bushes. Reaching the clearing, she didn't see Pipsqueak. The dog was still following her, catching up, but where was—

On instinct, Zoe looked up.

The cat was climbing a pine tree. When she was halfway up, the tree began to tilt from her weight. As Zoe ran past, she cried, "Watch out!" She shoved Harrison aside as Pipsqueak landed on the ground between them and the dog.

Hissing, she whacked the dog's nose with her claws.

Yelping, the dog fled.

Zoe and Harrison rushed to her. "That was amazing!" Zoe cried.

Harrison echoed, "Incredible! Wish I could have videoed it."

"Are you hurt?" Zoe asked the cat.

Pipsqueak was licking her fur all over. "Of course not. Cats always land on their feet! I read it in a book." She paused in her licking. "Are you?"

"We're fine," Zoe said.

Pipsqueak studied them for a second, then licked their heads, as if they were kittens she was grooming.

"Ew!" Harrison cried.

Laughing, Zoe wiped her cheeks and said, "Um, thanks? I mean, really, thanks!"

"You chased off a wild dog—or something. Whatever it was!" Harrison said.

"You were awesome," Zoe told her.

Pipsqueak preened. "Yes, I was! Wasn't I? Rest a little now. I'll watch over you. And the weird, adorable mouse."

From a tree above them in the darkness, the mouse piped up, "I'm adorable, and you're awesome."

"Yes, you both are," Zoe said.

They waited for a while, watching the shadows around the clearing, but the strange dog didn't return. When they finally felt safe enough, Zoe and Harrison climbed into their sleeping bags.

Lying down, Zoe didn't think she'd be able to sleep, but eventually her brain stopped whirling in circles and she fell asleep, with Harrison snoring beside her.

# CHAPTER 12

**Zoe woke, convinced she'd slept** on top of a hundred rocks that she hadn't noticed in the dark when she'd put down her sleeping bag. Still fuzzy with sleep (or lack of sleep), she blinked open her eyes and . . .

Saw a green dog.

It looked like the same dog from the night before, terrier-size with a scruffy face, and as green as a leaf. Its jaw was closed, hiding the terrible teeth. Zoe opened her mouth to scream, but before she could let out even a peep, the dog bolted and was gone.

"Harrison! Pipsqueak!"

Beside her, Harrison sat up and pushed his glasses onto his face. "What's wrong?"

"The dog was back!"

Fully awake, he scrambled out of his sleeping bag.

Alert, Pipsqueak prowled through the trees around the clearing. A few moments later she returned. "If it was here, it's gone now."

Keeping an eye on the trees, Zoe brushed her teeth with a little water from her canteen and tried to drag a brush through her hair.

She felt her hair frizz around her like a halo. Her legs ached like . . . well, like she'd been riding a giant cat all day.

They packed up camp and continued on.

Though she kept an eye out, she didn't see the dog again.

Over the next several hours they fell into a rhythm. They stuck to the trees, waiting to cross any streets until the roads were as empty as possible and then racing across at top speed. The flying mouse would zoom ahead first to watch for cars. It took Pipsqueak only three strides to reach the safety of the other side, and then they'd all disappear into the woods again. They avoided towns as best they could, but when the towns bled into one another too closely to bypass without going too far out of their way, Pipsqueak would leap onto the roofs—that was Zoe's favorite part.

They didn't notice when they crossed into New Hampshire, realizing it only when they caught a glimpse of a highway sign through the trees as they veered closer to a road. To save their phone batteries, they tried to resist checking the map more than once an hour.

"Wish Pipsqueak came with an odometer," Harrison said.

"Cats definitely don't come with odometers," Zoe said.

"I have whiskers," Pipsqueak offered.

Riding on top of Pipsqueak's head, the mouse said, "You have lovely whiskers!"

"Yeah, that's not the same," Harrison said. "If I knew how fast we were going, I'd know how long this is going to take."

"Are you trying to ask if we're there yet?" Zoe guessed.

"Well . . . yeah."

"We're not there yet."

Aunt Alecia lived fairly far north in New Hampshire, nearly to the White Mountains. They had a lot farther to go.

"Where are we going again?" the mouse asked.

"My aunt's house," Zoe said. "She'll be able to help us."

"Oh, I remember! You told me that! And I told you, you already helped me!" the mouse said, performing a loop above Zoe. "Look at me! No more cage! I'm free!"

"She'll free you more?" Zoe guessed.

*Maybe the mouse doesn't need any help,* she thought. He seemed happy, and he was small enough to hide easily. Petting Pipsqueak between her enormous ears, Zoe wished that the kitten's changes were easier to disguise. But a giant talking cat . . . *We can hide the talking, but not the size.*

What if going back to normal meant that Pipsqueak would stop talking too? She wouldn't have to lose that ability, would she? *You don't know that's even a possibility,* Zoe scolded herself. *You don't know anything. Except that she can't stay as she is.*

They kept going.

As the day wore on, the novelty of traveling by cat began to wear off, and it became clearer that they weren't going to reach Aunt Alecia's before nightfall.

"I want a shower," Zoe said as they skirted another town. "With soap. Lots and lots of soap. Also, a real bed with a thousand pillows."

"I want to repack," Harrison said. "My grandma . . . I didn't do as good a job as she always did. I think she'd be disappointed. Especially since we camped and didn't eat a single s'more."

"We were nearly attacked by a wild green dog," Zoe said. "Not so much time for s'mores. I think your grandma would have understood."

"Maybe," Harrison said, but he bit off the word, as if *he* didn't understand.

"Well, I'm having fun," Pipsqueak said. "We're seeing things I read about when I was hiding in the shed. We're having an adventure! Our own incredible journey!"

The cat did seem happy, sniffing her way through the woods, running parallel to highways. Many of the places they found were beautiful: streams that tumbled over rocks, meadows that whispered with wind, empty stretches of road that were dappled with sunlight poking through leaves. They continued to avoid towns as much as possible, which grew easier the farther north they went.

"I need to charge my phone," Harrison said. "And I think the grilled cheese went bad. It doesn't taste right. How about we stop for dinner?"

"You need to stop eating non-refrigerated cheese," Zoe said. "You're going to make yourself sick."

Pipsqueak spoke up. "Please don't vomit in my fur."

"Do you have any more snacks?" Harrison asked.

Zoe handed him a bag of Goldfish and an apple. "Maybe we

could stop at a restaurant or a store, since we're not going to get to Aunt Alecia's today. How much money did you bring?"

"Five dollars and eighty-six cents."

"Are you serious?"

Harrison looked defensive. "I have to buy my own video games, you know, and birthday money only goes so far. Especially if you add in Carvel Flying Saucers, which I do. How much do you have?"

"Eighteen dollars."

That could buy them some food.

"So we just stop at a McDonald's?" Harrison asked. "With a giant cat? The mouse is inconspicuous, but Pipsqueak . . . not so much."

*Yeah, that wouldn't be a good idea,* she thought.

The highway had a few rest stops along it, but even if they found Pipsqueak a dumpster or something else big enough to hide behind, if Zoe and Harrison showed up without a car or parents or any adults . . . Two kids traveling on foot—they'd look suspicious. But Zoe was starting to worry. They needed to check in with home, and their phone batteries were seriously low. Worse, they were also low on both food and water, despite trying to pack as much as they could. Pipsqueak had already eaten the bulk of the dry cat food Zoe had crammed into her backpack. She hadn't realized that Pipsqueak would be using more energy traveling and would need to eat more for each meal. And the cat was continuing to grow.

Taking a tiny sip of lukewarm water, Zoe thought, *I'd trade my arm for a soda. Or at least a finger or two. Maybe just a fingernail clipping.*

At last they spotted a store that wasn't so exposed: the Hammermill Country Store. One of those gingerbread house–type New England stores, it was off the highway, tucked between trees. On the front porch were wood carvings of bears and rabbits and beavers, like the kind her aunt made, each of them as tall as Zoe. A sign in the window said they sold fresh maple syrup and fudge. The curtains were lace, with apples printed on them, and only one vehicle sat in the parking lot, a pickup truck that probably belonged to a store employee.

"This could work," Zoe said. "Pipsqueak, can you stay hidden? And can you keep an eye on the mouse without totally traumatizing him?"

"Of course!" Pipsqueak said, sounding offended that Zoe would question her mouse-sitting skills. "He's too cute to chase."

The mouse squeaked, "We are friends! She was there when I ascended to freedom! Glorious winged freedom!"

"That's right," Pipsqueak said. "Your wings are very nice."

Sliding off Pipsqueak's back, Zoe left her backpack with the cat and mouse, then climbed onto the porch and peered in through a window. In the corner, she saw a refrigerator filled with sodas, Vitaminwater, and Gatorade.

“It’s open,” she reported.

Also shedding his backpack, Harrison joined her on the porch. “What do we say if anyone asks who we are and where we’re from?”

“The truth,” Zoe said. “At least some of it. We’re on a camping trip.”

“Maybe they’ll let us charge our phones.”

Zoe glanced back at the trees to see if Pipsqueak was hidden. She thought she saw a glimpse of something dog-size, furry, and green darting through the bushes, but it was only for a split second.

A bell rang on top of the door as they went inside.

The store was stuffed with tourist knickknacks: little snow globes with (plastic) wood bridges inside them, oven mitts shaped like lobsters, place mats with a picture of the Old Man of the Mountain. Lots of fake license plates with sayings on them. A bunch more of the wood carvings.

“Welcome to Hammermill,” a bored woman at the cash register said without looking up. She was perched on a stool and playing on her phone.

“Hi,” Zoe said as she headed for the fridge with the sodas.

Harrison lingered by the fudge display. “Fudge for dinner?” he asked hopefully.

“Why not?” Zoe said. “I don’t think they have grilled cheese.”

They paid for a chunk of fudge, two sodas, and two prepackaged sandwiches.

"Can we charge our phones?" Harrison asked the employee.

"Sure," the bored woman said. She nodded toward the back of the store, where quilts hung on racks. "Outlet by the bathroom."

They plugged their phones in, then took turns using the bathroom. Zoe was very happy to have toilet paper again.

Sitting on the floor next to the electrical outlet with Harrison, Zoe checked her phone. She'd missed only one text, from Surita, saying that she'd seen a news report about a mountain lion sighting at their elementary school and that she hoped they were far away from there. Zoe wrote back, promising they'd be more careful. And then she took a deep breath. "Ready? I'm going to do the call."

Surita had advised that they call as well as text sometimes, to add to the believability. Keeping her phone plugged in so it would continue charging, Zoe held it to her ear as it rang.

Alex answered. "Hello?"

Hearing his voice, she felt a flood of missing him. She hadn't expected it, and for a second, she couldn't speak. She squeaked out, "Hi, Alex."

"Zoe? Are you okay? You sound weird."

"Just . . ." She took a breath. ". . . miss you. That's all." She rushed on: "But I'm having a great time. Camp is . . . everything I hoped it would be."

"Good. Glad to hear it." His voice grew distant as he called, "Mom? Dad? Zoe's on the phone!" Then: "Yeah, camp let her call.

It's not a prison." Another pause; then he said to Zoe, "Everyone wants to know if you're having fun."

"Yeah. Everything's great." She had to think of a detail, something specific, but not too elaborate. Surita had said there was a lake. "Swam in the lake today. It was nice."

"Any fish nibble your toes?"

"Just a Loch Ness Monster."

"Tell him you taste better with ketchup," Alex said. "Oh, wait. Here's Mom."

There was a scuffling sound. She waited and then heard her mom's voice. "Zoe? Are you doing okay? Do you have everything you need? Have you gotten poison ivy yet?"

"No poison ivy." She began to feel more confident. They seemed to fully believe she was at camp. *Maybe this is working.* Harrison offered her a piece of fudge. She shook her head—not until she was done with the call. "I was just telling Alex I went swimming in the lake today."

"Really? With all the rain?" Mom asked.

*Rain?*

"Surita said it poured all day, and everyone was stuck doing arts and crafts in the lodge."

Zoe forced a laugh. "Hah! Today? Did I say today? Obviously we didn't swim today. Way too much rain. We're going to swim tomorrow."

"Good. If you're ever swimming and you hear thunder, get out of the water immediately. And don't touch anything with three leaves. And wear your sunscreen." She sped up. "Wash your hands a lot so you don't get any germs and—hold on, your father wants to say hello. Love you."

"Love you," Zoe said, and then her dad was on the phone.

"Zoe!" Dad said, his voice warm. "Do you miss us as much as we miss you?"

In the background, she heard Alex say, "Dad, that's the opposite of what you're supposed to say."

Then, muffled, Dad to Alex: "Why can't I say that?"

Alex, muffled: "She's supposed to . . . *mumble, mumble* . . . great time so . . . *mumble, mumble* . . . September . . ."

Dad came back: "Are you having a great time? Making memories you'll treasure forever?"

She glanced at Harrison, who had fudge smeared on his cheeks. He was texting his family. She hoped he heard her say it was raining at camp. Certainly wasn't raining here. "Yeah, I am. Vermont is great!"

"Good. You concentrate on having a good time and not getting eaten by any lake monsters."

"I'll be careful," she promised.

"And you'll have fun?"

"That too." She was passed around one more time to say bye to each of them, and then she hung up. Her eyes felt wet. She hadn't expected that.

Harrison studied her face, and she knew he had to see her almost-tears. She hoped he didn't ask, because then she was sure she'd start crying. Thankfully, he didn't.

He held out a chunk of mushed chocolate. "Fudge?"

She took it and shoved it all into her mouth.

It made an excellent dinner—fudge first, then sandwiches.

When they finished, they headed for the door. They thought they'd made it out without any issues, but then the woman from the cash register hurried after them onto the porch. "Wait, please," she said.

Automatically, Zoe paused. Then she thought: *We should run.* But that would look suspicious. She studied the distance between them and the woods.

"Are you in some kind of trouble?" the woman asked. "Have you run away from home?"

Zoe glanced at Harrison, who was trembling like a leaf. *No wonder she followed us. We look like two scared kids.*

*Which is accurate.*

She wondered how much of their phone conversations the woman had heard. *Probably all of it, including when I said "Vermont."* Zoe wished they'd been more careful. With luck, the cashier would assume they were attending a nearby camp. Without luck . . .

"We're fine!" Harrison squeaked. "All fine here! Thanks!"

The woman stepped toward them. "Let me call someone who can help—"

Before she could finish speaking, Pipsqueak leaped from the roof of the country store and landed in front of them with a *whoomp!* Dust and fur billowed up.

The employee screamed.

"No!" Zoe yelled.

"Jump on!" Pipsqueak cried. "I will rescue you!"

The woman ran, screaming, toward her truck, clutching her phone as she dialed. Probably 911, Zoe guessed, not whatever number you'd call to help two pathetic lost children. The woman was shouting into the phone as Zoe and Harrison climbed onto Pipsqueak's back.

Pipsqueak bounded toward the woods, trumpeting, "I am awesome!" She crashed over bushes and weaved between the trees, pausing only long enough for them to pick up their backpacks. The mouse flew alongside them, flitting between the leaves.

"Pipsqueak, that was *not* good!" Zoe said.

"But . . ." Pipsqueak slowed. "I saw your face! You looked scared, the same way you did when I protected you from the green dog with teeth. I thought you needed saving."

"Well, we didn't," Harrison said.

Stopping, Pipsqueak twisted around to look behind them. "Should we go back?"

"We can't," Zoe said. "She's seen you. And heard you!"

"You scared her half to death," Harrison said, and Pipsqueak cringed as if she'd been smacked on the nose. "We have to get as far from here as possible."

"And hope that no one believes her," Zoe said.

# CHAPTER 13

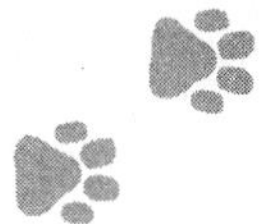

**THEY SPENT A SECOND NIGHT OUTSIDE,** in another forest out of sight of a road.

None of them talked much as they set up camp, and they all fell asleep nearly instantly to the sound of the winged mouse snoring in tiny squeaks.

When Zoe woke at dawn (thankfully, without seeing the green dog this time), she was still worrying about what had happened at the country store. She felt extra anxious about reaching Aunt Alecia. The sooner they could turn Pipsqueak back into an ordinary cat, the better.

She hadn't realized her worrying had rubbed off on Pipsqueak until they were underway, traveling in silence, and the cat suddenly asked, "Are you mad at me?"

"Of course not," Zoe said.

The mouse piped up. "Who's mad at who?"

"No one," Zoe reassured him. "We just . . . can't let Pipsqueak be seen by anyone else, that's all." *Or heard,* she thought. And then she wished she hadn't thought that. She didn't want Pipsqueak to stop talking! Just . . . it wasn't safe for other people to hear her.

"Because I'm scary," Pipsqueak said miserably.

Zoe didn't like hearing her so upset. "You scared that woman; you're not scary. There's a difference. One is how you act, and the other is how you are." Except that Pipsqueak hadn't been acting scary on the school playground. Yes, she'd intentionally scared the country store cashier, but the mother with the toddler had reacted because of the cat's size.

"She wouldn't have been scared if I hadn't grown so huge."

"We'll make you small again," Zoe promised. "Before anyone else sees you."

"I don't want anyone to be scared of me."

Circling over Pipsqueak's head, the mouse said, "I'm not scared of you. Yes, I was, the first time I saw you, but now that I know you, we're friends! I think people—and mice—just need to get to know you."

"Maybe—but maybe not," Pipsqueak said, and then fell quiet, brooding.

Zoe replayed the conversation in her head, wishing she'd said things differently. Sure, Pipsqueak had made a mistake, but Zoe didn't want her feeling bad about herself.

"You know what's best?" Harrison said, breaking the silence. "Grilled cheese with tomato. Now, I don't normally like tomato, on account of the inner squishiness, but with cheese . . . Yum. Also, bacon is a classic, but try any other meat and it's not grilled cheese anymore. It's a panini. And I don't want a panini."

Zoe almost laughed. Trust Harrison to come up with an absolutely random conversation topic to change the mood. "Everyone likes paninis."

"The problem with paninis is the ooze. You see, it's squished in a panini press, and when it comes out, the flattened bread can't contain the innards. Grilled cheese, on the other hand, has the perfect ratio of bread to innards—"

The flying mouse squeaked as he flew loops over Harrison's head. "Cheese is good!"

"Exactly," Harrison agreed.

"Once, a boy gave me a bite of string cheese from his snack box," the mouse said. "I will love him forever. Is grilled cheese as glorious as string cheese?"

"I like string," Pipsqueak said.

"String cheese," Harrison corrected. "It's mozzarella."

And they were off discussing the merits of various cheeses. It seemed to be successfully distracting Pipsqueak from worrying. *Thanks, Harrison,* Zoe thought.

But she couldn't stop wondering what was going to happen when they reached Aunt Alecia's. Would her aunt be happy to see them? Would she be able to shrink Pipsqueak right away? What would she do about the mouse?

After a while, when the cheese conversation flagged, Zoe

checked her phone. "Seven miles left." No more highways. No towns. Just smaller squiggly roads.

Pipsqueak slowed as they approached a field. She poked her nose out between the trees. A motionless tractor sat beside a large roll of hay.

"Should we go around?" Harrison asked.

"I don't see anyone," Zoe said. They could skirt the field, but the trees looked thin to the west and there was a road to the east. Straight across might be best. "How fast can you run?"

Pipsqueak twisted her neck to give them the cat equivalent of a grin. "Let's find out!"

Zoe grabbed on tighter to a wad of fur as Pipsqueak broke into a run across the field. She felt the sun on her back and heard the wind rush past her ears. Harrison hung on tight behind her. Pipsqueak's pace, unlike that of a galloping horse, was smooth and soundless. The grassy field whispered around them as the stalks parted. Zoe wanted to cheer. With the wind in her face and her heart pounding in her chest, once again she felt as if she were flying.

Midway across the field, Zoe heard the squeal of tires. She glanced toward the road. A man and a woman were climbing out of a pickup truck. "We've been seen!" she said.

"Faster!" Harrison cried.

The trees were only a few yards away. Zoe and Harrison flattened down on Pipsqueak's back as the giant cat barreled between the trees, smashing the bushes, and then slowed down to weave between the tree trunks. Zoe wished she could tell her to keep running.

"Wow, that was fast," Harrison said queasily.

"Was it fast enough?" Pipsqueak asked.

"Absolutely." The truck had been far away. If they'd gotten a picture, it couldn't have been a good one. "Pipsqueak, I think you're the fastest cat ever!"

Pipsqueak let out a pleased purr.

"We should stick to the woods, though, to be safe," Harrison said. "And maybe not go quite so fast?"

"Please don't vomit in the fur," Pipsqueak and Zoe said simultaneously.

Harrison waved them off. "I'm fine," he said. "At least I don't feel as green as that dog looked. Did you see it back there? I think it's still following us."

Zoe twisted, looking all around them. "Where?"

"I'm pretty sure it's gone now," Harrison said. "But it's out there somewhere."

"I keep seeing it too," Zoe said. "You know, I'm not sure it's actually dangerous. It did growl at me in the woods—at least I thought that's what I heard. Anyway, it didn't attack. I just ran when I saw its teeth. Maybe I shouldn't have."

"It showed its teeth," Harrison pointed out. "That's reason enough to run."

"But . . . I don't know." It had been following them for a while now and hadn't tried to attack or even approach them. Maybe it was just curious. Or something.

"Do you think it's always been green and toothy, or do you think it, you know, *changed?*" Harrison asked. "Like Pipsqueak and the mouse . . . Mouse, you really need a name. Do you have one?"

"The class voted to name me Squeakers," the mouse said. "But I don't think that's an awesome enough name for a mouse with wings."

"How about Mickey?" Harrison suggested.

"Taken," Zoe said.

"Bat-mouse?"

"Cute, but they're more like butterfly wings," Zoe said. "Buttermouse?"

"Buttermouse." Harrison nodded.

"I love Buttermouse!" the mouse cried. "And I love my butterfly wings!"

Zoe studied the mouse as he flew above them. She thought his fur was beginning to change color: hints of blue, green, and purple peeking through the white. She wondered if the dog had changed color the same way. Maybe he'd once been an ordinary animal too. Or he could be an entirely different kind of impossible creature.

As they continued through the woods, Zoe kept an eye out for the green dog. A few times she thought she saw something, but then a squirrel or a bird would emerge from the branches. About a mile away from Aunt Alecia's house, Harrison asked, "Do you think your aunt is really going to be able to help?"

"She said she would," Zoe said. "She knows about giant cats."

"What happened between your mom and her sister?"

Zoe knew only what she'd overheard, but that was a fair amount. "They used to be close. Visited all the time. Talked a lot. But then . . . I don't know. Fewer visits. And then when Mom started talking about taking a new job at the mayor's office, they had an argument. My aunt claimed that one of her horses was actually a unicorn. Or a unicorn in a horse's body. And my mom said she had to stop saying weird things like that because it would reflect badly on people who knew her . . . Mom's new job is out in the public eye, and she has to be more careful of what people think." *She's embarrassed by her own sister,* Zoe thought, *so embarrassed that she's not speaking to her, just because Aunt Alecia believes in things that can't exist. Like a giant cat. I was right not to tell Mom about Pipsqueak.* "Anyway, Aunt Alecia didn't like that, and they didn't talk much after that."

"Do you think she really has a unicorn?" Harrison asked.

"We have Pipsqueak and Buttermouse," Zoe said. "I don't think it's impossible." She considered it, trying to imagine a real, live unicorn. All she could picture were cartoon unicorns, like She-Ra's rainbow-maned winged unicorn. "Do you think it burps cupcakes?"

"Almost certainly," Harrison said. And then he burped, as if to demonstrate that he did not belch cupcakes. Both of them laughed. Buttermouse, back on Pipsqueak's tail, his favorite perch, squealed with mouse laughter.

And then Pipsqueak halted.

Zoe felt the cat's shoulder muscles tense beneath her, and Pipsqueak's nose twitched.

Harrison whispered, "What's wrong?"

Quietly Pipsqueak spelled, "D-o-g."

Ahead of them, between two bushes, stood the green dog. It was smaller than Harrison's Fibonacci, with fur that stuck out at all angles. It didn't look scary, especially while Zoe was up on Pipsqueak's back. Its tail was tucked between its legs, and its mouth was closed, hiding its many teeth.

"It's a terrier," Harrison whispered. "And it can't spell." He amended, "Probably?"

"It must have followed us," Zoe said. But why? "I'm going to make friends."

"Are you sure that's a good idea?" Harrison asked. "Remember the teeth?"

She couldn't forget the sight of those teeth. Still, in daylight, the dog looked harmless, more frightened than vicious. *Maybe I was wrong about it. Like the mother and the cashier were wrong about Pipsqueak.*

Sliding off Pipsqueak's back, Zoe crept toward the dog with her hand outstretched, palm up. "That's a good boy. Stay. Good boy."

The dog was even greener than Zoe remembered, with green eyes too. *Definitely unusual,* Zoe thought. It began to wag its tail. Or . . . tails? "Are those extra tails?" She didn't remember seeing multiple tails, though it had been dark.

Buttermouse had perched on one of the branches above them. "I see three!" he cried. Sure enough, the green dog had three fluffy tails.

Zoe stepped closer, and then Pipsqueak stuck her head past Zoe to look at the tails.

The dog yelped, turned, and ran.

"Sorry," Pipsqueak said. "I just wanted to see it better."

"Should we follow it?" Harrison asked.

Returning to Pipsqueak, Zoe shook her head. "We don't want to scare it more. Maybe it will approach us again if we don't act threatening. Let's just get to Aunt Alecia's and worry about the dog later."

The map on Harrison's phone led them to a rustic house beneath a circle of pine trees. Made of uneven wood, it looked like a beautiful patchwork quilt, every slat stained a different color. Outside, there were three sheds and all sorts of equipment strewn about—a riding lawn mower, various saws, several workbenches, as well as a huge pile of chopped wood leaning up against one side of the house. And many lawn ornaments made out of carved wood: lots of bears, several eagles, a few wolves. Pipsqueak approached slowly, keeping near the pine trees.

There weren't any neighbors close enough to see, which was good. Zoe looked for signs of movement inside. Maybe Aunt Alecia was at the back of the house.

"She likes boxes," Pipsqueak said approvingly, sniffing the

nearest shed and poking at it with her nose. It creaked as it tilted to the side, and she withdrew. "I didn't do it."

"Yes, you did," Zoe said, climbing off her back. "Try not to break anything, okay? I'm going to knock on the door."

"What should I do?" Pipsqueak asked.

Zoe was suddenly nervous. *This is it!* "Hide somewhere, at least until we know whether she's alone." They'd made it all the way here. It would be terrible to mess up at the very last moment.

"Good idea," Harrison said. "What do you think she's going to say when she realizes we're here on our own?"

"Worst case, she calls my parents." Though she tried to say it as if that was no big deal, she privately thought it would be a disaster. If Aunt Alecia broke her silence to report that Zoe had lied about camp and was wandering around New Hampshire, Zoe's parents would be beyond upset. *Let's hope she really doesn't want to talk to Mom.*

*And that she's willing to talk to me.*

Zoe squared her shoulders, approached the house, and knocked on the door.

She waited.

No one answered.

Standing on her tiptoes, she tried to peer into the window at the top of the door. All she saw was the hint of a hallway. Green wallpaper. A mirror. A few mobiles made of forks and spoons and feathers. Zoe knocked again and called, "Hello? Aunt Alecia, are you home?"

Behind her, she heard a crash.

She turned to see Pipsqueak standing next to a knocked-over shed. She'd tried to hide behind it, and it had collapsed like a house of cards, but hiding hadn't worked well anyway. She'd grown on their journey and was now the size of an elephant. The shed's roof had skidded off the walls, and all the walls themselves lay in a heap. It exposed a half-finished wood sculpture of a moose.

"Is anyone home?" Harrison called.

"I don't think so." Zoe tried the door, and it swung open easily. She poked her head inside. "Hello? Aunt Alecia? It's your niece, Zoe. You said to come . . ." She trailed off.

Propped up on a table across from the door was an envelope with two names on it: "Evie and Zoe." Mom and Zoe . . .

"Aunt Alecia's not here," Zoe said, loud enough for Pipsqueak and Harrison to hear her. Disappointment tasted bitter. It hadn't occurred to her that they could make it all the way here and Aunt Alecia might not be home. "Maybe she'll be back soon? She left a note."

She must have believed that Mom would bring her and Pipsqueak. She couldn't have guessed that Zoe would come on her own. *Well, not quite on my own.* Hesitating for only a second, Zoe darted in and opened the letter.

Harrison trotted into the house. "What's it say?"

Pipsqueak poked her nose through the doorway to listen.

"It's addressed to my mom and me."

*Dear Evie and Zoe,*

*I apologize for not being here when you arrived, but I wasn't certain when (or if) you'd come, and I had business that couldn't wait. There's been a sighting of an unusual animal, and I need to see if it needs my help.*

*As for your giant cat problem, bring your cat to the location marked on the map, and you'll find the help you seek. In the meantime, please make yourself at home. There's food in the kitchen and cat food in the pantry.*

*Love,*

*Aunt Alecia*

With a sinking heart, Zoe unfolded a map behind the letter. It showed the White Mountains to the north, with a star drawn in the middle of the wilderness, far from the towns and ski resorts. Many miles away. She held it up for the others to see. "She wants us to take Pipsqueak into the mountains."

# CHAPTER 14

**EVERYONE WAS SILENT FOR AN INSTANT.**

And then Harrison exploded as if he were a soda bottle that had been shaken. "She said she'd help! This isn't helping!"

Zoe agreed. She felt hot tears prick the corners of her eyes, and she blinked them back. "She was supposed to be here." Aunt Alecia was supposed to shrink Pipsqueak and make it so they could return home and live normal lives.

"Yes!" said Harrison. "Come to my house, she said, and we did. And we went and we went . . . And now we're supposed to go off into the mountains by ourselves, following a map—to what? She doesn't even claim she's going to be there when we arrive!"

"What *will* be there?" Buttermouse asked.

"We don't know!" Harrison shouted. "*This* was supposed to be the goal! All we had to do was reach her house, she said. We're supposed to get answers, not a cryptic note and an x-marks-the-spot map! I want answers now!"

*Me too,* Zoe thought. And she wanted the promised help. She tried not to let the disappointment overwhelm her. After all, they did have a map to . . . somewhere? Aunt Alecia's note said they'd find help there. Maybe that help would tell them what to do. "I want answers *and* help."

"We made it!" Harrison said. "Isn't that enough? I don't want another journey!"

Zoe agreed one hundred percent. Aunt Alecia had promised she'd help them if they made it to her house, which they'd done.

*We can't stop now, though!* Zoe thought. *We made it this far. We can make it farther!*

"Maybe your aunt doesn't know what she's talking about," Harrison said. "Maybe this map doesn't lead anywhere. Maybe she doesn't have any answers, and there's no solution to the problem of a giant cat."

Pipsqueak made a little worried *prrt* sound.

"There has to be!" Zoe said. They couldn't have come all this way for nothing. "We can't just bring Pipsqueak back home the way she is. Best case, she'd have to stay hidden in the shed all the time, and that would be a terrible life. Worst—and much more likely—case, she'd be discovered and taken away"—probably to somewhere awful, and where they certainly wouldn't love her the way Zoe did.

Pipsqueak whispered, "Dog."

"Exactly!" Zoe said. "The flying poodle was found, and it was chaos! If we go back now, without knowing anything about what to do about what's happening to my kitten—"

"Dog in the yard," Pipsqueak said louder.

Zoe and Harrison quit arguing.

Stepping outside, they saw the green dog in the yard, sniffing at the wreckage of the shed that Pipsqueak had accidentally destroyed. The dog now sported *six* gloriously fluffy tails, all splayed out like a peacock's feathers.

"Wow, that's a lot of tails," Harrison said, awe in his voice.

"Beautiful tails," Buttermouse said approvingly. "Almost as beautiful as my wings."

"Don't scare him off," Zoe whispered. Each time she saw this dog, she was more and more convinced he was just frightened, not dangerous.

"There must be a reason he's been following us," Harrison whispered back. "I want to know what it is."

"Feed him," Buttermouse suggested. "That's how I knew you were friendly."

"Good idea. If we feed him, he might stay," Zoe said. "I'll see if there's any dog food."

"Cat food too, please," Pipsqueak requested.

Zoe called gently to the dog as she backed through the door. "Don't be scared. It's okay. We won't hurt you. That's a good boy. We'll get you some food. Would you like that? Food?"

He didn't run away, which Zoe took as a good sign.

"Keep an eye on him," Zoe told Harrison.

She hurried through the house, looking for the kitchen, which she found quickly—it wasn't that big a place. It felt a bit like a log cabin. Everything was made of wood, and there was a wood-burning stove in the center of the kitchen. She plugged her phone into an outlet on the counter. In a pantry, she found huge bags of cat food and dog food, as well as rabbit, hamster, and bird food, and she hauled the relevant food to the front of the house, wondering why her aunt stored so much animal food when there didn't seem to be any pets. Then she filed that question low on her mental list of things to ask her aunt, if she ever got the chance.

Outside, Zoe gave some hamster pellets to Buttermouse, poured out some of the dog food, and opened the cat food for Pipsqueak, who plunged her face into it. Zoe retreated to where Harrison stood, just inside the doorway, and watched as the green dog crept toward the porch, hesitating every few steps.

At last the dog reached the food, sniffed it, and began to eat, chomping with his multiple rows of teeth. Wagging his many tails, he looked up and said in a growly voice, "Thank you."

"He talks!" Harrison said.

"At this point it probably would have been more surprising if he didn't," Zoe said. "What's your name? Where did you come from?"

Shoving his muzzle deeper into the food, he didn't answer.

"I bet your name is Oz, for the Emerald City," Zoe said. She kept her voice as light as possible, hoping a casual conversation would make the dog feel more comfortable. She didn't want him to flee as soon as he finished eating. If he was following them for a reason, she wanted to know what it was. *He might need help.*

"Or Hulk? The Hulk's green," Harrison offered.

"Yoda?" Zoe suggested.

"Mike Wazowski."

"Shrek," Zoe said. "Or Beast Boy."

"Green Lantern?" Harrison said. "Except he's not green. Ditto Green Arrow."

"Gamora," Zoe said. "Except he's not a girl dog."

"Wait! I've got it! Kermit."

Zoe tried it out. "Kermit the Dog. Love it." She asked the dog, "What do you think? Do you like it? Do you want to tell us what your name is?"

The dog nosed the empty food dish. "I like Kermit."

Harrison poured him more food. "Why were you following us, Kermit?"

Swallowing, he said, "I . . . don't know. I felt like I should. Like you're my pack, and I'm supposed to be with you."

"Then why did you try to attack us in the woods?" Zoe asked.

"I didn't! I wanted to talk to you, to ask if you were my pack, to ask if that's why I felt like I should follow you. But then the cat chased me away . . ."

"I'm sorry," Pipsqueak said meekly. "I won't chase you away now."

"Thank you," Kermit said. He resumed eating.

After a few more minutes of watching Kermit and Pipsqueak happily chowing down, Zoe returned to the kitchen and filled three more bowls of varying sizes with water for Pipsqueak, Kermit, and Buttermouse.

Harrison helped her carry the bowls outside.

Zoe and Harrison didn't talk to each other as they checked Aunt Alecia's cabinets and refrigerator for food they could eat. Harrison helped himself to a hunk of cheddar cheese, fed some to Buttermouse, who had followed them to the kitchen, and ate the rest with bread. It wasn't exactly a grilled cheese, but it was close. Zoe found raspberry jam and made herself a jam sandwich.

"Guess we have another unexplained mystery," Harrison said. "Why did that dog feel compelled to follow us?"

Taking a chunk of cheese from Harrison's plate, Buttermouse fluttered up to the ceiling and perched on one of the kitchen rafters. "Because you feel like friends. I felt the same way." His blue wings opened and shut as he nibbled on his feast. "I could have flown anywhere once I had my wings of freedom, but I chose to stay with you."

Harrison shook his head. "It feels like there's more than that. I mean, you talked with us before you decided to stick with us. You had a chance to see that you liked us. The dog said he followed on instinct. Why would that be his instinct, especially after Pipsqueak scared him? If your aunt were here—"

"But she's not." Zoe took a deep breath. "I made Pipsqueak a promise that I'd take care of her, and I'm not going to break that promise. Even if it means going farther. Do you . . . Would you . . . What do you want to do?"

For a long moment Harrison didn't say anything. He stared at a bit of faded wallpaper in a way that made Zoe think he wasn't seeing the wallpaper at all, that he was lost in his thoughts. At last he said, in a much quieter voice, "It's just that this is it. Tomorrow's Wednesday. It took us almost three days to get here, and it'll take us the same amount of time to get back. Six days total. This new journey looks like another two days in the opposite direction from home . . . The math doesn't work. If we don't start heading home soon, like tomorrow, we won't make it back by the time camp ends. Surita will have to return home without us, and our parents will know we lied."

Zoe hadn't thought about that. She crossed to where her phone was charging and checked it. It displayed a series of texts from her family, all about how they were looking forward to seeing her on the weekend. Camp was halfway over.

*If we turn around right now, we'll make it back in plenty of time.*

*If we* don't *turn around . . .*

Her family would be furious—and worried.

On the other hand, if they didn't continue, what would happen to Pipsqueak?

But they didn't all have to go. Maybe she could keep Harrison from getting into trouble. "You could call Surita and have her come get you, and I'll take Pipsqueak and the others north. At least then your parents will never know you weren't at camp." She watched his face, hoping he'd say of course he'd come too, no matter what the risk.

He snorted. "Yeah, but when you don't come home, they'll know I let my best friend disappear."

"We'll think up some excuse. Or Surita will."

He was silent again, thinking, and she knew he was tempted. His parents were laid-back, but this was on a whole other level.

"Before, there was a chance we'd find Aunt Alecia and get back home without anyone finding out. Now that chance is over. But there's no need for both of us to get into trouble," Zoe said. It was her cat and her idea. "If you want to call Surita, I'll understand."

"You know she doesn't like to be my taxi service." Harrison managed a wan smile. "Besides, given how long the trip will take, we should have plenty of time to figure out how to tell our parents where we went instead of camp."

Zoe felt herself smiling back at Harrison. "You'll come to the mountains with me, even though it means extending our trip and pretty much erasing any chance we had of getting through this without our parents noticing?"

"Yeah."

"You're sure?"

"We still don't have answers. How can I return home before we know why? *Why* Pipsqueak? *Why* Buttermouse? Maybe even *why* the dog followed us." He shrugged. "Besides, you're my best friend. No way am I making you do this alone."

She felt as if she'd never stop smiling. "Then we'll keep going north until we know why all of it is happening." *And what to do about it.*

They spent the night at Aunt Alecia's house. The next morning, before they left, Zoe texted Surita: "We might not be back by Friday." And then she texted her family, in hopes they wouldn't be too worried: "Having fun! Love you so much!" Plus a bunch of heart emojis.

Before she could shut it off, her phone binged. Surita. "YOU CAN'T BE LATE!!! What do I tell your parents?"

Zoe texted back: "Don't know."

Surita texted a bunch of irate emojis.

Zoe: "Sorry."

Then she turned the phone off.

"Let's go," Zoe said.

She and Harrison climbed onto Pipsqueak's back.

"Do you want to come, Kermit?" Zoe asked.

He barked. "You're pack! Yes!"

They helped him up onto the cat's back, where he curled up between them. Buttermouse rode too, nestled in the fur on Pipsqueak's head.

Loaded with passengers, Pipsqueak headed down the dirt driveway.

Harrison consulted the map, matching it against the map in his phone. "Looks like we have a few fields to cross."

"Feel like running again?" Zoe asked Pipsqueak.

"Oh no," Harrison moaned.

"Oh yes!" Pipsqueak shouted, leaping forward.

Laughing, Zoe held on to the cat's fur. Harrison gripped both Pipsqueak and Kermit, and Buttermouse lifted off, flying alongside them.

Eventually they reached the forested slopes that marked the start of the White Mountains. It was slower going here than through the trees along the highway. These woods had never been tamed for houses or fields—they were just slope after slope of pine trees and birches. And a lot of rocks. So many rocks. *No wonder they call it the Granite State,* Zoe thought. She hoped Pipsqueak's paws were okay after walking so many miles over so many rocks.

At the base of one of the mountains, they traveled alongside a stream. Pipsqueak carefully kept her paws out of the water as she minced from stone to stone. Zoe saw the shadows of fish in the frothing water.

"Any idea how close we are?" Zoe asked Harrison.

"No coverage here."

"Use the map, not your phone."

"Oh, right. Forgot." He unfolded the map Aunt Alecia had left them and studied it. Then he waved it in front of Zoe. "I think we have to pass this ski resort first. Looks like a small one, but still . . ."

"Good thing it's summer," Zoe said.

As they traveled, they saw cows grazing on the slopes, chewing on patches of grass between the old stone walls. The cows didn't seem to notice them. But as Zoe and her friends drew closer to the ski resort, houses began to appear. Gas stations. Antique shops. More antique shops. They stuck to the woods, skirting the tiny town.

"We need to get to the other side of the ski mountain," Harrison said. "I don't think we can follow the road around it. It's too exposed. We'll be seen. I think we'll need to go over the mountain."

They passed the lodge with its empty parking lot. Soon Zoe saw the chairlift. Unused in summer, it looked like a sleeping spider, with its web stretching up the side of the mountain. They slowed as they approached it. "Wish it were running," Zoe said. "It would be a lot easier to cross the mountain if we could just ride up."

"I've never ridden a chairlift," Harrison said.

"I have. Once." Her family had tried skiing. She remembered Aunt Alecia had gone with them. This was long before Mom's new job. "I fell at the top."

"Then it's probably good we aren't riding it," Harrison said.

"I only fell because I was wearing skis."

"I think you've identified the major flaw with skiing," Harrison said.

It was too bad they couldn't use the chairlift. It went straight up through the trees. Zoe eyed the wires, an idea forming. "Cats have really good balance, don't they?"

"Yes," Pipsqueak said. "Why do you ask?"

"Could you walk on that?" Leaning forward on Pipsqueak's back, she pointed at the chairlift wires.

Harrison squeezed her arm. "Zoe, what are you suggesting?"

"We can't ride it. But maybe Pipsqueak doesn't need to."

Pipsqueak trotted to the chairlift, then jumped on top of the base building with Zoe, Harrison, and Kermit clinging to her back. She sniffed at the wires running out of it. The empty, stationary chairs swung in the wind. Placing one paw on the wire, she tested it.

"This is a terrible idea," Harrison said. "What if it snaps?"

"It's made to hold thousands of people on hundreds of chairs. It can take our weight." *At least I think it can,* she thought, then shook off the worry. *Of course it can.*

"What if she falls?"

"I'm a cat," Pipsqueak said reasonably. "I always land on my feet."

She stepped onto the wire, and it sagged beneath her. But Zoe was right—the ski lift had been designed to carry hordes of happy skiers, and now it had to hold only two people plus one elephant-size cat and a dog. Taking a careful step forward, Pipsqueak spread out her weight.

At first she wobbled, stepping over the top clamp of each chair and pausing on each pole, but then she found her footing and began tightrope walking along the bowed wire with assurance.

"She's doing it!" Harrison said.

"Yes, I am!" And Pipsqueak continued on faster, with increased confidence.

In summer, the ski slope looked like a green river. It cut through the pine trees, twisting and turning. A few snow-grooming machines were parked on the sides, looking like slumbering monsters. At trailheads, each green river was marked with a green circle, blue square, or black diamond.

Twisting around, Zoe looked at the view behind them, thinking that all of New Hampshire was visible at once. She saw mountains, fields, farms, towns, rivers. And probably a hundred antique shops. It was the best view she'd ever seen.

And it only got better.

At the top, Pipsqueak leaped off and landed in a crouch beside a map of ski slopes. She trotted a few yards to the bare peak of the mountain, beside a closed lodge. Before them lay the White Mountains.

Zoe felt her eyes widen, as if that would help her see it all at once. Green mountains, blanketed with evergreens, overlapped one another. Beyond them, the green faded to blue, then to purple. Blurred by clouds, the farthest mountains looked as if they were painted. Pipsqueak sighed happily. "I've read about mountain views. It's even more beautiful than I imagined."

"Almost like climbing Mount Everest," Harrison said. "You know—if there were ski slopes and giant cats in the Himalayas. But I imagined a view like this, where it feels like you can see the entire world."

"Which way from here?" Zoe asked. Harrison had Aunt Alecia's map.

Opening it, he studied the map and then pointed. "I think we need to go that way—"

Without waiting for him to finish, Pipsqueak bounded down the opposite side of the mountain, landing many yards down the slope and then leaping again. Zoe whooped as if she were on the best roller coaster ever.

She loved every second of it.

# CHAPTER 15

**The deeper into the White Mountains** they went, the easier it was to avoid people. Zoe wondered if she should worry about wolves, bears, or Bigfeet instead. *Or, as Surita would say, Bigfoots,* she thought.

Reminded of home, Zoe powered up her phone, planning to send a quick text to her family about how great canoeing was today, but there was no signal. She put it back in her pocket and hoped her parents hadn't already started worrying. *We're not late yet!*

Soon, though . . .

Pipsqueak crossed the next slope on silent paws, setting the pace. She seemed more determined than Zoe had ever seen her. Maybe the extra cat food had energized her, or her success with crossing the mountain.

They traveled on and on, between pine trees, across fields, uphill and downhill.

Eventually, though, even Pipsqueak began to flag.

"Anyone else tired?" Harrison asked. They'd been traveling with only a few breaks since they'd left Aunt Alecia's house, and it was deep into twilight. "I'm tired. Can we camp?"

The cat took a few more steps into a clearing and flopped sideways onto the ferns and moss. She'd grown even larger and looked a bit like a very furry elephant lying down for a nap. Zoe, Harrison, and Kermit tumbled off her back. As they scrambled to sit up, they saw Pipsqueak stand, knead the moss and flattened ferns with her claws, and then lie down. She repeated this three more times.

Zoe and Harrison unrolled their sleeping bags. This was their first official night beyond civilization. Sure, they'd camped before, but the other times, they'd known that a highway and the next town weren't far away. Tonight there were only trees and stars and mountains.

It was shockingly loud.

Crickets. Leaves rustling in the wind. The babble of a nearby stream.

Tired all the way down to her pinkie toes, Zoe climbed into her sleeping bag. Bone-deep tired. *I never knew what that phrase meant before.* Every bit of her ached. She closed her eyes.

"Do you think there are bears?" Harrison asked.

"I don't know," Zoe said. "Probably."

"Wolves?"

"Sure."

"Mountain lions?"

"We have a giant cat," Zoe said. "We don't have to worry. They'll all be avoiding us."

"Unless we're in their territory," Harrison said. "Or unless we get between a mama bear and her cubs. Every single survival show ever made says not to do that."

"Pipsqueak, can you tell him not to worry?" Zoe asked.

Pipsqueak laid a paw gently on Harrison's face and licked his hair. "Hush, dog boy."

They lay in the darkness, which wasn't really dark, just as the silence wasn't really silent. In between the branches of the pines, Zoe saw more stars than she'd ever imagined existed. At the apex of the sky, a few looked fuzzy, as if a streak of cloud had stopped moving. "Is that the Milky Way?"

She expected Harrison to answer. He was the one who camped out in his backyard so much, but it was Pipsqueak who said, "Yes. I read about it in *A Beginner's Guide to the Universe*. No cats in it, but there is a constellation called Leo."

Harrison pointed up. "That one's the Big Dipper."

"You can follow the stars in the Big Dipper to find the North Star," Zoe told Pipsqueak. Demonstrating, she traced a line of stars. "See? Right there."

They all stared up at the stars for a while.

"I like seeing the things I read about," Pipsqueak said. "When Aunt Alecia changes me back to a kitten, will I still be able to read?"

"I . . . don't know," Zoe said. "I hope so." Surely Pipsqueak wouldn't have to give up reading. Or talking. Or would she?

They fell silent again.

"The crickets are loud," Harrison complained.

"So are you," Zoe said.

"Good idea. I'll drown them out." He raised his voice and started to sing, "'Row, row, row your boat, gently down the stream' . . ."

Zoe joined in, making it a round. "'Row, row, row your boat' . . ."

After they'd sung it twice through, Pipsqueak began to yowl in harmony with them, or loosely in harmony. Kermit the Dog howled along. Then Harrison switched to yowling instead of words, and Zoe changed to "Meow, meow, meow-meow meow . . ." They kept going in meows and dog howls until Zoe and Harrison were laughing too hard to sing.

"I was right about you being my pack," Kermit said, sighing contentedly. "A pack is supposed to sing together and be happy together. I'm glad I followed you."

"I still don't understand why you did that," Harrison said to Kermit. "You said it was instinct, but what did you mean by that?"

"Was it because of Pipsqueak?" Zoe guessed. "Did you think she was like you? I mean, different from others?"

"I . . . don't know." He told them about how a few days ago, after a visit to the vet, his owner went to let him out of the car and saw the dog had sprouted extra rows of teeth and his fur had turned green. "He was scared of me. Started screaming that I was a monster and yelling at me to get away from him. He looked like he might even start throwing things. So I ran away. I was alone in the woods, until I felt pulled to you."

"We're glad you found us," Zoe said.

Harrison, Pipsqueak, and Buttermouse all chimed in to say yes, they were on this adventure together, and it was good he'd joined them.

"I'm glad too," Kermit said.

"Yay, we're all friends! And we're all magnificent!" Buttermouse cheered.

"I think . . . maybe the mouse is right," Pipsqueak said. "Kermit's owner may not have seen it. And the person at the store and the mother at the school didn't see it. But . . . I think we are all magnificent. Even the dog boy."

Harrison sighed. "It's Harrison."

Pipsqueak let out a purr-laugh. "I know."

Side by side and happy, they all looked up at the stars, especially the North Star. After a while, Kermit spoke again. "So, where are we going? And who's Aunt Alecia?"

They took turns telling the story of their adventure so far, from the day Zoe found Pipsqueak as a little kitten, alone and scared by her garage. Zoe told him about Aunt Alecia's letter and the note they'd found in her house, and Harrison described the route they'd taken and how they'd avoided being seen, mostly.

"You left home so that Pipsqueak can return home?" Kermit asked.

"Yes, that's right," Zoe said. She hadn't thought of putting it exactly that way, but Kermit was right. They weren't trying to find a way to get *away* from home; they were trying to find a way to *be* home, safely together. *We left in order to stay.*

"But your parents . . . They won't understand, like my owner? Even if you succeed, you'll still be in trouble?" Kermit let out a whine, as if the thought distressed them.

*It distresses me too,* Zoe thought.

"Yeah, we haven't figured out what to do about that yet," Harrison said.

They fell asleep soon after that, with Kermit curled up next to Harrison, Buttermouse nestled in a patch of moss, and Pipsqueak's fluffy tail encircling all of them. Zoe dreamed about giant mice, towering mountains, and furious parents.

It started raining shortly after dawn.

Zoe woke to water drops splatting on her face. She groaned and scooted farther into her sleeping bag. Beside her, Harrison was waking up too.

"Okay, this isn't fun," Zoe said, peeking out of her bag.

Beside her, Pipsqueak was awake and licking her fur everywhere a drop of rain landed. "Make it stop!"

"I can't," Zoe said. "It's rain."

"I know what rain is! I want you to make it stop!"

"Really not in charge of that. I don't want it to be raining any more than you do."

Harrison raised his hand. "I want it even less. There's a wet dog in my sleeping bag."

As if on cue, the green dog stuck his nose up, flinched as a drop of rain landed on his muzzle, and then retreated. "You smell wet," Kermit said, muffled within Harrison's sleeping bag. It wasn't clear whether that was a complaint or a compliment.

Zoe felt a flutter against her elbow, shrieked, and then realized it was Buttermouse. He'd crawled into the sleeping bag with her. She noticed the colors in his fur were even brighter, albeit damp. "Oh, hi. I didn't see you there."

Half asleep, Buttermouse said, "I want my box back."

"It's in my backpack," Zoe said. "I'll get it for you." To everyone she said, "Do we find someplace to hide and wait it out, or do we continue on?" There weren't any buildings for miles, but maybe there was a ledge they could duck under. The trees weren't helping. In fact, they seemed to be dumping even more water on them every time the wind blew.

Crawling out of her sleeping bag, she found Buttermouse's old shoebox. He scurried in, and she tucked it into the top of her backpack, safely cushioned by clothes. She rolled up her sleeping bag, hoping the water wasn't going to soak through. She did not want to sleep in a mass of wet down.

Harrison rolled his up too. "I should've packed the tent. We weren't supposed to be camping this long or be this far north. It wasn't supposed to rain on the days I planned for. I should have at least packed a raincoat."

The rain began to come down harder.

"Or a scuba-diving suit," Harrison said.

Zoe and Harrison climbed onto Pipsqueak's back. Her fur was wet, and the water seeped through Zoe's shorts. The cat started forward. Every few paces she paused to shake—more of a shudder—and Zoe and Harrison had to hang on extra tight. Keeping pace beside them, Kermit looked like a used mop.

It rained intermittently through the day, and as the rain increased in the late afternoon, it became more difficult to see. The mountains faded into a sheet of gray. Zoe's clothes clung to her, and her hair was plastered against her cheeks. "We have to find someplace out of the rain!"

Pipsqueak tried huddling against a tree, then behind a rock. At last she found a narrow outcropping of rocks that acted almost like a roof. Zoe and Harrison climbed off her back. All of them huddled against the rock wall, looking out at the rain. Kermit the Dog whimpered, shivering.

"If my grandmother were here, she would make a campfire so we could all dry out," Harrison said. "Though I'm not sure she would have approved of us being out in the rain in the first place."

"Did you pack matches?" Zoe asked.

"Of course, but what would we light? Everything's soaked."

"It's summer," Zoe said. "We'll dry out." She tried to make her voice sound upbeat. Really, she was wishing they were home. Drawing out her phone, she powered it up. The battery was at four percent.

Worse, there was still no signal.

She had no way of knowing whether her parents thought they were still at camp, whether Surita was still covering for them, or whether her parents were panicking because she hadn't texted since they were at Aunt Alecia's.

She powered the phone off, wishing she could talk to them and tell them how she felt out here in the rain, not sure of how much farther they had to go.

*Maybe I should have talked to them from the very beginning.*

They could have helped her. Maybe they would have. If she'd tried trusting them, they could have surprised her. After all, she was certain they loved her. *As Kermit would say, they're my pack.*

On the other hand, maybe they would have panicked and called Animal Control or someone who would have taken Pipsqueak away from her. *I made the right decision. Didn't I?*

Pipsqueak looked miserable. Her whiskers drooped, and her

wet fur was matted into clumps. Every few seconds she licked a different part of herself, but it didn't seem to help. "I want to go home," she said. "This was fun and exciting and nice and new, and now it's not. I don't want to be wet anymore!" Pipsqueak shook herself, shedding water and fur.

"When this is all over, I'm going to crawl into bed—my bed, with all my blankets and every pillow in the house—and sleep for three days," Harrison said in a dreamy voice. "I'm going to get a bag of potato chips and bring it into bed with me. And if I ever talk about climbing Mount Everest again, yell at me."

"I want to tell my family I'm sorry," Zoe said.

"Really?" Harrison said. "I'm not going to tell mine anything."

"I didn't say I'm going to do it," Zoe said. "I just want to." She especially wanted to say it to Alex. She'd never kept such a secret from her brother before. She'd never had such a giant chunk of her life that he wasn't a part of. She wondered if there were things he didn't tell her—there probably were. He'd had girlfriends she barely knew about, and she didn't know what he did when he went off with his friends. She'd never really asked. She'd only cared that he was spending time with her at that moment. What he did in the other moments hadn't mattered. But she didn't like having secrets from him.

*I wish I could tell him.*

*I wish he were here. Or better yet, I wish we'd found Aunt Alecia, fixed Pipsqueak, and gone home, where we'd be safe and sound and dry.* But they were a long way from that happening.

Moodily, they all watched it continue to pour as the sky grew darker and darker, and the miserable day turned into a miserable night.

Somehow, Zoe slept, even wet and uncomfortable against a wall of rocks. She woke, her eyes feeling gummy and her mouth tasting like peanut butter. The rain had stopped, and everything was dripping and hazy. The humidity was thick enough that it looked as if the trees were smoking after a fire. Around her, the others woke too.

"Maybe we take a break from traveling and just lie in the sun for a while?" Zoe suggested.

"Yes!" Buttermouse cheered. "I want to feel the sun on my wings! All those months in a cage in a dark classroom . . . I saw the sun through the window, but I never knew I'd feel it on my fur and wings, out in the beautiful mountains! I am a lucky mouse."

"Have you always been this cheerful?" Harrison asked. "Or is it new, like the wings?"

"I am still who I am. Just with extra awesomeness." Examining himself, the mouse pointed with a paw to his belly fur. "Look, I'm even more rainbow!" His fur boasted brighter blue, green, and purple than it had before.

"Very pretty," Zoe told him.

He preened.

Zoe and Harrison rode Pipsqueak until they found an open meadow. It had an exposed rock in the middle that was perfect for lying in the sun. After they dismounted, Pipsqueak stretched out on the rock while Kermit shook the remaining water from his fur.

Zoe lay on her back and let the sun soak into her. It was going to be a hot day, but right now that was what she wanted. She tried to imagine just turning around and going home. Of course, they couldn't do that. It was sheer luck that she'd been able to keep her family—not to mention the rest of the town—from noticing the giant cat for as long as she had.

She tried not to think about the fact that today was Friday, the last day of camp. They were supposed to be home with Surita by the end of the day.

A few minutes passed, and then Harrison's voice drifted across the rock. "Hey, Zoe? Pipsqueak? We haven't been in this field before, have we?"

Pipsqueak didn't move. "No. It's north of where we were. We're *going* north. We haven't *been* north."

Zoe sat up. She saw Harrison squatting in the grass and staring at the ground. Kermit sniffed at the grass. "What is it?" Zoe asked.

"Come see."

Pushing herself up with a groan, she crossed to him. She stopped and stared. There, in the ground that had been softened by rain, in the opposite direction from where they'd come, was a cat paw print.

A giant cat paw print.

Zoe stared at the print. She knew she wasn't an expert on animal tracks, but it looked like one of Pipsqueak's. "Pipsqueak, could you come here?"

"One minute. I'm finally warm again." The cat rolled onto her back, displaying her belly to the sun.

"I just want to measure this paw print." Zoe eyeballed it. It seemed to be the right shape and size.

Pipsqueak shot over to where the others were. "What print? Oh. Whoa. *That* print." She laid her own paw into it. The track was slightly broader, but it was the same exact shape.

*Another giant cat,* Zoe thought. *Could it be?*

It had to be! The evidence was right here!

Pipsqueak sat abruptly. "I'm not the only one. Maybe?"

"You're not!" Zoe beamed at Pipsqueak. "You have a brother! Or a sister. Or a long-lost cousin. Or something. And he or she is nearby. She may have walked right by us, and we didn't see each other because it was so rainy."

Pipsqueak sniffed the track. "I don't know how I didn't notice another cat's scent. Maybe because the two of you stink so badly."

"Hey!" Harrison said.

*She's not wrong,* Zoe thought. The rain should have helped, but after a night sleeping under the stars, they both smelled like a wet dog that had rolled in a bog.

Pipsqueak trotted across the field, her nose sniffing the air. Zoe and Harrison hurried after her with Kermit and Buttermouse. At the next paw print, she lingered to sniff more, and they caught up to her. As soon as they reached her, Kermit started sniffing too, eager to help. Then Pipsqueak was off again, stopping only when Zoe and Harrison called to her. Fidgeting impatiently, she bent so they could climb on.

Following the paw prints in the soft earth, they tracked the other cat into the woods and a quarter of the way up a mountainside. Once, Pipsqueak paused and sniffed the air so hard it looked as if she were eating it. Zoe wondered what she was thinking and feeling, knowing there was another who was like her somewhere nearby. Did he or she talk too? Had he or she grown fast like Pipsqueak?

Zoe was so excited she didn't even notice that the sun had dried her out. She didn't care that they hadn't eaten breakfast. She even forgot that she hadn't peed since she woke.

Every once in a while, Pipsqueak lost the trail, when dirt switched to rocks or when they had to hop across one of the zillion streams. But then she found it again.

"If you were a wolf, you could howl, and then he'd come find you," Harrison said.

Pipsqueak tried out a yowl. It sounded as if she were being squeezed. She cut off mid-screech. "I don't think that's going to work."

"You could call out," Zoe suggested. "You know, with words, not howls." She shouted, "Hello, other giant cat! Are you out there? We want to meet you!"

Pipsqueak joined her. "Hello! Where are you?"

And Harrison: "We're friendly!"

Zoe shouted, "Come be our friend!"

Harrison broke off shouting. "Really? 'Come be our friend'? That's what you went with?"

"Well, we want to be his or her friend, don't we?" Zoe said. Pipsqueak obviously wanted to meet someone like herself. And Zoe had bunches of questions she wanted to ask.

"Yeah, but isn't that a little too . . . I don't know. Needy?"

"It worked with you." Grinning, she elbowed him. When she first met Harrison, they were in kindergarten. According to their parents, at recess one day, shortly after borrowing his green crayon, Zoe had marched up to him and said, *You should be my friend.* Harrison had studied her quietly for a little while, then supposedly said, *Okay.* Zoe didn't specifically remember this, but she'd been told the story so many times that it felt true.

*Funny how it only takes a single moment to change so much.* If she hadn't become friends with Harrison . . . Well, a lot would be different. She'd taken a risk then and won a best friend. She hoped the risk they were taking now would pay off too.

"Fair enough," he said, then shouted, "Be our friend!"

When that didn't work, they continued to follow the track silently until Pipsqueak halted.

"What is it?" Zoe asked.

"The tracks . . . They stop."

Harrison got out the map. "So if that's this mountain . . . And if we're facing north, which we are, given the sun . . ." He squinted at it and then looked up at the empty clearing. "We're here."

"We are?" Taking the map from him, Zoe stared at it and then handed it back. He stared at it too, twisted it sideways, then upside down.

"Yeah, this is it," he said.

"I know," Zoe said.

"It's, um, not really anywhere."

"I know." She tried to ignore the worry that was clawing its way into her throat. If the map led nowhere . . . If there were no answers to be found and no help to be had . . . *But Aunt Alecia promised,* she thought. She had to trust that.

Beneath them, Pipsqueak shifted. "Are you sure this is right?" The cat sat down, and Zoe and Harrison, with their packs, slid down her fur to the ground.

"This is where the map says to go," Zoe said, hearing her voice waver. She saw nothing but more trees. Mostly pine trees. A few of those white-bark trees. And a lot of rocks. But that was no different from the rest of New Hampshire.

Kermit the Dog trotted past them as if he smelled something. "Ooh, ooh, ooh!" Wagging his tail, he sniffed a rock.

Maybe they'd misread the map and missed the location, and Kermit sensed that. Maybe he could lead them there! "What did you find?" All of them stared at Kermit, waiting for him to bark or chase after a scent or do something.

He lifted his hind leg and peed on the rock.

"That was less helpful than I expected," Harrison commented.

From his perch on Pipsqueak's head, Buttermouse flapped his wings and rose into the air, wobbling in the breeze and then righting himself. He had continued to change colors. In addition to his blue, green, and purple belly, he now sported a pink snout, red ears, and a yellow and orange neck.

"Nice colors," Harrison said.

Buttermouse twisted in the air to admire himself. "Oooh, I'm even more beautiful!"

Zoe listened to the forest. She heard wind rustling the leaves but nothing . . . Wait, maybe she did hear something. "Aunt Alecia?" she called.

"Do you think she's here?" Harrison said. "She didn't say she would be. She just said we'd find help here." He turned in a slow circle, scanning the forest. "I don't see any help."

Pipsqueak let out a plaintive "Mew!"

Zoe hadn't heard her meow in a while. She put her arms around Pipsqueak's neck. "It'll be okay. We'll figure out what to do. I promise somehow we'll find a way to change you back."

Kermit barked. "Stranger!"

All of them tensed and turned as a woman stepped out of the woods. She looked a bit like Mom, the same eyes and nose, but she had a pointier chin and pointier cheekbones.

Aunt Alecia!

"Change her back?" Aunt Alecia said. "Why on earth would you want to do that?"

# CHAPTER 16

**ZOE HOPPED OFF THE ROCK.** "Aunt Alecia?"

Circling her, Kermit sniffed. "She smells nice."

"Thank you, dear." Aunt Alecia bent to pat him on the head, but he skittered out of the way. She didn't look either surprised or offended by that. She smiled at Zoe and held her arms out. "Zoe, you've grown since I last saw you! Happy twelfth birthday! I'm sorry I wasn't there to celebrate with you."

Zoe ran to her aunt and hugged her. "How are you here?"

"I heard reports of an unusual animal, and I came to help it find its way to Sanctuary." She said the word *Sanctuary* as if it were the name of a place, like a town. "If I'd known when you were coming, I would have waited for you, but I didn't even know *if* you were coming. Where's your mother?" She looked around the clearing. "Evie? Show yourself!"

"It's just us," Zoe said. "This is my friend Harrison, and this is Pipsqueak." She went around, introducing everyone. "We came because—"

"Your mother isn't here?" Aunt Alecia's face fell. She looked so disappointed that Zoe felt terrible, and then her aunt's eyes widened. "Did you children travel all the way here on your own? Do your parents know where you are? How did you get here?"

"Really long story, but first, please, we need your help with Pipsqueak!" Zoe said.

"And we're hoping for answers," Harrison put in.

Pipsqueak stepped forward, crunching a bush. "Zoe's aunt . . . Could you tell me why I've grown so much? Am I going to grow more? Why is this happening to me?"

"And me?" Buttermouse asked, doing a figure-eight loop in the air. "What did I do to earn such glory?"

"Yeah, why did Buttermouse sprout wings?" Harrison jumped in. "And why does Kermit have shark teeth, green fur, and extra tails?"

"Why can we talk?" Pipsqueak asked. "And read?"

"Ooh, we can read?" Buttermouse asked. "I want to read! That sounds fun!"

"It's as wonderful as wings," Pipsqueak told him.

Aunt Alecia studied them. She opened her mouth as if to answer, and then she glanced up at the sun. It was still high in the sky, flooding the mountains and forest with light. "We have time for a proper explanation. And tea. Let's make a fire. Rest yourselves, and I will answer every question I can." She lowered the bag on her back to the ground. "Could you help me gather wood? I'll also need stones to keep the campfire safely contained."

Kermit the Dog loved that idea. He raced around the woods,

fetching every stick he could find. Harrison joined in, collecting rocks and twigs.

Zoe helped too, but she couldn't stop herself from getting more and more nervous. She trusted her aunt, but what about the explanation was so big that it required them to sit down and have tea? *Maybe it's just a long explanation,* she thought. *Or . . . it could be an upsetting one.*

"I found sticks for s'mores!" Harrison announced.

"Excellent," Aunt Alecia said with approval. "But I don't have marshmallows or any of the other ingredients."

Harrison rummaged through his pack. "That's okay! I do!"

"Wait—you have more food in there, and we didn't eat it?" Zoe said. She knew he hadn't picked up s'more supplies at Aunt Alecia's. He must have brought them from home, which meant he'd had them the whole time, even when they were so low on food that they'd risked stopping at the country store.

"You can't eat raw s'mores," Harrison said as he tossed out a bag of marshmallows, a box of graham crackers, and several Hershey bars.

He'd been lugging all of that since Massachusetts? "Harrison! You can absolutely eat 'raw' marshmallows, crackers, and chocolate!"

"But then they're not s'mores," Harrison explained patiently. He helped Aunt Alecia build a pyramid of sticks in the center of the circle of rocks, and soon they had a fire going.

All the animals crowded around it as Zoe joined Harrison and

Aunt Alecia. "All right," Zoe said. "We're calm. We're sitting down. Can you please tell us what's going on with Pipsqueak? And all of them?" She tried to keep her voice as steady and even as possible, but she'd already waited so long! She just wanted to know, regardless of whether it was good or bad! What had happened to her friends? Why had they all transformed? And how could they change them back so that Pipsqueak could come home with her and be safe? "Please, Aunt Alecia, what's wrong with Pipsqueak, and how do we fix it?"

A marshmallow in her hand, Aunt Alecia sighed, sounding exactly like Mom. "There is nothing wrong with your cat. She's become exactly who she was always meant to be."

Pipsqueak looked as confused as Zoe felt. "But . . . But cats aren't supposed to be the size of elephants," Pipsqueak said. "I've read biology textbooks. I know I'm unusual."

"Most cats stay significantly smaller," Aunt Alecia agreed. "And if you'd never met Zoe, you most likely would have stayed the size of an ordinary cat. Zoe changed you."

"Me?" Zoe squeaked.

Beside her, Harrison sputtered, "Wh-what?"

"I didn't do anything!" Zoe said. That was absurd. She didn't know how to make a cat grow so fast. *This makes no sense!* "What about the mouse and the dog?"

"They changed after they met you, didn't they? All it required was your proximity. And, of course, your twelfth birthday." Aunt Alecia slid her marshmallow on a stick and held it out to Zoe. Automatically Zoe took it. "Relax, have a s'more, and I'll explain."

Buttermouse switched from Harrison's shoulder to Zoe's. He laid a tiny paw on Zoe's cheek, as if trying to comfort her. Her thoughts seemed to be swirling faster than a whirlpool. She was glad no one was speaking right now. She needed to try to think. As though sensing her spinning thoughts, Kermit cuddled closer to her, and Pipsqueak wrapped her tail around her.

Aunt Alecia poured water from a canteen into a small kettle and nestled it near the fire. She then accepted another marshmallow from Harrison. The flames licked over the thicker twigs, spreading into a nice-size campfire.

Harrison stuck a marshmallow onto his own stick. "The key is don't put it into the flame. Hold it *near* the flame until it browns and bubbles." He sounded overly cheerful, as if he were trying not to freak out, or were trying to keep Zoe from freaking out.

She only half heard him. Making s'mores was the furthest thing on her mind. What Aunt Alecia had said . . . It didn't make sense. *How can* I *have changed any of them?* "Aunt Alecia . . ."

"You're a Catalyst," Aunt Alecia told her.

"A what?" Zoe asked.

Pipsqueak nudged her with her nose. "You're a Cat-alyst," she said. "A Cat. A list."

"But . . . what does that mean?"

"A catalyst," Harrison said, "is something that causes change. Right?" He stared at Pipsqueak and Kermit. "You did this, Zoe?"

Zoe shook her head. "It wasn't me. I'd know if I did this." Then she studied Aunt Alecia's face. She didn't look as if she were joking. "Wouldn't I?"

Aunt Alecia shook her head. "Your powers aren't conscious; they're a part of you. They flow through your veins as naturally as blood—"

Harrison looked as if he wanted to cheer. "She has powers? Like magic? Zoe, this is awesome! What kind of magical powers? Wait—that's obvious. You have cat-embiggening powers. And dog greening? Unusual, yes, but still awesome . . ."

"This can't be possible," Zoe said. "What—"

Lunging forward, Harrison caught Zoe's wrist and lifted her marshmallow stick out of the fire. Half the marshmallow was blackened. "Here, eat mine." He held out a perfectly browned marshmallow. "You put it between graham crackers and a few squares of chocolate."

"Harrison, I really don't—"

"It's fine. I like burnt."

"No!" Zoe sucked in air and tried to stay calm. She felt tears pricking the corners of her eyes. This was just too much. "Aunt Alecia, please. I don't understand. How could I be this . . . a 'Catalyst'? I don't have 'powers'!"

"Yes, you do. Your animal friends are proof of it," Aunt Alecia said. "I know it's a lot. Take a minute to absorb." Aunt Alecia poured her tea into a mug, took graham crackers and chocolate, and made a s'more. Harrison did the same, handing the s'more to Zoe before making one for himself out of the burnt marshmallow.

"I don't want a s'more!" Zoe didn't understand how they could be acting so calm about this. Aunt Alecia had just dropped the hugest bombshell in her lap and now was pouring herself tea and making campfire snacks? Zoe wanted to scream in frustration.

Before she could, Pipsqueak leaned over the fire and said to Aunt Alecia, "You're scaring my friend, and that is not okay. I will drool on all your snacks if you don't explain more." She held up her paw and extended her claws. "And pop your marshmallows."

Zoe laughed. She couldn't help it. It was the most ridiculous, most perfect threat. And one of the nicest things anyone had ever said on her behalf. "Thank you, Pipsqueak." She crossed her arms and glared at her aunt.

Aunt Alecia put down her tea and her s'more. "I was trying to give you a moment to adjust, but very well. Magic doesn't exist in this world. But it *does* exist in the Sanctuary, which is a . . . Scientists would call it a 'parallel dimension.' It's like a world *beside* our world. Similar, but full of magic."

"Yes! I called it!" Harrison whooped. "I knew there was another dimension."

Zoe shot him a look. "No, you didn't."

"I said there could be. Distinctly remember that."

"You also had about a hundred other guesses. Including aliens."

"But magical other world was one of them," Harrison said. "Hah."

Aunt Alecia continued. "Magical creatures who live in Sanctuary grow up naturally with all their powers. But magical creatures who are born *here* . . . There's no magic in this world to trigger their magical selves. They grow up like nonmagical animals, often never even knowing their heritage—unless they encounter a Catalyst. Like you, Zoe. You carry inside you the magic of Sanctuary."

"I . . . do?"

"That's why these animals were drawn to you," Aunt Alecia said, gesturing at Zoe's friends. "There aren't *that* many creatures in the world with the potential to become something extraordinary. It happens only when a magical creature leaves Sanctuary and starts a family on Earth. His or her descendants carry the potential for magical transformation inside them. Your cat, the dog, the mouse—all of them must have had a parent or grandparent or great-grandparent who came from the magic world, and that latent potential drew them to you, which is why you've encountered so many in such a short period of time, despite their rarity in our world. Their potential sensed your potential, and it pulled them to you."

Kermit lifted his head. "I knew I should follow you, but I didn't know why. But it started before that. When I saw you outside the vet's, I wanted to go to you."

Zoe looked at Pipsqueak, who shrugged her cat shoulders. "I

was a kitten. I don't remember how I ended up at your house. But maybe this explains it? We didn't find each other by chance; I was drawn to you."

"But why?" Zoe asked. *Why me? Why magic? Why all of this?*

"You were born with magic inside you," Aunt Alecia said. "It's like having blue eyes. Pops up in some families, always emerging into full bloom when the Catalyst turns twelve. Tell me, when did your cat begin to grow? Was it on the morning of your birthday?"

*It was,* Zoe realized. Pipsqueak hadn't grown right away—she'd only begun on the day Zoe turned twelve. And that was the day she'd taken her to the vet. She remembered seeing a terrier there, in the parking lot. He'd been eager to play with them. Was that Kermit?

"This ability has appeared before in our family, which is how I know about it, even though I'm not a Catalyst myself. Your great-grandfather, in fact, was responsible for making the portal to Sanctuary that I use."

Zoe thought of her family. She didn't think Mom, Dad, or Alex was magical. *It must be a recessive gene,* she thought. She remembered drawing Punnett squares for science, the diagram showing how blue-eyed parents could have a brown-eyed child and so on. Of course, none of those squares ever included magic. "Is that why you and Mom argued? Because you know about all of this, and Mom thinks it's . . . quirky?"

Aunt Alecia gave her a bittersweet grin. "Well, basically yes. It all culminated in an argument over a potential unicorn. The creature had the mind and body of an ordinary horse, but I believed it was more, or could be more. I wanted to show your mother, to share all this with her."

"What happened?" Zoe asked, although she could guess.

"She refused to even come see it. Said that she needed me to stop believing in fairy tales, that it was time for me to grow up. She said her new job would have her in the public eye, and having a sister who believes in unicorns and other nonsense could damage her career and the causes she's fighting for. So I told her to stuff it. Then I brought the horse here to your great-grandfather's portal and sent it through to Sanctuary. Once it was exposed to Sanctuary's magic, it transformed, and now it's living happily and safely as a unicorn on the other side of the shimmer." Aunt Alecia took a bite of her s'more. "Mmm, delicious. So would you like to see it?"

"I don't . . ." Zoe felt as if her head were thick with a million thoughts, all of them bashing into one another. Aunt Alecia had been right—it was a lot to absorb. Sitting down had been a good idea.

Harrison jumped in. "Yes, we absolutely want to see a unicorn!"

"Not just the unicorn," Aunt Alecia said. "Sanctuary. The magic world. It's why you're here, isn't it? To bring these extraordinary creatures to their new home, the place where they belong?"

Zoe wanted to jump to her feet. "No! We came to find a way for me to take Pipsqueak home. You were supposed to reverse this and fix everything!" She threw her arms around one of Pipsqueak's legs.

Aunt Alecia sighed. "There you go again, talking about changing them. They are all exactly who they are meant to be."

"Well, yes, I know you said that," Zoe said, still hugging Pipsqueak. "But a giant cat living in Eastbury—"

"Even if it were possible to change her back, which it isn't, you would be depriving your cat of who she was meant to be. Because she met you, she is able to realize her potential. Without you, she'd have been unhappy, always missing a piece of herself without knowing why. Unable to grow to her destined size. Unable to speak. Or read. But now . . . look at her! She's whole."

Leaping into the air, Buttermouse performed a flip. "And me! You gave me wings, Zoe! You made me extraordinary! Thank you!"

Kermit spoke up. "I was sad when my owner wanted me gone, but you all made me happy again. You gave me a new pack." He thumped his many tails hard on the ground.

Zoe looked up at Pipsqueak. *If she hadn't changed, she never would have been able to talk with us. And we never would have had this adventure.* "But if she stays like this, how can she ever be with me? I promised her we'd be together!"

Pipsqueak wrapped her paw around Zoe's waist. "I might be unhappy if I were changed back, but I'll also be unhappy without Zoe. That's all I want, to be Zoe's cat and for her to be my human.

That's what this journey was for. Also to find answers." She paused. "And to splash in swimming pools, climb up ski lifts, and sing under the stars!"

"None of which would have happened if you'd stayed a tiny kitten," Zoe said. She *knew* that, but . . . "If we can't change her back . . ." *Or if we* shouldn't *change her back.*

Wow, that was something she hadn't even considered.

But maybe she should.

All this time, she'd been so focused on "fixing" Pipsqueak that she hadn't really thought about who Pipsqueak had become . . . Her size, her intelligence, her ability to talk and to read—it was all a part of her.

*Harrison said from the beginning that Pipsqueak was amazing,* Zoe thought. *I wish I'd listened to him better.*

She stroked Pipsqueak's paw, marveling afresh that it was larger than her hand. Changing Pipsqueak back now would mean losing everything she had become.

*Maybe Aunt Alecia is right.*

Zoe started again. "If we can't—shouldn't—change her back, is there anything we *can* do? Besides send her through some magic portal, even if it was made by my own great-grandfather?"

"You won't be sending her," Aunt Alecia said. "You'll be going with her. Once you see the other world, you'll understand. Pipsqueak will be safe and happy there, and you'll be able to return home knowing you've helped an extraordinary creature."

"Come on," Harrison whispered. "This is a chance to see *another world!*"

"I . . ." Zoe looked up at Pipsqueak, who was gazing at her with the same full-of-trust expression she'd had as a kitten. Zoe wanted to jump on her back and ride her all the way home. She wished they'd never come. She should have found a way to hide her, a way to help her . . . but there hadn't been a way. Coming to Aunt Alecia was the only idea she'd had. And now Aunt Alecia had dumped all these impossible revelations on her . . . *Me, magic?* And her late great-grandfather had created a portal to another world? A magic world?

Everyone was looking at her.

"Well, we've come all this way," she said. "I guess it wouldn't hurt to see it."

# CHAPTER 17

"**KERMIT, COULD YOU PLEASE** put out the fire?" Aunt Alecia requested.

Standing, Kermit trotted to the fire, lifted one of his hind legs, and . . . put out the fire as Zoe and Harrison both scrambled away.

Kermit congratulated himself. "Good dog."

"That's right," Aunt Alecia said, patting his head. "You're a good dog."

He wagged his many tails.

"Uh, okay, that worked, I guess." Harrison picked up his backpack.

Fetching her pack too, Zoe told herself they were just going to *look* at this Sanctuary place, to see if it all was true. Maybe while they were there, they'd think of a way Pipsqueak could come back home with her. "Is it far?"

"Very close," Aunt Alecia said, gathering her supplies and carrying the still-hot kettle. "I marked it on the map. You were right near it. It's just hard to see, nearly impossible in fact, if you don't know what you're looking for." She led the way, and they all followed.

They tromped through the forest to the next clearing, where Zoe was sure they'd been before. Or mostly sure. They'd seen a lot of mountains and woods, and the scenery was all blurring together.

Stopping, Aunt Alecia said, "Here we are."

"Is it hidden with a magic shield?" Harrison asked. He immediately began walking around the clearing, holding his hands out in front of him as if he expected to bump into an invisible wall. "Cloaking device? Please say it's a cloaking device."

Aunt Alecia laughed. "Close. The entrance to Sanctuary *is* invisible—"

"Knew it!" Harrison whooped.

"You did not," Zoe said. "You thought the map led us nowhere."

Aunt Alecia pointed. "If you look at it just right, unfocus your eyes a bit, and look at the background instead of the foreground, you can see it."

Kermit's green tongue lolled out of his mouth. "I think I smell it," he said.

Following her finger, Zoe saw a shimmering up ahead. It looked like heat above a barbecue grill—the air seemed to waver—but when she looked directly at it, it vanished.

Buttermouse landed on Zoe's shoulder and said, "Look! It's shiny!"

"Yeah, I see it too!" Harrison said. "Sort of."

Reaching up, Zoe stroked Buttermouse's back between his wings. The little mouse didn't seem scared or even worried, which was reassuring. "How did you know what to look for the first time you found it?" she asked her aunt.

"Your great-grandfather. Remember I said the magic had popped up in our family before? He left a diary that explained how he made this portal, though it took me years to find the right spot. He was vague on *where* he'd made it."

Zoe wished she could have met her great-grandfather. She had a lot of questions for him. Maybe he would have known what to do about Pipsqueak. *There has to be something I can do besides say goodbye!*

"Go ahead," Aunt Alecia said. "Look around a bit. Get your friends settled. We can talk more when you get back."

All of them stared at the crack between worlds. It looked, Zoe thought, like a knife had cut the air. You could see the pine trees on the opposite side of the slit, but they were wavy and blurred.

"So we just . . . walk through it?" Harrison asked.

Kermit whined. "Will it hurt?"

"Not at all," Aunt Alecia said. "Here, I'll show you how easy it is." She strode up to the shimmer. "It doesn't hurt even a—" And she vanished.

Zoe had been expecting a slow fade. Or a sparkle. Or some kind of special effect like you'd see in a movie. But mid-sentence, Aunt Alecia stepped into the wavering air and disappeared.

One second there, the next gone. *Like magic,* Zoe thought.

*Of course like magic.*

"Wow," Harrison said.

"Yeah," Zoe agreed.

They waited what felt like an eternity but was only a few seconds, and then Aunt Alecia reappeared just as suddenly. Zoe hadn't even blinked.

"See? Easy." Aunt Alecia beamed at them. "I'll wait here until you're done." She dropped her pack, settled herself on a rock, and poured herself another cup of tea from the kettle.

"You look scared," Pipsqueak said to Zoe.

"I am," Zoe admitted.

"Aren't you curious? Curious as a cat?" Pipsqueak lowered her head and bumped it gently against Zoe. "There are answers through there."

"But there might not be a way home."

"Maybe once we see, we'll figure out a way."

*I hope so,* Zoe thought. Reaching up and petting between Pipsqueak's ears, she stared at the portal and couldn't sort out how it made her feel. She felt jumbled inside.

On the other side of that hazy bit of air was supposedly a whole magical world, maybe filled with giant talking cats . . . *If we go through that shimmer . . . Will we discover that Pipsqueak belongs there instead of with me?* "It's just—what if . . ."

"Ride on me," Pipsqueak suggested. "We'll go through together."

That was the perfect idea. Zoe wrapped her arms around Pipsqueak and climbed up onto her back. She held out her hand and helped Harrison up behind her. Buttermouse flew over to them and landed on Pipsqueak's head.

Together, they rode up to the shimmer, with Kermit following. Zoe could hear Kermit murmuring to himself, "You can do this. You're a good dog. Brave dog. Yeah, who's a good dog? You are."

Stopping in front of the portal, Pipsqueak stuck her paw into the hazy air. It vanished.

Harrison yelped. "That! Is! Freaky!"

Pipsqueak yanked her paw back. She licked the pads and between her toes and then extended her paw again. It vanished a second time. "Your aunt is right—it doesn't hurt."

"Still looks freaky. Half of me wants to turn around and run the other way," Harrison admitted with a melodramatic shudder.

"And the other half?" Zoe asked.

"The other half wants to shout 'Tallyho!' and ride through."

Zoe's lips twitched. It was hard to be scared of anything when Harrison was with her, making her laugh. His enthusiasm was contagious. "Seriously? Tallyho?"

"Try it, Zoe," he urged.

Together, Zoe, Pipsqueak, and Harrison shouted "Tallyho!" and Pipsqueak plunged forward, carrying them through the shimmer.

• • •

The forest blinked around them, and they were in a meadow. Zoe inhaled, and the air made her feel dizzy. It smelled, even tasted, different, as if a thousand flowers had been wadded together and dipped in honey. The bright sun, after the dappled forest, made her squint as the scenery resolved itself: a meadow, a stream, a few distant mountains, groves of trees.

It was the White Mountains. But it wasn't. Aunt Alecia wasn't here. Breathing in, Zoe again tasted the difference, even though she couldn't see it. *Maybe the magic is in the air,* she thought.

"It's the same," Harrison said. "Sort of."

"Pretty!" Buttermouse cried.

"It *feels* different," Zoe said. She couldn't exactly put her finger on why it felt different. It was a bit like the way your head felt if you stood up quickly. A little dizzy, but not in a fall-down way. She twisted around and saw the portal behind them, wrinkling the air.

Kermit the Dog popped out of the shimmer. He immediately began sniffing everything: rocks, bushes, flowers. "Everything smells good!"

"Very good!" Buttermouse squeaked. He wiggled his nose, sniffing the air, and then flapped his wings, rising up from Pipsqueak's head. Zoe watched him wobble in the air as he joined a flock of other winged mice. They landed on fat pink flowers that swayed beneath them. "Yay, more friends to meet!" sang Buttermouse. "I am the luckiest!"

"Guess we came to the right place," Harrison said.

Zoe felt Pipsqueak stiffen beneath her, and then the cat sat down. Zoe and Harrison slid off her back. Coming around to her head, Zoe asked, "What is it?"

Pipsqueak let loose a yowl so loud it could have shaken a football stadium.

She bounded across the meadow, and Zoe saw, by a grove of trees, another giant cat. This one was long-haired, with black and white fur in splotches. She saw the strange cat's tail arch up and then settle down as Pipsqueak skidded to a halt.

They were too far away for Zoe to hear what they were saying, but they were clearly talking. Pipsqueak was circling the other cat, examining him from every angle, but her tail was relaxed and she didn't look scared.

"She's really not the only one," Zoe said, awed.

Everything Aunt Alecia had said was true!

*Even about me?* she wondered.

*And even about Pipsqueak belonging here?*

Watching Pipsqueak frolic in the meadow with the black and white cat, Zoe began to laugh. She didn't know why she was laughing. It was only that Pipsqueak looked so free and happy that she couldn't *not* laugh. It bubbled up inside her.

After a few minutes, Pipsqueak trotted back toward them, with the other cat following. Both were roughly the size of elephants.

The black and white cat was narrower, and its fur draped from its belly to the grass. "Zoe, meet . . ."

"Cow," the other cat said. Reaching them, he added, "When I was half grown, I got lost. I accidentally fell through the portal and found my way to a farm. There were cats there, but they were ordinary size and afraid of me. So I didn't spend time with them. I spent my time out on a field, with the cows. The farmer *did* think I was one of them, at least until he got closer. Anyway, when Alecia rescued me and brought me back to Sanctuary, Cow became my name."

"Nice to meet you, Cow," Zoe said.

Harrison grabbed her arm. "Look! Bigfeet!" He pointed toward the trees, where several hairy man-shaped creatures were lumbering by. "Bigfoots? We can ask them which it is."

Cow craned his neck to see where they were looking. "You won't get much of an answer out of them. They mainly grunt. But you can try if you like. I can promise you, though, I'm a much better conversationalist. How about you tell me your names, where you come from, and why you're here?"

"Oh." Zoe studied the cat for a moment. "Aunt Alecia . . . my mother's sister . . . she guided us here." She watched Kermit race across the meadow, fetch a random stick, and then run back.

"You're Alecia's family! Excellent news! She has been missing her family. She told me so herself during my most recent visit to your world."

"The cat paw prints we saw!" Harrison burst out. "They were yours!"

He displayed his paws. "Must have been."

"I'm Zoe. And this is my friend Harrison. You met Pipsqueak. That's Kermit"—she pointed to the dog and then the flying mice, though she wasn't sure which mouse was theirs—"and that's Buttermouse."

"You found so many!" Cow asked. "Highly unusual!"

"Aunt Alecia says I'm a Catalyst. Do you know what that means?"

Cow began to purr. "Oh, that explains everything! How wonderful! It means you have reunited more families than just your own. They were drawn to you, and you brought them here. Pipsqueak, Kermit, and Buttermouse, welcome! You will be safe here! Your families will be found, and you will flourish in your new home!"

"Oh, Pipsqueak and I are just visiting," Zoe said quickly. All she had to do was figure out how she could keep Pipsqueak safe at home without changing who she'd become. "Right, Pipsqueak?"

But Pipsqueak didn't reply. She was marveling at the flock of winged mice flying by, with Buttermouse at the center, performing figure eights in midair.

Cow showed them around.

Sanctuary looked like their world in every way, except for the presence of magical creatures. Same sun. Same sky. Same mountains blanketed in evergreens. Zoe, Pipsqueak, and Harrison walked along a stream that burbled over stones, and while Cow pointed out a herd of unicorns grazing on wildflowers, he told them that farther to the south, there were cities with people.

Stopping, they stared at the unicorns, so distant you could see their horns only as slim shadows rising from their foreheads, but the signature horns were unmistakably there.

"Our friends will be safe here?" Harrison asked.

"This world is called Sanctuary for a reason," Cow said. "Everyone here understands the rule of 'Do no harm.'"

"This place is amazing!" Pipsqueak said. Nearby, Kermit clearly agreed. He was racing back and forth beneath the flock of mice, zigzagging as he followed one and then another.

*Pipsqueak seems happy,* Zoe thought. *And she'd be safe here, and unafraid.*

"So all these creatures"—Harrison waved at the unicorns and the flock of flying mice—"they were born in this world, surrounded by magic, so they grew up magical. Except for the ones whose distant relatives got stuck on Earth. They didn't change until they got here, or until they met someone like Zoe. Or, more accurately, were drawn to someone like Zoe. Yes?"

"Correct," Cow said.

"Cool."

They watched the mice and the unicorns. Kermit was digging a hole for no apparent reason. His tails were wagging so hard with joy and excitement that his whole body was vibrating.

"Magic is real," Zoe said, trying out the words.

"Yep. I believe in magic," Harrison said. "One hundred percent believer here. Going to move all my fantasy books to the nonfiction shelf."

Pipsqueak agreed. "I believe too."

Harrison jerked his thumb at the cat. "The giant talking cat agrees. I don't think you can get more definitive proof than that."

Zoe shook her head, trying to find the right words. She *did* believe what her eyes were telling her about this world and what Aunt Alecia and Cow had told her about their animal friends, but she didn't feel like *she* was magical. She felt like herself—ordinary Zoe, who was going to be in so much trouble with her parents when Surita came home from camp without her and Harrison. "Am *I* really magic?"

"You are to me," Pipsqueak declared. She lay down and tilted her head so Zoe could pet between her ears. "It wasn't just my body that changed. My whole life changed because you found me. Because of you, I've had adventures. I've jumped across rooftops and climbed up chairlifts. I've seen the world! I've seen *two* worlds! I've made friends that I never would have been able to talk to before. You. The dog boy. Even the girl who called me a rodent. And Buttermouse and Kermit, of course."

"But if this happened only because you met me . . ." Zoe felt her eyes grow hot, as if she was about to cry. "You could have led a normal life as an ordinary cat. You wouldn't have had to be scared. We wouldn't have had to lie to my parents and leave home to hike through the wilderness . . ."

Placing a paw on her head, Pipsqueak began to lick Zoe's hair. To Zoe it felt like sandpaper every time her tongue caught a bit of cheek or forehead.

Zoe ducked away. "What are you doing?"

"You're upset," Pipsqueak said, rising to her feet. "I'm calming you. Are you done being ridiculous?"

Harrison was smothering a laugh. "She's certainly done being dry."

"If you hadn't helped me change, I wouldn't be me," Pipsqueak said simply.

That was true. Zoe thought of how amazing it was to be able to talk with her kitten, to have adventures with her, to share all these new memories. Still . . .

Pipsqueak bent down and licked harder, and Zoe started to laugh. "Hey, that tickles!"

Arms spread wide, Zoe launched herself at Pipsqueak's side. Pipsqueak pretended to be knocked over, and they slid down a grassy slope. Harrison joined in, and they rode the cat like a sled until they slowed in a heap, laughing, next to a blueberry bush.

Zoe leaned her cheek against the cat's side. "Thanks, Pipsqueak."

"Hey, it's true for me too," Harrison said to Zoe, panting from laughing so hard. "You changed me by being my friend. If I didn't know you, I'd be home, playing video games, rather than here, playing with a giant cat and learning that life is way bigger and stranger than I knew. Because of you, I'll have a best friend forever. And because of you, I'll be grounded for the rest of my life when our parents discover we never went to camp."

Also true.

"I hate to say it, Zoe," Harrison said, "but we don't have long before our parents know we didn't go to camp. We have to figure out how we're getting home and what we're going to tell them when we get there."

"Pipsqueak . . ." Zoe's throat felt clogged. Aunt Alecia had been right: seeing Sanctuary made it clear. This place was perfect for a giant cat. Zoe could see how happy Pipsqueak was here, with Cow, with an entire new world to play in. *She should stay,* Zoe thought.

"I know," Pipsqueak said. "It's time to go home."

Cow made a meowlike yelp and said the words Zoe didn't want to say: "You already are home! You'll never be safe in her world! This is where you belong!"

*She* does *belong here,* Zoe thought.

This was what the entire journey had been about: finding a way to keep Pipsqueak safe and happy.

And she'd found a better answer than she'd ever imagined.

*I brought her home,* Zoe thought.

Pipsqueak would be happy here. She deserved to be somewhere

she could be herself, with a whole world to explore, filled with other giant cats to befriend and plenty of strange mice and birds to play with. This was a giant cat's paradise. She didn't deserve to spend her life in hiding, crammed into a shed in the backyard, and she certainly didn't deserve to be shrunk down and made less than who she was supposed to be.

"Out in the nonmagic world, what is there for you?" Cow asked. "Being chased by farmers who don't understand what you are? Having to hide every day of your life? Never being free to be yourself?"

All true, true, and true.

But Pipsqueak looked torn. She swiveled her head between Zoe and Cow. Her claws kneaded the grass. "I . . . I . . ."

Taking a breath, Zoe did the bravest thing she'd ever done.

She said goodbye.

"Cow's right," Zoe said. "This is what we were trying to find: a way for you to be safe, a place where you belong. You'll be happy here." She threw her arms around the cat's neck and hugged her again. "I'll miss you."

It was the right thing to do, she knew, even if it hurt. She had to do what was best for Pipsqueak. Zoe tried hard not to cry into Pipsqueak's fur. "I'll never forget you," she promised. "And I'll visit whenever I can."

Pipsqueak nuzzled her head. "But I'm not ready to say goodbye!"

"Me neither." She'd hoped she wouldn't have to say goodbye at all. *But if I'd gotten what I wished for, and Pipsqueak became an ordinary cat again . . . that would have been a goodbye too.*

"Promise you'll visit?" Pipsqueak's voice was small.

That was an easy promise to make. "Yes!"

"If our parents ever let us out of the house again," Harrison muttered.

He was right. Her parents were going to be furious that she'd lied to them and come here instead of camp. They would never understand. *Especially if I don't tell them the truth.*

*What if I* did *tell them the truth?*

She thought of her mother and Aunt Alecia. Aunt Alecia had tried to tell Mom the truth, and Mom hadn't believed her.

"Zoe? You will be able to visit, won't you?" Pipsqueak asked.

"I . . ." How could she convince her family to believe her? Without proof . . . If only she could show them Pipsqueak . . . *Could I?*

"You're worrying me, Zoe," Pipsqueak said, still kneading the grass.

"Come home with us. Just briefly. I'll explain everything to my family and show them how you've changed, and they'll see how amazing you are, and then Aunt Alecia can bring you back here where you'll be safe. My family won't keep me from visiting if they understand why I had to help you!"

Pipsqueak nuzzled the top of her head. "Of course I'll come."

Breaking away from the flock, Buttermouse zoomed toward

them. "Ooh, I want to come too! So long as we can return to this place."

Kermit wagged his many tails. "Me too! You're my pack! I want to help! If your family meets all of us, maybe they won't be angry. Maybe they'll understand."

Harrison waved his hands. "Wait, wait, wait! You're talking about showing your family? What if someone sees and posts about Pipsqueak online? What if everything we were afraid of comes true?"

"After my family meets her, she'll come back to Sanctuary, and it won't matter if anyone saw her or not. She'll be safe. They all will." *And I won't have to say goodbye just yet.*

Cow frowned at them, clearly concerned. "Are you certain you want to do this?"

"Yes," Zoe and Pipsqueak said at the same time.

Cow led them back to the portal. The shimmer was still there, a hard-to-see wrinkle in the air. It reminded Zoe of a tear in a piece of cellophane.

"Come back soon," Cow said.

"We will," Zoe said, though it hurt to say it. She knew she was only delaying the inevitable. But maybe she could make some things right at the same time.

# CHAPTER 18

**Zoe and Harrison tumbled out** through the shimmer, back into the ordinary world. Immediately, Zoe saw the pine trees, the blueberry bushes, and her aunt sipping tea.

Putting down her tea, Aunt Alecia jumped up and clapped her hands. "Now you understand! See how amazing it feels? Helping creatures find where they belong! This is your destiny! Now that you—"

Pipsqueak, Kermit, and Buttermouse trotted out of the shimmer behind them. "Very nice other world," Pipsqueak said politely. "But we're not ready to say goodbye to this one yet."

"You . . . what?" Aunt Alecia's eyes bulged. She pointed to Pipsqueak, then the shimmer, then back at the animals. "But . . . it's Sanctuary! The perfect place, where you'll be accepted and loved and safe, where you belong! Why would you come back?"

"We're going to help our pack!" Kermit said.

"Yes. They helped us, and now we get to help them," Buttermouse said, and then did an aerial somersault.

"Family helps family," Harrison said.

Zoe thought the Acharyas' family motto—and the broad way they defined family—made perfect sense. She smiled at all of them.

Aunt Alecia sputtered. "But . . . but . . ."

"Don't you know cats always want to be on the opposite side of any door?" Pipsqueak said. "Zoe helped me become who I am. She came on this journey with me, all to help me. Maybe it didn't turn out the way we thought it would, but now I want to help her and tell her parents *why* she came north instead of going to camp." She leaned against Zoe.

"And then she'll come back here," Zoe said, even though she hated saying it.

Her mouth hanging open, Aunt Alecia tried to form words. "I . . . I don't . . . Zoe . . . People aren't prepared for the reality of magical creatures. My sister least of all! Zoe . . . Your mother pushed me away when I tried to share all this with her."

"You didn't have proof to show her." Zoe waved her hand at the animals. Buttermouse, as if on cue, flew in a circle, displaying his lovely blue wings and rainbow pelt.

"She didn't want to see it," Aunt Alecia said. "She could have come here, to the portal. She could have seen for herself, but instead she decided I was an embarrassment."

"You don't know how she'll react when she's faced with real proof," Zoe said. "I don't know either. I didn't give my parents or my brother a chance." But that was going to change. *I didn't even try before,* Zoe thought. *I just ran.*

"But you've already reached safety! Think of the risk!"

Harrison chimed in. "People do lots of things all the time that aren't guaranteed safe. They decide it's worth the risk." He was on Pipsqueak's opposite side, hugging her furry leg. "Like flying in airplanes. Riding in cars. Swimming with sharks. Hiking on volcanoes."

"Eating food," Zoe added.

"True," Harrison said. "Why are we designed to breathe and eat through the same tube? It's ridiculous. A little flap is supposed to keep us safe? Why not have one mouth for breathing and another for eating? But we don't stop eating . . . Wait, where was I going with that?"

"It *will* be safe, if you help us," Zoe said to her aunt. "Can you give us a ride home and then bring Pipsqueak and the others back when we're done?"

"I . . ." Aunt Alecia looked as if she wanted to argue more but had run out of words.

"By car, it's half a day instead of several days," Zoe said. "The sooner we can get home, the less worried our parents will be. And the lower the risk of being seen." Her parents would still be furious when they realized she'd lied to them and hadn't gone to camp, but *less* furious would help. She wanted the chance to say she was sorry and make everything right. She wanted them to be able to understand—and, hopefully, help her keep Pipsqueak and the others in her life. That chance was the gift Pipsqueak, Buttermouse, and Kermit were giving her before they said goodbye. "Please, Aunt

Alecia. If I can make them understand, maybe they'll let me come visit!"

This way, she might not lose Pipsqueak entirely. She'd still be able to see her. *She'll still be mine, and I'll still be hers.*

Aunt Alecia took a deep breath, as if she were about to argue once more, and then she deflated. "Of course I can drive you. My truck is nearby. But you need to be the one to explain to your parents. I'm not going to argue with my sister again. I'll drop you off and wait in the truck until Pipsqueak, Buttermouse, and Kermit are ready to leave."

Zoe hoped Aunt Alecia would want to talk to Mom, but she wasn't going to force her. If she didn't want to risk another argument with her sister . . . Well, Zoe had kept the truth from her parents and her brother, so how could she criticize? *It's up to me to tell the truth.* "That's fine."

They trooped through the woods until they reached a battered pickup truck with a horse trailer hitched to it. It was more rust than paint. Aunt Alecia patted its hood as if it were her trusty steed. "Everyone in!"

Coming around the truck, Aunt Alecia opened the back of the trailer. Pipsqueak sniffed it the way she'd sniffed the box fort in the shed, and then she squeezed herself inside. She filled most of the trailer. Contorting herself, she managed to turn around, settling in and leaving a tiny space for Zoe. "Nice box."

Zoe started to climb in with her, then paused and looked back at Harrison. He was eyeing the trailer, and she remembered that he got carsick when he felt bounced around too much. "Can you ride in the front with Kermit and Buttermouse?"

He looked relieved. "Yes, I can do that!"

"Ooh, a ride!" Buttermouse squeaked. "I've never been in a truck before. Or a car. Or a plane. Or a helicopter. Or . . ."

Wagging his many tails, Kermit jumped first into the cab of the truck. "Can you roll the window down so I can stick my head out?"

"Only until we reach the road," Aunt Alecia said.

Settling into the trailer with Pipsqueak, Zoe petted the cat between her ears, the way she liked. Pipsqueak began to purr as the truck lurched forward, the entire trailer rattling as they drove. Zoe got a glimpse of trees and sky through the narrow windows at the top. *At least if I can't see out, no one can see in.*

"What do you think my parents will say?" Zoe asked.

Pipsqueak stuck her broad tongue out and licked a stray tuft of fur on her leg. "I think they'll say, 'Wow, that's a big cat.'"

Zoe laughed and then felt like crying. "Pipsqueak . . ."

"I know."

Zoe nestled herself in against the fluff of Pipsqueak's shoulder as the trailer bumped over the terrain. Pipsqueak curled around her.

They talked about everything and nothing. Zoe cried. Pipsqueak licked her hair. They planned visits, as many as Zoe's parents would allow, to Sanctuary. This wasn't a permanent goodbye. Just . . . a change.

Pulling out her phone, Zoe turned it on and checked the battery: one percent. Just enough for a final text. She sent it to Surita: "Coming home. All of us."

She just wished they were all coming home to stay.

Several hours later, after one stop by a secluded forest spot for a bathroom break, Zoe felt the trailer lurch to a halt and heard the engine shut off. She elbowed Pipsqueak. "I think we're here."

Pipsqueak yawned, bumped her head on the roof of the trailer, and then hissed. "Not asleep. Awake the whole time."

Zoe grinned. "Sure you were. Stay here until the coast is clear, then hide in the backyard, okay?" She unlatched the trailer door and pushed it open. Motioning for the cat to stay behind her, she peeked outside. It was dusk, and her parents' cars and Harrison's parents' cars were in their respective driveways.

Aunt Alecia had parked on the street in front of Harrison's house, and Surita—who must have been watching for them—rushed out.

As Harrison climbed out of the front of the truck, Surita grabbed him in a half hug, half shake. "Do you have any idea how worried I was?"

"Sorry!"

"But you made it!" She hugged him again without any shaking. "Knew you could do it. Or hoped you could. Or . . . Anyway, Grandma would be proud."

"Thanks," Harrison said, hugging her back. "Yeah, I think she would have been. Even made her famous s'mores."

"You cut it close, though. Another hour, and your parents would have quit believing my excuses and called the police," Surita scolded him. "Don't ever make me lie like that for you again!"

"Are they mad?" Harrison asked.

"Not yet. I told them that you and Zoe were getting a ride home with a friend. They're not thrilled you didn't call or text to ask permission, but they haven't guessed the truth. You may have gotten away with this, thanks to me," Surita said. "Did you at least find what you were looking for?"

"Well, we found Zoe's aunt, plus a portal to a magical dimension," Harrison said. "So yeah, I'd say we did." He shot a grin at Zoe, but she couldn't grin back. Soon Pipsqueak would be returning through that portal. She tried, again, to remind herself it was for the best.

Surita let out a whoop. "I knew it! Well, I didn't know it, but it was a possibility. What's it like? Did you see it? Was it amazing?"

Going back to the truck, Harrison opened the door, revealing Kermit to Surita. "This is Kermit the Dog," Harrison said. "I think he'll get along with Fibonacci. I promised to introduce them."

"Whoa . . . he's very green."

"It's not easy being green," Harrison agreed.

"And those are a *lot* of teeth."

"Don't worry," Kermit said. "I'm friendly!"

Eyes wide, Surita whispered, "Awesome."

"Let me tell my parents I'm home and fine," Harrison said. "Let Kermit and Fibonacci sniff each other out of sight in the garage, and then we can go to Zoe's house. We'll explain everything there. Can you help me make sure no one's watching while I bring Kermit in?"

Zoe saw Aunt Alecia peek at them in the side-view mirror of the truck. She didn't look like she'd changed her mind about not talking to Mom, but Zoe couldn't wait to go in and see her family, even if they were furious with her. She broke into a jog, reaching the front door at the same time as it opened.

"Alex!"

"Zoe!" He scooped her up in a hug, swung her in a half circle, then set her down. "I think you grew."

"Hah-hah, very funny." Zoe lightly punched his arm.

He wrinkled his nose. "I also think you need a shower. Maybe even before Dad makes dinner. How rustic was this camp?"

"Very."

As Harrison let Kermit in through his garage, Alex called, "Welcome back, Harrison and Surita!"

Surita gave him a wave, and Kermit wagged his many tails as he trotted into Harrison's garage. Both Surita and Harrison were trying to shield Kermit from view from the street, but his greenness and his tails were visible from Zoe's house.

"Hey, what's up with that dog's tail?" Alex asked. "And his fur?"

"Long story," Zoe said. "I was kind of hoping to tell you all at once, with Harrison."

"After you shower?"

"It's kind of important." *This could work,* she thought. Sure, a few people who had seen Pipsqueak on their journey north had panicked: the mother on the playground, the store employee, whoever was driving that truck. But Surita had been ecstatic. And everyone had to agree that Buttermouse was adorable, right?

After one more glance back at Aunt Alecia's truck, Zoe went inside, with Alex's arm slung over her shoulder. He bellowed, "Zoe's home! Smelly, but here!" He shepherded her into the living room, where Dad put down the book he was reading and jumped up. Mom had her laptop balanced on her knees, but she set it aside.

"Finally!" Mom said.

All three of them hugged her at once.

"You, young lady, were supposed to be home an hour ago," Mom scolded. "Surita told us you were getting a ride home with a friend . . . You know better than to change driving arrangements without clearing it with us. Why didn't you text us? We don't like you driving with strangers."

"I wasn't driven by a stranger," Zoe said. "And I'm fine. Sorry for worrying you. My phone battery was drained." She took a deep breath. Despite spending the whole drive down obsessing over it, she still didn't know what she was going to say. There wasn't a good way to break the news. It was going to be a shock no matter what words she used. She just had to go for it. "I, um, have a new friend. Actually, you've met her already, but she's a little . . . different now. She grew."

"Zoe, what are you talking about?" Dad asked. "Who drove you? What new friend?"

Harrison burst into the room, with Surita and Kermit in tow. All three of them were panting, as if they'd run full speed across the lawns, which they most likely had.

"Did I miss it?" Harrison asked. "Did you tell them yet?"

"Are you sure this is a good idea?" Surita asked, nearly simultaneously. "Remember all those movies where everything goes wrong! Remember the reporter who came to your house!"

Mom had stood up. "Zoe, what are you trying to tell us? And what on earth is wrong with that dog? It's *green!* And look at its tails!"

"Never mind its tails," Alex said. "Look at its teeth!"

Zoe saw movement out the window behind Mom. She smiled encouragingly at Pipsqueak. *They're going to love her,* she thought. *I hope.*

Loudly, through the glass, Pipsqueak said, "Hi, Zoe's family!"

Alex leaped into the air.

Mom turned, saw the cat, and screamed.

Everyone began shouting at once, with Surita saying "I told you so!" and Harrison and Zoe trying to calm everyone down. *They have to listen!* Zoe thought. *This will never work if they won't at least try to listen!* "Please, let me explain!"

Alex shouted, louder than everyone, "Let Zoe talk!"

Amazingly, her family calmed. Maybe it was because of Alex. Or maybe it was because the giant cat outside the window had disappeared instead of attacking and it was easier to pretend they'd all imagined it. All of them turned to look at Zoe.

She, with Harrison adding comments, told them everything.

# CHAPTER 19

**AFTER SHE FINISHED EXPLAINING,** Zoe led the way out the back door. She'd expected more questions, but everyone just wanted to see the proof. And there was the giant cat, curled up beside the barbecue grill.

"Um, do you want a burger?" Dad offered. His eyes were so wide they seemed like they were about to pop out, cartoon-style. He was looking from the giant cat to the green dog and back again. "Either of you?"

"Seriously, Dad?" Alex said. "There's a giant magic kitty and a mutant dog in our backyard, and you want to know if they want dinner? Aren't there better questions to ask?" He faced Pipsqueak. "Uh, hi, Pipsqueak? Guess that didn't turn out to be the most accurate name. Ha-ha."

Pipsqueak lashed her tail sideways and glanced at Zoe.

"She likes her name," Zoe said quickly. She could tell that Pipsqueak was just as nervous as she was. Her fur was extra fluffy, and her pupils were wide. But the rest of Zoe's family might see a large, angry feline swatting her tail.

"Great! It's perfect then," Alex said.

Her tail stopped. "Zoe, would I like a burger?"

"They're delicious," Zoe assured her.

After starting the grill, Dad rushed to the kitchen and returned with hamburger meat. He shaped it into a few patties while they all stared at Pipsqueak, and she stared back at them. Slinking closer to the grill, Kermit lolled his green tongue out and drooled.

Mom looked like she was trying to decide between terrified, awestruck, and furious. "How could you . . . You just wandered off into the wilderness? All the way to New Hampshire? With . . . Zoe, I don't know what to think or say!"

Despite not knowing what to say, Mom opened her mouth to talk more, but Pipsqueak beat her to it. "Zoe and Harrison just wanted to help me and keep me safe. And find answers, which they did."

Crossing to Pipsqueak, Zoe plunged her hands into the cat's neck fur and began to pet her neck and cheek. Closing her eyes halfway, Pipsqueak began to purr. "Alex? Want to pet her?" Zoe asked.

"Um, sure?" He tiptoed closer, his hand outstretched.

"Can I pet her too?" Surita asked. She was so excited, she was dancing from foot to foot, her hands clasped over her heart.

Leaning closer to the cat, Zoe whispered, "Do you mind if they all pet you?"

"That's fine," Pipsqueak whispered back. "They don't seem angry. Except your mother. But she seems mostly confused."

"You can pet her," Zoe told Surita.

Surita scurried over with Alex, and both of them began petting the giant cat. "She's so soft!" Surita gushed. Alex looked enchanted, with a goofy smile on his face.

When they stopped, Pipsqueak began meticulously licking her fur where they'd ruffled it.

Dad solemnly offered her a burger on a paper plate. "Bun? Lettuce? Tomato?"

"I'm a *cat,* not a rabbit." Pipsqueak delicately plucked the burger off the plate and swallowed it in a single gulp. "Oh, Zoe, you're right! Delicious!"

Dad gave her a second one and also one to Kermit, who devoured it instantly with *num-num-num* sound effects that caused Dad to stare at him. "Did he just . . ." Dad began.

Finishing her second burger, Pipsqueak declared, "It was a good decision to come back."

"You were living in the shed, right under our noses," Mom said. She asked Zoe, "Is she why you and Harrison built a box fort?"

"Cats like boxes," Zoe said.

Mom nodded, as if the pieces were all fitting together. "Ah, I see . . ." Her voice sounded a bit strangled, as if she were doing her best to stay calm. Zoe was impressed that she hadn't lost it yet. So far, Zoe wasn't even grounded. *Maybe when she has a chance to think about it more, she'll be angry. Or upset. Or confused. Or . . . maybe Mom just doesn't know what to feel.*

"I wish you'd trusted us enough to tell us," Alex said.

"I'm telling you now," Zoe pointed out. It had taken her a while to see this was the right thing to do, but at least she'd seen it. "I wanted you all to understand. I shouldn't have ever lied to you. I should have believed in you and given you a chance to help. But I'm doing that now. I'm asking you to understand. And to let me visit Pipsqueak and Kermit and Buttermouse in Sanctuary. Please, can I visit them?"

She looked to her parents, but it was Alex who spoke. "I want to visit too. Every time I'm home from Paris, I'll take you to New Hampshire."

She hugged him. "Thanks, Alex." Maybe that wasn't as good as Alex never leaving home, but it would be amazing to share this with him. She remembered what Dad had said back when all of this began: *Zoe, things never stay the same. That's just the way life is. It doesn't mean it's all bad. Change can be good. Even exciting!*

Maybe he was right.

"I don't know what's harder to believe," Mom said, "that my daughter is some kind of magical Catalyst or that my sister was telling the truth about her impossible creatures."

Zoe glanced toward the front of the house. There was Aunt Alecia, holding a shoebox, standing in the shadows, listening to everything. Zoe smiled. "If Aunt Alecia were here now, what would you want to say to her?"

"I'd start with an apology. At the very least, I owe her one of those."

"Write to her," Dad suggested. "What harm could it do to try?"

"What if she doesn't want to hear from me?" Mom buried her face in her hands, and Dad wrapped his arms around her shoulders.

Reaching her head out, Pipsqueak licked Mom's hair.

Mom shrieked. Pulling out of Dad's arms, she patted the licked portion of her hair, which stuck together in wet clumps. "Robert . . . I've been so wrong about her."

Dad kissed the part of her hair that hadn't been licked. "We can fix this."

"Aunt Alecia drove us home," Zoe blurted out.

Everyone stared at her.

"Remember I said I wasn't driven home by a stranger?" Zoe said. "It was Aunt Alecia. And I think"—Zoe continued—"if you wanted to talk to her . . . she'd want to talk to you too." Glancing over Mom's shoulder, Zoe expected Aunt Alecia to duck back behind the house. But instead she took a tentative step forward.

Seeing her, Mom looked as shocked as she had when Pipsqueak peered in through the window. *Maybe even more shocked,* Zoe thought.

"Alecia . . ." Mom began.

"Oh no, Buttermouse!" Harrison slapped his forehead with his hand. "I forgot! So sorry, buddy! Let's get you out of there." He darted forward to take the box from Aunt Alecia. He opened it, and the winged mouse fluttered up, saw the crowd, and did a loop, showing off his marvelous wings and multicolored fur.

"Whoa, cool," Surita said.

"Hello, new friends!" Buttermouse squeaked.

"Aunt Alecia will be driving them back to Sanctuary," Zoe said. "But they wanted to come and meet you and tell you it's all real. And that everything's all right."

While Mom and Aunt Alecia talked, cried, and hugged a lot, Zoe helped Dad make more hamburgers for all the humans and nonhumans in their backyard. The people sat on various lawn chairs, and Pipsqueak curled up next to the shed, while Kermit flopped down against her furry belly. Buttermouse perched on top of Pipsqueak's head.

"A magical paradise," Mom marveled. "How did you find it?"

"You remember our grandfather?" Aunt Alecia asked. "Well, he wasn't just odd, like our parents always said. He had magic. He created a portal to Sanctuary in the White Mountains, but the notes he left about its location were cryptic at best. I had been searching off and on for years, but on the day I found the portal, I . . . well . . . I was looking for Bigfoot."

Surita let out a little happy yip. "Your aunt is my idol," she whispered to Zoe.

"It was quite an adventure. I wish . . . I wish you'd been there," Aunt Alecia said to Mom.

"I . . . should have been," Mom said.

"You didn't understand. I should have showed you. Like your daughter did."

Mom glanced against at Pipsqueak. "She did make her point effectively."

She still sounded a little dazed, but she smiled tentatively at her sister, who smiled back.

"Tell us what this all means for our daughter," Dad said.

Alex jumped in. "Is my sister a superhero now?"

Harrison raised his hand. "If she's a superhero, I'm her sidekick. She's definitely going to need a sidekick, especially one with proven camping skills."

Zoe grinned at him. "If I'm a superhero, you're my number one sidekick."

"I'll be sidekick number two," Surita volunteered. "But only if you introduce me to Bigfoot. And can I ride a unicorn? Can I ride a unicorn *with* Bigfoot?"

Aunt Alecia answered Dad. "Your daughter is a Catalyst. It's not an active power. She isn't casting a spell or shooting beams of magic out of her eyes—"

"Aww," Surita and Harrison said simultaneously.

"She simply *is* magic. And when she is in the vicinity of a creature with latent magic inside it, she activates it. Think of it like waking up a dormant gene. From there, the change cascades within the creature until the transformation is complete." Aunt Alecia waved her hand at Pipsqueak, Buttermouse, and Kermit.

"Am I complete?" Pipsqueak asked. "Will I grow more?"

"From what I've seen of other giant cats, you are full size," Aunt Alecia reassured her. To all of them, she said, "The tricky part of being a Catalyst is helping the animals through their transition. It can be a shock to suddenly sprout wings."

Buttermouse squeaked, "I love my wings!"

Mom jumped, and Dad dropped his burger. He picked it up and dusted it off. "I forgot it could talk," Dad said. "Guess I'll have to get used to that."

He moved to throw his burger away, but Alex intercepted it. "Five second rule!"

"Alex . . ." Mom began.

Alex bit into the burger.

"At least some things don't change," Dad said with extra cheer. Mom didn't look amused.

"We can search for new creatures that could be magical," Surita suggested. "Volunteer at animal shelters. Offer to dog-walk people's pets. Visit petting zoos. Farms. Aquariums. Expose Zoe to as many animals as possible!"

Mom held up her hands. "Hold on! I don't want her seeking out new magical creatures. It's one thing if they're drawn to her, but actively looking for them? Zoe and Harrison—they're only twelve. And Surita . . ."

"My parents think I need more extracurriculars," Surita said.

"You can't put this on a resumé!" Aunt Alecia sputtered. "It's highly secret, for the protection of all the extraordinary creatures!"

Zoe said, "Surita can keep a secret. She kept our secret about camp . . ." She trailed off. Maybe it wasn't the best idea to remind her parents of that little detail. "Anyway, you can trust her."

Pipsqueak spoke up. "I trust her."

Surita looked like she wanted to cry. "Oh! Thank you!"

Mom pulled the conversation back on track. "Zoe, I don't want you endangering yourself to help magical creatures. No more trekking off to New Hampshire on your own."

Aunt Alecia agreed. "Yes. When you find any extraordinary creatures, notify me, and I'll take them to Sanctuary myself."

Zoe promised she would.

"I can't believe we're even discussing this," Mom said, shaking her head. "Why is this happening to us? Why our Zoe?"

"She got it from your side of the family," Dad said.

Mom glared at him.

"He is technically correct," Aunt Alecia said. "She inherited her power from our grandfather—"

"It was a rhetorical question," Mom said.

"Zoe has always wanted to rescue animals," Alex pointed out.

Zoe gave her brother a grateful smile. Even faced with such an unexpected surprise, he was still on her side. "In a way, this isn't so different," she said. "I'm just helping unusual animals."

"I know all of this sounds very exciting and wonderful," Mom said, "but—"

Kermit wagged his many tails. "It *is* exciting and wonderful! We all want new friends."

Everyone stared at Kermit. "Does *everything* talk?" Mom said, exasperated, and then shook herself. "As I was saying, all of this sounds like a great plan when Zoe is older, but right now, she's too young to have to worry about seeking out magical animals. And there are still reporters, scientists, tourists, and many other people searching for unusual creatures—"

"Creatures will be drawn to her whether she seeks them out or not," Aunt Alecia said. "What matters is deciding how to handle this new normal."

"I'm a Catalyst," Zoe said. It was the first time she'd said it, and it felt strange to say out loud. "I guess, maybe, I've always been one?"

She wished being a Catalyst didn't mean having to say goodbye to all these amazing creatures so soon after she met them. She was going to miss them all, not just Pipsqueak.

*If only the portal weren't so far away!* she thought. She wished her great-grandfather had created it closer. Of course, he'd probably picked the White Mountains exactly because it was far from any town or city . . .

*Could one be made closer?*

She wondered, for the first time, *how* her great-grandfather had created the portal. Aunt Alecia had just said he'd done it, and she'd used his journals to find it. If he'd discovered a way to make a portal . . . could that same way be used to make another one?

Aunt Alecia continued, soothing Mom. "Keep in mind that magical animals are rare. There hasn't been a Catalyst in this area in years, so these creatures were waiting for Zoe's power to emerge. She may not encounter another like them for a long time, even if she tries to look for them."

"Good!" Mom said. "Life is complicated enough without—"

Zoe interrupted, her voice shaking with nervousness. *Please, let me be right!* "Aunt Alecia, you said my great-grandfather was a Catalyst. He had the same magic as me."

"Yes, that's right." She studied Zoe. "Why?"

"You also said he made the portal." Zoe's heart was pattering faster and faster. If she were right . . . If she'd inherited her great-grandfather's power, all of it . . .

Harrison immediately grasped what she was thinking. "Wait. You mean to say that Catalysts can make portals? Zoe, could you make a portal *here?*"

Everyone turned to look at Zoe, who looked at Aunt Alecia.

"Exactly what I was wondering," Zoe said. "Can I?"

Aunt Alecia's eyes widened, and she started to smile. "You have the same magic. You should be able to do anything he did. Including make a portal."

"Awesome!" Harrison said.

Pipsqueak began to purr.

# CHAPTER 20

**Zoe and Harrison sat with Pipsqueak** in front of the shed. Everyone else had gone inside—Surita back to Harrison's house to tell his parents he'd return soon, and Mom, Dad, and Alex in the house with Aunt Alecia, Kermit, and Buttermouse. It was Aunt Alecia's idea to give Zoe space to concentrate.

"You sure you don't want me to go too?" Harrison asked.

"Definitely not," Zoe said. "You have to help me figure out what to do."

Aunt Alecia's instructions had been cryptic and kind of poetic: *Open yourself to the magic, welcome it into your heart, and slice the sky.* She'd recommended opening the portal within the shed, just inside the doors, so it could be hidden.

"I'm supposed to have a passive magic," Zoe said. "No spells or anything. It's just inside me." She squirmed as she said it. It still felt weird to think of herself as having any kind of power.

Next to her, Harrison poked her shoulder. "That means no sparkles. Or saying 'bibbity-bobbity-boo.'"

She glared at him. "You're not helping."

"Maybe you're just supposed to think about magic a lot?" he suggested. "Try focusing on feeling magical."

"I don't feel magical," Zoe said.

"But you *are* magical," Pipsqueak said. "Accept that."

That could be what it meant. She was supposed to accept that she was different from the way she thought she was and that the world was different from what she'd been taught it was too.

She thought of her mom, how convinced she'd been that her view of the world was right and Aunt Alecia's was not, and how she was inside right now coming to terms with the fact that she'd been wrong and, even more, that her daughter's future was going to be different from what she had envisioned for it. She thought of Alex and how he was starting a new adventure in September, even though it wasn't the adventure he'd originally planned. And she thought of everything that had happened to her and Harrison since the day she found Pipsqueak shivering and alone by the garbage cans—the new journey, the new friends, the new world.

"I do accept it," Zoe said.

Things changed, as Dad had said, and sometimes that was hard, and sometimes it was wonderful.

"And do you welcome it into your heart?" Harrison said. "Whatever that means. Sounds like a chapter in a super-cheesy self-help book."

Zoe thought about it. Really thought. Did she welcome the way her life had changed since she met Pipsqueak? It hadn't been easy, and it wasn't going to be — she didn't know what was going to happen when she started transforming more animals. Aunt Alecia claimed they weren't that common, but Zoe was bound to find more, especially if they were drawn to her. Next time she might not be as lucky as she had been; people might notice. All that she feared, with reporters and an Internet circus, could still happen, and people might try to take the animals away or keep her from helping them reach Sanctuary. She'd have to be careful.

But she didn't wish she'd never met Pipsqueak, and she was happy she'd helped Pipsqueak become who she was meant to be. She didn't regret any of that. "I'm glad I met you," she said to her cat.

Pipsqueak nuzzled the top of Zoe's head. "Me too."

*I'm glad I'm a Catalyst,* she thought. *It brought us all together. Me, Harrison, Pipsqueak, Kermit, Buttermouse.* It wasn't just the animals who had changed. She was different too. Just a few weeks earlier she'd thought all she wanted was for everything to stay the same, and now here she was — at the very center of change. For the first time, she felt as if the world wasn't just something that happened to her; she happened to the world. Stepping up to the shed, Zoe took a deep breath. "I welcome it."

"Now what?" Pipsqueak asked. "How do we slice the sky?"

The shimmer in New Hampshire had looked as if someone had ripped through the air, Zoe remembered. She glanced at Pipsqueak. "Use your claws."

Pipsqueak tilted her head. "What do you mean?"

"Ooh, yes!" Harrison said.

Zoe put her hands on Pipsqueak's closest paw. "I'll think about magic while you cut the air with your claw. My magic combined with your extraordinary self."

She concentrated on all the ways Pipsqueak and the others had changed—and all the ways she'd changed—as Pipsqueak raised her paw, claws extended, and slowly scratched the air within the shed doorway.

The air began to shimmer in front of them.

"Whoa," Harrison said. "You're doing it!"

Zoe breathed in and tasted the air of the other world as Pipsqueak kept slicing through the air until the shimmer was as long as she was tall. She lowered her paw, and Zoe exhaled. Laughing, she sprang up and hugged Pipsqueak's neck. "We did it!"

"You know what this means," Harrison said.

"It means no goodbye," Zoe said, feeling a smile rise up from inside her.

Pipsqueak nuzzled the top of her head.

"Yeah. Any time Pipsqueak or Kermit or Buttermouse want to hide, they can go to Sanctuary. Any time they just want to run around or explore or play, they can go to Sanctuary. Also, any new magical animal we find can go straight to Sanctuary."

"And any time *we* want to visit a magic world . . ." Zoe nodded to the shimmer.

"Should we make sure it worked?" Harrison asked, grinning at her.

"We should." She grinned back. "Tallyho?"

"Tallyho," Harrison agreed.

They climbed on Pipsqueak's back, and together they walked into the shed and through the shimmer. The backyard and shed and patio vanished around them, replaced by an orchard of apple trees. Zoe guessed it was what their neighborhood would look like without the houses.

"Is this Sanctuary?" Pipsqueak asked. "Did it work?"

Breathing in, Zoe tasted flowers in the air.

"Yep, it worked," Harrison said, pointing to a unicorn a few yards away.

"Cool," Pipsqueak said.

They marveled at the magic world for a few minutes more, and then Pipsqueak's stomach rumbled, vibrating her fur. "Do you think your dad has any more of those burgers?"

"Probably," Zoe said.

"Great," Pipsqueak said. "Let's go home."

And together, they did.

# ACKNOWLEDGMENTS

My first cat was named Fluffy. So was my second cat.

I named Fluffy Two after Fluffy One because I missed the first Fluffy, because cats are soft, and because I was four. Since then, I haven't been trusted to name any pets on my own.

I've always loved cats. There's a photo of me as a baby lying on a blanket while a cat walks around me as if protecting me—that was Barny, a stray calico who used to live in our neighbor's barn (hence the name) until we started to feed it. I have a huge smile on my face in that photo.

Growing up, we had other animals too. Labrador retrievers, just like Harrison's Fibonacci. We also had a barely ridable horse, an anxious guinea pig, and a hive full of bees. I loved all of them (except for that one bee who stung me), but it was the cats who sat on my lap while I read book after book after book, who slept with me at night, curled up with my many stuffed animals, and who kept my secret when I whispered to them that someday I wanted to be a writer.

I wrote this book with the help of my current cat, Gwen. She sat on me while I typed, and she napped on the manuscript while I was trying to revise it. Writing can be lonely sometimes—just you and your laptop for many hours. A cat can fix that loneliness.

Gwen is a beautiful gray cat. She's as soft as a chinchilla and as sweet as milk chocolate. She's also a klutz. Once, while she was careening around the house at high speed, she tried to leap from the kitchen counter to the top of our refrigerator, missed, and collided with my face instead. Gave me a black eye. It was very embarrassing, for both of us.

Cats are worth it, though.

I'd like to thank Gwen, as well as all the other cats who have been a part of my life—Fluffy, Fluffy, Barny, Mittens, Sawyer, Jezebel, and Perni—for the years of cuddles and purrs.

I'd also like to thank all the wonderful non-felines who helped bring Zoe and Pipsqueak's story to life: my phenomenal editor, Anne Hoppe, and my incredible agent, Andrea Somberg, as well as Amanda Acevedo, Lisa DiSarro, Candace Finn, Eleanor Hinkle, Catherine Onder, Frank Radell, Sharismar Rodriguez, Opal Roengchai, Jackie Sassa, John Sellers, Tara Shanahan, Dinah Stevenson, and all the other awesome people at Clarion Books and Houghton Mifflin Harcourt. And a special thank you to the fantastic Brandon Dorman for the fabulous art that graces the cover.

Much love and many thanks to my husband, my children, and all my family and friends—you are each magnificent, awesome, and extraordinary. Even better than a whole pack of talking cats! But please don't tell Pipsqueak I said that.